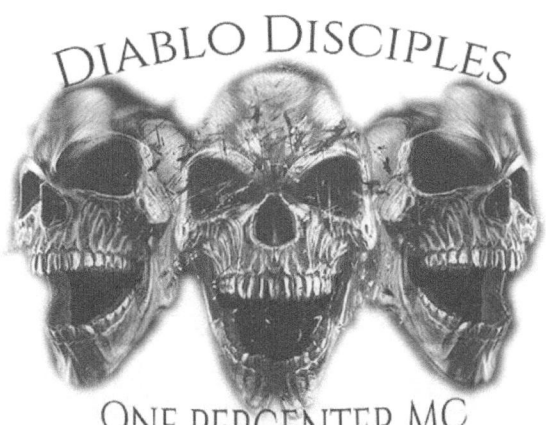

TOMB

DIABLO DISCIPLES
ONE PERCENTER MC

By V. THEIA

Tomb

This is a work of fiction. Names, characters, places, and events are the products of the author's imagination or are used fictitiously. Any resemblance to persons, living or dead, is coincidental.

Names and characters are the property of the author and may not be duplicated. The use of any real company and/or product names is for literary effect only. All other trademarks and copyrights are the property of their respective owners.

Tomb

Cover photo: Depositphotos.com

Cover Design: V. Theia. ©2023

Published by V. Theia 2023

All Rights Reserved

DEDICATION

To my girlies who don't mind falling in love with a married man.
This one is for you!

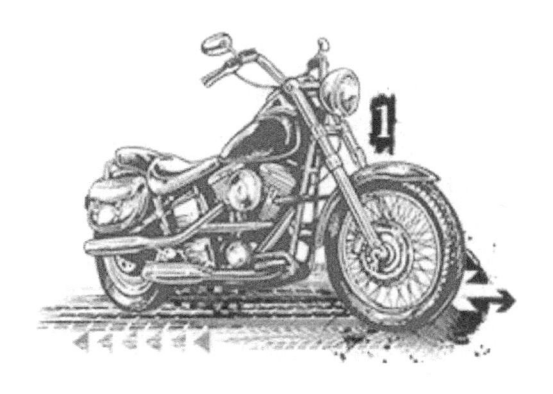

Nina

It was an awful, sickening pain in Nina's heart to know before the day was out, she would tell her husband she wanted a trial separation.

Want was a loose term since she was still madly in love with Tomb.

But the decision hadn't been straightforward. It was long thoughts and sleepless nights alone in their bed. Something she'd agonized over for months. If she left it any longer, she'd change her mind just like she had five million times already because her heart was weak.

This time, Nina was letting her head rule.

And her head was telling her their marriage wasn't maturing at all. Two years in, and it was as if they were two single people who fucked a lot but then went back to their separate lives. Approaching forty-one, Nina should have been shrewder to realize that getting married didn't change a person.

She loved that man. God, did she.

Some days, her love for Tomb felt like it would break her rib cage open, too big to keep inside her chest. If she could solve world hunger with the love she felt for Tomb, then no one would starve ever again.

If love was a beautiful, perfect thing, people chased their whole lives, why did it hurt so much?

She'd seen him and wanted him instantly.

According to Tomb, it had been the same for him.

They were in bed only hours after meeting. That showed the level of chemistry they had. What they still had.

It was that chemistry and sexual attraction that gave Nina pause for weeks. How could she be so unhappy and yet get laid regularly with the best orgasms? Some women would call her a greedy bitch for wanting more from the relationship.

Maybe she was.

Maybe she was damn ungrateful.

Tomb wasn't a wife abuser.

He was far from greedy with his money. Whatever she wanted, she could have. He was a friendly guy, and everyone loved Tomb. Easy-going, funny, and the best protector.

It could be she was expecting the complete package when that didn't exist outside of movies and books.

Sighing, she stopped in her wide hallway in front of the mirror by the front door. It was her last chance to check her appearance before she left the house for the day.

Nina knew Tomb loved how she looked. The banked flames in his eyes told her how attracted he was to her petite five-foot-one height, golden blonde hair down to her shoulders, helped only a little with low lights. Pursing her lips, she slicked on a thin, clear gloss coating to make them shine. She smiled absently, remembering Tomb's face covered in her red lipstick not so long ago.

Not only his face wore the red color that night. But she couldn't think about his wonder dick or how he used it to mesmerize her into submission.

She headed out the door with everything she needed, remembering to set the house alarm.

The stomach ache she'd carried all week like it was a symptom of her guilt, irritated Nina most of the morning until she drowned it in enough coffee to sink a ship.

Carrying bucket loads of guilt because she felt like a failure.

She'd obviously failed at being a wife.

It could be some people weren't meant to be married.

Now, she contemplated leaving him because it took two to make a marriage work.

When he'd proposed, her answer had been uncomplicated, like she'd waited her whole life for that question.

Now, she didn't know if she'd made the right decision.

More than ever lately, she'd enjoyed the quietness of the salon once she'd opened up. Not that Tomb was home to cause noise. He'd already left before she was awake.

She felt like she was turning into a silent nag, racking up negatives in his marriage tally. Not spending any peaceful time together each morning was one of them.

If they weren't having sex, Tomb was often out of the house doing his own thing.

She'd sold her condominium to live in his spacious three-bedroom bungalow. And though she had free rein to redecorate, it was sometimes like she was just an overnight visitor. A booty call with space in the double walk-in closet.

Lost in her racing thoughts, she jumped at the knock on the door. Esther was always early.

"Holy hell, it's hotter than Satan's armpits. We're gonna fry today, doll." she dumped her purse and coffee tumbler on the work side. Esther was in Nina's age bracket, with three kids and a deadbeat boyfriend, long in the past. They'd been fast friends ever since Esther interviewed for the position of nail technician.

Not long after the pair set up the salon for the day, Nina's other stylist arrived fashionably late, as always. Ross greeted them as enthusiastically as he did every morning. "Hello, you sex kittens. What kind of day are we having today?"

"Not sex kittenish, that's for sure." Scoffed Esther, rolling her eyes as she prepared her workstation.

"Didn't get laid again?" asked the twenty-something, brushing black hair out of his eyes. Ross claimed it was his God-given queer right to butt into their sex lives. Or non-existent sex life, in Esther's case. There were many failed attempts to set Esther up with blind dates, but Ross wouldn't give up trying to find her a man.

"If you mean I drove one kid to a basketball game and another to a gamer convention and then watched five episodes of True Crime while painting my toenails, then yeah, I got laid."

Ross clicked his tongue, shaking his head. "It's a sad day when you're not getting that body rocked at least twice a night, cupcake."

"My rocking days are behind me."

"Bullshit. This one," he pointed at Nina, who was minding her own damn business but always got brought into their spats. "is your age and is getting her world rocked by the hottest man on earth." Ross wasn't finished. "She walks in here bow-legged. He's that damn good."

"Nina is married." Answered Esther.

Ross made a sarcastic noise from his throat. "That means fuck all, cupcake. Tell her, Nina."

"Don't bring me or my sex life into it. I've hardly sipped coffee yet. And stop calling my husband hot, or I'll tell Bastian what you're saying."

"Bas would agree; he fancies Tomb, too. We've agreed if Tomb ever comes to our side, he will be our throuple."

Choking on a sip of coffee, Nina coughed before she met the humored eyes of her soon-to-be-fired colorist.

"At least that put color in your cheeks. What's up, cupcake? You're not your usual lively self this morning." He winked.

"Less of the cupcake," she tried to reprimand, but smiled with it. "Remember, I'm your boss; I could fire you anytime."

"Not when I'm the best colorist this Podunk town has ever seen. Now answer, madame boss lady. Everything okay?"

"Everything is fine, Ross." Nina was saved from further explanation when the receptionist and intern arrived. Minutes later, the salon team assembled, and the day was ready to start.

Thank God for her thriving business, which meant Nina was kept busy. It was what gave her a purpose. Nina's salon was coming up on its tenth year, and thankfully, she'd come through dips and scares with the economy. But like death and taxes, everyone always wanted their hair to look nice, so while other shops around her on Main Street had come and gone, Nina's survived.

On a break, she half listened to Ross and Bethany, her quiet yet hardworking intern, when a text buzzed.

She frowned, seeing who it was from.

Tomb: Princess, gotta go on a run. I'll be home late.

Her heart sank as she kept her eyes on the screen to see if he'd send another text. Maybe love or kisses, or he'd miss her. Nothing came.

They weren't ships passing in the night at this point. Their boats weren't even in the same fucking ocean.

Nina: No problem. I'm going out with the girls. Be safe. XX

She missed that man more than she could say. And she had to wonder if he missed her at all. Slipping the phone into her back pocket, she tried to push aside the hurt.

Something had to change, and soon, before she lost herself to a deep-seated depression.

But Nina didn't know if she could put into motion something that would break her heart. It was unimaginable to think of hurting Tomb, not when he owned her completely. It was unthinkable to make her big man frown.

It hadn't always been this way.

Not in those first few days and weeks when they'd been so obsessed with each other.

She wanted that back.

She wanted more. And Nina didn't believe she was wrong about needing more.

Did she try, or did she give up?

Nina
BEFORE

Who'd expect to meet someone while reading in the neighborhood diner?

The first Nina knew she wasn't alone at her corner table was when a shadow masked the sunshine streaming through the window. She cocked her head, expecting the server to ask if she wanted more coffee. She did. But her mouth dried when she saw it was a mountain of a man, smiling at her.

Nina prided herself on never being flustered, by men especially. They didn't tongue-tie her; she could flirt with the best of them. Her last date was eons ago, as was her previous relationship, but her skills were still razor-sharp.

Until now.

The man continued to smile while she found her tongue.

Holy shit.

He wasn't conventionally handsome, but something was appealing about his rugged features.

Biker, she amended. Not just a man. He wore a leather vest decorated with fine stitching and three patches on the front. Underneath, he wore a long-sleeved undershirt pushed up his hairy forearms. He had a thick body all over. Christ, he was broad; her mouth suddenly filled with moisture as she skimmed her eyes down his long legs encased in navy jeans. She looked up to see a pair of aviators hung like jewelry on the neck of his shirt. Around his wrist was a black leather cuff, and a beaded bracelet. On the other wrist, he wore a silver watch. Two silver rings, one around his thumb, finished his ensemble. The biker was naturally masculine, and the sight of him caught her breath. Straight up arrested it in her throat.

It could be that was why she only gawped without offering a fast quip. She felt disconnected from her smart brain in front of the guy with his incredibly carved jawline, dusted in brown face scruff and lips that looked like sinning artists painted them.

You couldn't live in Utah, especially Laketon, the home ground of the Diablo Disciples MC, and not know about the biker gang. A decade ago, Nina moved to town to open her salon and was immediately told about the Diablos. Some were in awe. Other people spat expletives about the biker men as if they were devils intent on ruining the town. The biker's wives and girlfriends were regular clients in her salon. Naturally, she'd heard all the gossip.

This was the first time having a face-to-face with one of them, and what a face it was. The bluest eyes crinkled at the edges. She cleared her throat and curved a questioning eyebrow, praying he didn't mention she'd been checking him out. He didn't mention it, but his smirk said he'd noticed.

"You mind if I sit down?" he asked in a sin-soaked, gravelly baritone. Her hormones gave a little zip of interest. Sexual hormones, which had been dormant for a while, came awake.

The biker had a voice straight out of a sexy audiobook. Intrigued, she nodded to the chair.

"Thanks." he put down the white cup and situated himself, filling the whole thing with his size. He had to be at least six-foot-five. Those shoulders could carry whole-ass donkeys. She'd bet on it.

Okay, horny bitch, focus.

"I've been watching you…"

"Have you?"

"Yeah," he smirked. "I wondered what you were reading to make you smile."

Huh. That was not what Nina expected him to say.

He nodded down to the Kindle she was holding. "Mind if I look?" he asked, looking at her expectantly like he was used to getting his way. He wore a slight smile around his lips. Making him impossibly more attractive. She noted the shape of his thumb when he rubbed a finger over the silver band. Veiny hands, tanned skin, and long fingers with even cut nails. *Nice.*

"Are you sure you want to do that?" two thick brown eyebrows shot up into his longish hair at the front of his forehead.

Chuckling, he wiggled his fingers at her. "Now, I gotta see this."

"Okay, then." She handed over her Kindle and watched him read.

The silence continued as he swiped pages until he zeroed his glinting amusement across the table. Nina was biting the inside of her cheek, knowing what sex scene he was reading. His gaze returned to the book.

He continued. At one point, he sat back and crossed a leg over his knee. Seeing him so engrossed swept the breath out of Nina, and she was dying to know what he was thinking.

"Well? What thoughts do you have?" she finally asked impatiently.

The biker raised his smiling eyes and handed over her Kindle. She closed out the screen and placed it by the coffee cup.

"I think I might need a minute before I can leave." He answered gruffly. Hot and sexy. Nina burst out laughing.

"I tried to warn you."

"You did. I'll believe you next time." he winked and made heat crawl up her chest. "Can't believe you're sitting here sipping coffee like ice wouldn't melt in your princess mouth, and you're reading porn."

"It's refined smut with an intricate storyline, thank you very much." Nina took a delicate sip of coffee, aware he watched her intently. The focus was unsettling because his eyes never wandered to check out her body, as men typically do.

"My mistake," his lips twitched.

It was then he asked if he could buy her another coffee.

Of course, Nina said yes.

He returned to the table with an array of cookies on a plate.

"I'm Rome King, but everyone calls me Tomb." He said, "thought I'd better introduce myself since I gate-crashed your table."

Smiling, Nina liked his straightforward style.

"I'm Nina. And you brought cookies. You're welcome to sit at my table anytime."

"Cookies," he smirked, "duly noted."

She couldn't believe she was flirting with an Adonis stranger in a leather jacket and scuffed biker boots.

"Cookies or carrying books."

"You a bookworm?"

"I don't get much time to read, but it's nice to relax."

"With smut…" Those gorgeous lips lifted again.

"Elite smut. I'm fussy. What about you, Tomb? Do you read?"

"Do mechanic magazines count?"

Now it was Nina's turn to grin as he shoved a whole cookie in his mouth, chewing with manners without dropping a crumb on himself.

"Sure. It means you're not illiterate." he chuckled a rich laugh and gained attention from women tables over.

Tomb didn't even glance over. Another check in the pro box.

The following words from his lips stopped the air in her lungs because, as well as her flirt game might be, she didn't expect this to go any further.

"Let me take you out for a beer, babe."

Oh, wow. She got tongue-tied, then offered a response. "It's lunchtime."

A hot, suggestive stare came her way. The man was so perfectly packaged that he took all her good sense away with a smile. "Later then. After you spend the day telling me about these sex books, you like to read."

It was a straightforward decision to say yes.

The attraction was there, sure. But Tomb was easy to talk to, and over the next few hours, they spoke about many varied things over coffee and cake.

Nina learned about his job at the Diablos compound and what it meant to be a road captain.

"When was your last road trip?" she asked.

"I went to Miami weeks back. That place was on another level of chaos." He said, tapping his silver-ringed fingers on the table.

She told him about her salon and her shambolic but lovable staff. Tomb shared about his family and club brotherhood.

The hours flew by. It was the best conversation she'd had in a long time. And when they parted, Tomb picked her up an hour later after she'd changed into jeans and a silver shirt paired with heels. It was worth it to dress fancier when his eyes heated as he stepped down off the big motorcycle and walked over to her door, where she was waiting.

"You're fucking stunning."

His eating stare made her steps stumble, but Tomb was there to catch Nina before she fell.

"Careful, princess." He rumbled.

"Thanks for the save. The first drinks are on me."

"When you're with me, you don't pay for shit." He announced, helping her onto the back of his bike.

True to his word, Tomb wouldn't let Nina pay. Though his biker brethren were in the same bar, he kept her to himself in a corner booth.

For the first time in years, Nina didn't want to be the woman who said no to second dates. As Tomb reached across the table to stroke a finger over her thumb, the chemistry ricocheted between them like lightning zaps.

"You're beautiful," he husked, his eyes piercing her down to the marrow.

Nina captured his thumb, holding it hostage. The moment she did, his eyes flashed heatedly, enjoying her touch.

That's how the next few hours went.

Nina didn't drink much, and though she'd only had two cocktails alongside fizzy water, she felt tipsy by Tomb's attention.

They talked so much that she could now identify every person close to him if they walked into the bar. They laughed and shared jokes; his were much dirtier than hers. He asked questions and seemed genuinely interested in her responses.

It was the best first date she'd had in forever.

Easily the best.

And then it got better when he pulled her up to dance.

"It's a bar, Tomb. No one is dancing," she protested, laughing, letting herself be pulled along.

"Who cares?" Eyes like the devil, inviting her to the darkness.

Of course, she went straight into his arms when a slow song came on the jukebox. The music he'd selected moments ago. Nina melted into his tall frame. God, he was thick all over, so solid and mouthwatering. Her arms naturally banded around his waist, stroking her fingers up the length of his back as he held her just as closely.

"I've been waiting to get you in my arms." He shared by her ear.

Their height difference was comical, but somehow, the biker made it work, swaying her gently.

"Christ, I could carry you around in my pocket," he rasped, bending low to nip at her ear, and Nina shivered as pleasure zipped down her spine.

"Your pocket princess," she joked in return, using the nickname he'd coined. He rumbled agreement, squeezing her tighter as the song continued, and the swaying lengthened into two more songs. The bar disappeared around them.

"Get a room, Tomb," someone shouted. Nina jolted in his arms, but Tomb didn't release her. He only spun them around to snarl at the grinning guy. "Shut your trap, Splice, before I shut it for you."

"Come on, my guy, all that bumping and grinding is doing things to me." the other biker laughed, and Nina chuckled into Tomb's beefy chest.

"Ignore him," he told her. "He's an asshole. They're all assholes."

They'd gained an audience. The table of bikers watching them.

"Duly noted." They weren't doing much dancing now, just holding each other. "And what about you? Are you an asshole?"

"I'm the exception," he winked.

Weirdly, she believed him. Or her hormones had taken the wheel, and she wasn't thinking clearly.

It had to be horny hormones because her following actions were nothing to do with being drunk. Nina was in her competent mind when Tomb lowered his head.

"Give me a kiss, biker."

He made a hot, rumbling noise that vibrated through his chest and into hers.

When Tomb's mouth slanted, it was game over after that.

She was obliterated by his expert, all-consuming kiss that set off a series of prickles that started at her toes and fired heat into the base of her spine.

Dear God, the biker could kiss. He deserved accolades and rounds of applause as he gripped the side of her face, turning her to the angle of his open mouth, seeking her tongue.

Nina might have started it, but Tomb was in charge, and it sizzled her blood into a hot boil. Men who took charge were her type. She didn't know why, but in all her sexual adulthood, she'd been disappointed by lovers and boyfriends when they inevitably gave up control under her authoritative nature. She'd craved someone who could overpower her senses. And the way Tomb commanded her tongue to follow his, he was all that and more. When they drew apart naturally, Tomb looked like he wanted to devour her.

Never had a simple kiss derailed her.

"Not here," he growled low, answering whatever unspoken question she'd said with only her eyes. Tomb slid a hand to his back pocket and fished out the wallet attached to the dangling silver chain around his hip. He left money on the table, took her hand, and hurried out of the bar without acknowledging his buddies.

Nina's heart flatlined in her chest, butterflies manically flapping excited wings as she followed at Tomb's side. Her fingers twitched inside his larger palm, and he sent her a sideways glance so full of longing she nearly stumbled.

She was not a clumsy girl. At all. She could hold her own in situations, but faced with a man who was so damn hot, so damn attractive in every way possible, she felt like a little girl with a first crush. It snatched tightly at her core as the cooler night air hit her face. It should have brought clarity to her whirling thoughts. But didn't.

Tomb started around the corner to his parked bike, but as soon as they were out of sight, he pushed her up against a wall. Dropping his head, she smelled the whiskey on his breath. His hand slid beneath her wave of hair and gently cradled her neck as his body crowded up against her, not caring about boundaries.

"I'm going out of my fucking mind wanting you, baby."

It was impossible to control how her heart skipped. And though she should have let Tomb know she didn't do one-night stands, all that came out of her mouth was. "Yes."

Tomb rested their brows together, and he squeezed the back of her neck. It was more than clear from the massive bulge pressing into her stomach how he wanted her. "Fuck. I love hearing you say yes to me. I always wanna hear you say yes to me."

The dizziness making her head swim culminated in the hottest kiss smashed to her lips as she reached up to rush her fingers through Tomb's hair. Gripping him tightly to hold on, or she might fall off the edge of the world.

He kissed her until she thought her lips might forever be swollen.

"Nina girl." He growled, biting her, tasting her, turning her into a wanton woman who clawed up a man to get closer to him.

Under his seeking hands, she felt like a girl again, not a jaded woman who didn't believe in dating and romance. She felt desired and *wanted*. Experiencing those intense feelings up close meant having sex against a wall with a man she hardly knew would not be a regret of hers.

Because his kisses sent her to heaven, and his masterful touch felt like nothing else had before. She was intoxicated by Tomb and the skill of how he fucked her. It all happened in a blur of clothes being moved out of the way but not removed altogether. Her jeans hung around her ankles. She heard the crinkle of a condom packet, thank God, because her head was in the fucking clouds to think about such mundane, sane things.

He treated her like a doll in his hands as he put her where he needed her, groaning her name when he'd stuffed his cock inside her.

She was split apart by bliss and put back together again.

"Sweet, sweet baby, Nina girl." He groaned, holding her entire body up against the wall.

And then Tomb fucked her in a way she'd never experienced before. Rough, tender, all-consuming. He praised her with filthiness and lavished her with kisses. He fucked her so good that he had to hold a hand over her mouth to stifle her screams of pleasure as he drilled an orgasm out of her so fast her vision blacked out.

"Sweet, sweet Nina girl." He rasped into her neck as he moved in heavy slams while she splintered apart. She had to bite into Tomb's palm to hold her screams inside. *Incredible*. And when it was over, she was floating outside of her body.

He took her home and stayed.

One night turned to two and four.

Then they were seeing each other every night for weeks.

Blinking back from that memorable night, Nina hadn't imagined it.

Their connection blazed brighter than a planet. It had flickered to life like Tomb had put a match underneath them.

She didn't know how; between that moment and getting married, that same connection had disappeared.

Was it dead for good, or could she find an ember of what it once was and bring their relationship back to life?

She didn't know. Or if she had the energy to try, if she was the only one feeling alone.

Tomb always seemed content, happy even.

He liked their relationship as it was.

Nina wanted the unattainable.

Being desired by her man, but knowing he enjoyed spending time together when they weren't in bed.

To crave the attention and non-sexual affection of her husband was a lonely feeling. And one Nina wasn't able to burden for much longer.

Tomb

There was no feeling like being out on the open road for a Road Captain, with the wind blowing in his face and an endless journey ahead.

Tonight was not unlike any other night when Rome 'Tomb' King was on a run for his club, the Diablo Disciples. Pick up a payment and drop it off at one of their business to funnel into legal channels. It was rinse and repeat, something he did twice a week, more if needed.

Being part of a One-Percenter lifestyle wasn't for the weak. It was thumbing your nose to what society deemed proper and morally decent, doing what you wanted to do.

He might land somewhere ambiguously in the middle on a scale ranging from good to bad. He'd met worse men than him and his club brethren.

Tomb loved the open road. He loved the sense of freedom, which no other job offered him until he'd walked into the Diablos compound and found home.

And then everything changed, like it had been aligned in the fucking clouds by someone who was on his side for once, the day he met Nina. That freedom he'd been searching for no longer seemed to matter.

He pulled into a gas station outside Laketon, Utah, waited for a Buick to fill up, and checked his phone to see if Nina responded to his text. How she didn't get sick of his ass, he didn't know, but he'd lucked out with her big time. She never complained, never bitched him out like some of the old timers and their old ladies. Their marriage was as sweet as he could want, a peaceful life.

Sure, they fought, but that was more foreplay than actual anger.

The smile dropped off his face when he thumbed open her message.

My Princess: No problem. I'm going out with the girls. Be safe. XX

That meant beers and dancing. And his woman attracted assholes who thought they could get with her. Her utter beauty brought every pervert to her orbit. Tomb felt the tightness in his back molars, angry he wouldn't be there to stare his warning at any fool who thought shooting his shot with her was an innovative idea.

His Nina was oblivious to her charms, but Tomb, sure as shit, saw men checking her out. Especially when the Diablos hosted parties for visiting out-of-town clubs, all eyes were on his woman.

He didn't fucking like it.

Young Bucks had no fear, and he didn't have time to break milk bones and bury those swaggering Gen Zs in the woods.

Growling under his breath, he took his turn to fill up the tank. Heading into the gas station to pay, he picked up a drink and gum before returning to his bike.

Feeling every second of his forty-year-old body when his back hurt from sitting so long on the Harley. Tomb swiped his fingers through his messy hair and pulled on the leather gloves from his pocket, the night air turning chillier. He caught a car full of college-age girls gawking at him. Bikers drew female attention like a free-for-all Magic Mike show. But Tomb had never been the type to mess around with random hookups once he reached his thirties.

He'd been in the biker lifestyle long before he even took a seat on Axel's council. It started with just a few friends gathering to ride along the coast in the summer. Axel had been two years into his reign as Prez when Tomb found the MC. Within a week, he'd left his dead-end construction job and was hired as a club mechanic in their expanding garage.

Half a year later, he was assigned his Road Captain patch and a seat on the council. When the club went on big rides, Tomb mapped the route, ensuring everyone arrived safely and on time. Since marrying, his duties had increased, which meant any time a brother was needed out of town, for pickups, drop-offs, or to visit another club for business, Tomb was the brother to ride.

Knowing his wife would be without him near to scare off the masses, Tomb experienced stinging guilt because it had been his idea to volunteer for the out-of-town jobs recently. His reasons were personal, and he fucking hated himself.

Ignoring the ogling car of women parked at the side of him, Tomb knew what they saw. He wasn't hit with the ugly stick by any means, yet he wasn't in Reno or Ruin's pretty boy lane. Before his Nina girl snapped his attention like a rubber band, he'd rarely been without female company when he'd needed it.

He wasn't fat, but he sure as shit didn't have a six-pack like the crazy twins or Diamond, who was an exercise freak. In the highlight of his twenties, Tomb sported washboard abs and bulky pecs. Today, he was solid, but preferred getting his workout with a gorgeous little blonde going to town on his lap. Since marrying Nina, she'd made him drop thirty pounds in sex sweat alone. Being six-foot-five, he carried his frame like an athlete who preferred slower sports, like golf and ten-pin bowling, channel surfing like a pro.

The club chicks said he had a dad bod. Whatever the fuck that meant, since he wasn't a dad, he'd rather swing from a tree by his dick than become a father.

The old biddy in the Buick sent Tomb a withering stare as he put the cell phone to his ear. *Yeah, yeah, lady*. He arched his brow. He knew the law was not to use devices in a gas station, but he wasn't about to blow himself up, so she could chill her fucking curlers.

"Yo, big man, what's hanging?" answered Splice on the other end.

"You're gonna hate me, brother."

He heard Splice groan. "Goddamn it, Tomb. Please don't say it. I have a date tonight."

His bud meant *date* in the loosest terms. The Sergeant At Arms patched brother didn't date, he fucked, and he didn't fuck the same women twice. This meant he had a lot of women in his rearview.

"I'll owe you."

"Fucking right, you will. When and where?"

Tomb gave him the info, and the pair hung up.

Still, his jaw was tight, knowing he was riding in the opposite direction toward Denver to meet up with Jamie Steele from the Apollo Kingsmen.

Hours after he arrived at the Kingsmen's compound, close to midnight, he checked the last update from Splice. He was dog-tired as he removed the helmet and gloves and stretched his back muscles. Shoving the phone away, he'd missed a goodnight text from Nina when she'd gone to bed.

It was too late to reply, or he'd wake his hardworking wife, but it didn't stop him mentally kicking his ass for not stopping sooner to check in with her.

Christ's sake, he was holding his baser self together by a fucking thread at this point. Two years of marriage, more years together before that, and his Nina girl didn't know the deviant motherfucker beneath his skin.

And if Tomb had his way, she never would. Because he'd lose her, and that was not happening.

A light flipped on over the doorway of the Kingsmen entryway. It was Amos, their VP, who came out. A cigarette dangling from the corner of his mouth and a ball cap worn backward. The pair shook hands. "You made good timing. We weren't expecting you for a couple of hours yet."

"My fucking knees hate me right now."

Amos chuckled. "I hear that, my guy. We have spare bunk rooms inside if you wanna stay for the night. But we'll get you fed and watered first. Jamie's inside seeing to some shit."

Curious, Tomb followed into their clubhouse, and warmth enveloped the chill in his weary bones. He'd zipped up his leather jacket to hide his Diablo patches. It wasn't the law, but most bikers followed the rules of respect by not flaunting their club on another MC's turf.

"You got shit?"

Amos cocked a brow over his shoulder and smirked. "Of the female kind. The worst kind, if you ask me." Tomb followed Amos through a hallway.

The last thing he expected to see was a half-naked, diaper-wearing baby carried in Jamie Steele's arms. Tomb wasn't an expert on babies, but it looked like a newborn with scrawny frog legs scrunched up under its body. Jamie patted the diaper butt to stop the squawking while the baby rooted its mouth around Jamie's chest.

"Told you already, you won't find milk in there."

Tomb chuckled. "Have you opened a creche since the last time I was up this way, Steele?"

The guy looked worn out even as he squeezed out a stare, still shushing the baby with small pats on the ass.

"His baby mama tried to hide his kid. Jamie is a *surprise; you're a daddy* to his two-week-old son, and he's got the baby mama locked up in the dungeon as punishment." It was Amos who spoke. Tomb wasn't sure if the guy was kidding as Amos threw himself on the couch, and Jamie assumed his seat.

"Do you ever tire of running that fucking mouth of yours?" snapped Jamie, staring a warning at the laughing VP.

"Come on. We haven't had gossip to share in ages."

"My son is not fucking gossip, now shut your trap."

Amos shut his trap.

"This is big news, my friend," offered Tomb. "I should have brought a congratulations cactus or something."

"Big news to me, too." Muttered Steele, but then he was all business in the next blink despite his glaringly obvious domestic problem in his arms. He reached into a desk drawer and offered a fat package of money, which Tomb thumbed through. They were in business together, but that didn't mean the Diablos mindlessly trusted anyone not to rip them off. Hell, it had taken them the best part of two years to shake the connection to the Mexicans, and in the meantime, Axel had his house blown up. They'd been extra vigilant since. However, the Kingsmen frontman was trustworthy. After slipping the money into his pocket, he gave Jamie the location of the next European shipment from their Irish contacts. The triad discovered that cooperation led to higher profits, but the Murphys only collaborated with the Diablos in this region.

"Sweet," he said, reviewing the list of cars being shipped across the ocean. Expensive as fuck and newly stolen. "Luxe will have fun driving these to their new buyers."

As that, the office door swung open. Tomb turned around to see a petite little thing dressed only in boxer shorts and what looked to be a man's oversized shirt. The sleeves rolled up her arms.

"I want my son, Jamie."

"*My son.*" He hissed, staring something close to heat *and* hate at the woman, if Tomb was reading the room right.

"I need to feed him."

"Do it here." Jamie relented and shot Amos a warning glare before he let rip with a laugh.

"You want me to get my boobs out in front of everyone?" she bit like she dared him to say yes.

He and his Nina fought over stupid things, but there was always a reason. Usually, it was so she could get into his pants and on his dick.

"Fine," Jamie sighed, as the woman approached him the same way she might face a firing squad, with her chin pointed high and a ready *fuck you* lashed around her tongue. Jamie's baby mama was pissed. Tomb fought a grin as they swapped the baby from his arms to hers. "Bring him back to me when he's eaten."

Tomb was sure she muttered, "Lick rust and die," under her breath before disappearing from the room.

Jamie sighed again and sat back in the seat.

"You got a handful there, my man." Tomb remarked helpfully.

"Tell me about it." he rubbed his face tiredly.

Tomb took them up on their offer of a room to sleep in. There was no way his fatigued brain would get him home safely. And was back on the road around five a.m. Eager to get home to Laketon, he kept to the speed limit and made it to his house within hours. But Nina wasn't around when he entered a quiet house.

The place never felt the same when she wasn't there.

He breathed deeply and inhaled her scent when he crossed into their bedroom. It was everywhere, and he fucking loved smelling her.

Tomb rushed to shower and change clothes because he detested the quietness without Nina. He went to the clubhouse. After dropping off the money at Axel's office, his gurgling belly took Tomb to the kitchen, where he ate breakfast until satisfied. Next, he tried to hit up Splice, but that brother was probably still sleeping off a sex-induced hangover. He reckoned if anything had happened last night, Splice would have called to let Tomb know.

Relying on someone else wasn't ideal.

He fucking hated it.

But what was the alternative? His wife saw his true self and headed for the hills. Not a fucking chance.

For now, Tomb held his shit in check at all costs. But he didn't know how long he could keep going the way he was. Denying himself something he craved like it was a second skin covering his bones meant he fought his inner demons on the daily.

Some days, like today, they sneaked out a little. He fished out the phone from his back pocket as he headed toward the garage in long strides.

Tomb: I'm home, princess. You good? Send me a picture.

The hunger to see what his wife was wearing chewed on the back of Tomb's skull, and until the phone pinged, he was wound tighter than a coil. That coil loosened something in his chest when he eyed the full-length mirror picture she'd sent. A vision in painted-on white jeans ripped along the thighs, a shirt designed to hug her tits, and a pair of sinful heels. *Fuck*, his wife was everything addictive, and Tomb rubbed a thumb over his lower lip as he ate up the picture.

"You mooning over the Mrs again, brother?"

A voice to Tomb's left asked, and he turned the phone away, savagely possessive of any sight of his wife, even from his brothers. He locked eyes with a smiling Diamond.

"I leave the mooning to you young stags, D." the pair bumped fists.

"Yeah, right, tell yourself that. I saw you at the last club party. Wouldn't even let me take Nina on a spin around the dancefloor."

No, he fucking wouldn't.

"My wife likes her feet unbroken, you clomping hippo." Diamond chuckled. He was a massive man, and that was coming from Tomb, who also tipped the scales and height chart. Diamond was built like a bodybuilder, which made it worthwhile for his security duties. People hired him as protection or to look menacing. "Where are you headed today?"

"Axel wants me down at the docks for the Murphy shipment. Gotta love the Irish. They always bring gifts." He smirked, running a hand over his shorn hair.

"You mean the wee lassies that might tag along with them? You'll get in trouble one of these days, D, if the Irish think you're messing with their baby-girl cousins."

"If not friend, why friend-shaped?" he shot back, and Tomb burst out laughing.

After checking the worksheet in the garage to see what needed working on, he jumped into his bay and got under a sedan to sort out a cracked oil pipe.

Only later recalling how Nina hadn't told him if she was good today.

And that shit didn't sit well with him.

Tomb

Being raised by a single mom instilled values in Tomb he'd stuck to his whole life. He left home at seventeen and remained close to his mom and younger brother. So, as he pulled into the carport outside of Nina's salon, he connected a call to his mother.

She was sixty-five going on twenty-one and had a wilder life than he did, but Tomb refused to know details. He and Austin agreed long ago that their parent didn't get up to the shit they got up to.

As soon as the call connected, he grinned when she demanded. "Why are you keeping my favorite daughter-in-law away from me, Rome?"

"Hello to you, too, Ma."

"Don't avoid my question. You might be enormous, but I can still whoop your ass."

"You and whose army, shorty?"

He heard her snort. "You're testing me? You wait. There's a big can of whooping with your name on it the second you step through my door. You'll be spitting out teeth for weeks." She warned in her sweet voice.

Amused, Tomb unclipped the helmet and hung it on the bars. He could see through the salon window, and his chest warmed, catching sight of his woman.

"Old woman, you'd break a bone. Now, is there anything you need?"

"Yes, more grandbabies and a date with Shaquille O'Neal."

He skirted the grandbabies' talk because it wasn't anything new he was hearing.

"You already have one toy boy," and the less thought about her younger boyfriend, the better. "Starting a harem?"

"I might. I have some free time on my hands." She sassed. "Now answer the question, Rome, you've missed the last two Sunday dinners. When are you bringing Nina to see me?"

"She's not my prisoner, Ma," he would like to tie her up, though. *Fuck.* Couldn't think about that now. "Nina can see you anytime, but the salon is busy."

"You're keeping her from me. I know it. I'll whoop your ass."

His lips twitched. "Fine, add it to the list. So, you're good? Do you need anything?"

"No, I'm fine. George is taking me to dinner soon, so I must make myself pretty."

"You're already beautiful. Make sure that jackass pays."

"He's not a jackass, and George never lets me pay."

Good. The younger stud lived another week. He knew he was a decent sort since he'd looked into him. There was no way he'd allow some milk-drinking punk, young or old, near his mom if he weren't. She'd put up with too much shit from his father to last a lifetime. George was a fifty-five-year-old retiree from Denver City. If he treated their mother right, Tomb and Austin would leave him alone.

"Have a good time," he told her, swinging his leg over the bike seat, eager to get inside and put eyes on his wife. "Hit me up if you need anything."

"Your brother said the same this morning. I don't know how I raised you two sweet devils. Talk soon, sweetheart. Give Nina a hug from me."

"Will do."

Chemical scents and music greeted him as he crossed the doorway. The desk girl smiled and didn't stop him from advancing into the black and pink decorated salon. Each time he walked in, he was hit with pride for what his wife built for herself. She was staunchly independent; he'd known that from their first conversation. She differed from the women he'd fucked around with before her because Nina hadn't been chasing his money or his biker clout. Because he understood that, he'd reined in every dark instinct he was made of, letting Nina be who she was, even when it went against his instincts. Even now, as proud as a husband as he was, if she told him she wanted to jack the salon in and be a stay-at-home dog mom, he'd be fucking tickled pink about it.

But until Nina decided, Tomb bit his tongue and let his feet walk as he approached. A pair of hairdresser scissors were in one hand and a comb in the other. The woman in the chair was talking when he got behind Nina. Her face blanked when she saw him in the mirror, and he couldn't work out what the look meant. But then she smiled as he kissed her head, inhaling the smell of coconut shampoo.

"I know you're busy, princess, just dropping in. What time are you finished here?"

It was not news to Tomb how fine as fuck his wife was because he was the deranged fucker who put a guy in check when he'd tried to pat Nina's ass one time. Thinking he had a shot with her. How fucking bright was he when he went home with a broken hand?

Of fucking course, Tomb was punching above his weight.

She could have had any guy she wanted, and she'd picked his sorry soul.

When she turned around, he flashed her a smile. Their size difference was funny, and he fucking loved it. Even though Nina was small, she had a lot of confidence and a fierce temper. The times she slept curled up on Tomb's chest, he realized she had fixed something he didn't know was broken. Sappy fuck, he was. Thank fuck he didn't spout that shit out loud, or he'd lose his masculinity.

"Oh, hey." She smiled softly. "About seven, why?"

"I'll pick up dinner."

Her eyebrows shot up. "You'll be home tonight?"

A pang of guilt hit his midsection. He couldn't blame her for the innocent question, remembering how often she must have eaten alone this week. And last week. Last month. Too many absent times to count.

"Yeah, I'll be at home. Is there anything you fancy to eat?"

When her forehead wrinkled, she hesitated to answer. Tomb relied on gut instinct, and the tight dread in his stomach said she was holding something back from him.

But then Nina smiled. "Whatever you want is fine with me."

"Walk me out, baby." He said, cuffing her wrist, not giving her a choice but to follow him outside. Only then, when they were out of eyeshot of the wide window, he pressed Nina into the wall.

Everything Tomb ever wanted was standing in front of him. But something was off with her. He just couldn't put his finger on what it was. And that wasn't his Nina. She was open with her thoughts and opinions.

Nina was beauty itself, not only the outside package. She was a complete knockout, but her heart was pure gold, and everyone warmed to her.

Unable to help himself, Tomb shot forward as if catapulted from a cannon and got his wife's mouth the way he'd been hungering to take it. By forcing her lips wide, he swallowed her startled gasp. Whatever hesitancy she'd had didn't matter when he invaded her. Then her tongue swirled around his, and her taste bolted heat to his dick.

When her sweetness saturated his tongue, Tomb realized it had been endless days since he'd kissed his wife.

She should be kissed every day, multiple times.

Especially when she mewled, clinging to his chest with hard nails digging through his shirt. *Fuck*, she whined for him in that way he loved, all sweet and yielding. He remembered they were in public and ended the kiss, but held her close.

"Missed you, princess."

"Yeah?" she blinked her opaque eyes.

"Yeah," he smirked, brushing a lock of hair.

"I should get back in. I left my client." Nina slipped out from the cage he'd made with his body and headed for the door, but looked back. "I'll see you at home." Again, she offered a smile, but it didn't reach her eyes like it usually did.

"Is something wrong?"

"What could be wrong?"

"I don't know, you tell me."

"I'll see you at home if you're there." Then she disappeared back into the salon. When Tomb looked through the window, Nina was her usual effervescent self as she fussed over her client and called out something to Ross.

I'll see you at home *if you're there*.

He wasn't hard of hearing. He caught her emphasizing the last part.

Now he was left to wonder what shit had his wife's panties in a twist.

Nina

If the Diablos owned half of Laketon, then Emilio Conti aspired to own the other half.

He repeatedly liked to brag about his rags-to-riches story about leaving Vernazza, Italy, for new beginnings in the States, as though he thought he was the Godfather himself.

Emilio was just an insignificant man with an inflated ego. Nina could see him for what he was, and that was a con man with exaggerated ideals and a lot of bullshit. Had she known who he was today, she'd never have leased a store from him, but back then, she'd been excited about her salon and didn't understand much about the commerce world, and he'd been offering reasonable prices.

Those low-rate prices were long gone under inflation and incredible fucking greed.

There was never an instance she wasn't irritated when he showed up. He had no reason to since she dropped off the rent check personally to his office every month without fail.

She was preoccupied with the thought of Tomb's unexpected visit and wasn't paying attention to a G-Wagon outside.

Sighing, Nina watched Emilio slide his tan loafers out and adjust the charcoal dress jacket. Gold dripped off every part of his body like he thought he was in a 90s rapper video. He wanted people to see his wealth, not understanding it was tacky.

Ignoring the double tap on the door, she prayed her landlord would go away, not in the mood for whatever lousy news he was toting with him. Once again, he tapped, louder this time, and she expelled air, turning to see him watching her with a simpering smile. If Nina had to pluck a man out of a stereotypical Italian mobster movie, Emilio would be that man. He spoke faultless English but hadn't lost his distinct accent.

"Mr. Conti. Is there something you need?" she asked at the door. The asshole stepped forward, forcing Nina to inch back and allow him inside. She closed the door but left it unlocked. She didn't get an unsafe vibe, but that didn't mean she wanted to be in a confined building with him.

"I've told you, Nina, call me Emilio. All my friends do."

We're not friends.

"You're my landlord. It wouldn't be appropriate." She told him and saw he enjoyed the fake respect.

"I insist." He looked around, feigning interest, but this was what he did before he dropped the hammer on whatever shit he had to deliver.

It began a few years back. The first rent increase. It was expected, but how he'd worded it made it sound like it was for protection. His *pay or else* was very much implied in his snake-like tone.

Women were born with dickhead radars, to survive in a world that seemed to hate them. It was instinctual to sense when a man wasn't being genuine. He gave off all the dickhead vibes. The rent increased every six months after that, with hardly any notice.

And now the salon was successful, making it even more challenging to consider moving location.

"I was just about to go home," she said.

"Of all my properties, this is the classiest, Nina," he remarked, adjusting his cufflinks at each wrist. "I say it every time. It's classy. You've done well for yourself."

"Thank you."

He smiled. It was like facing a hungry predator within striking distance. Having grown up dirt poor without a nickel to her name most days, owning a business meant something to Nina. Despite feeling uneasy, she'd dealt with bigger bullies in the past and would let no one intimidate her as Emilio took an envelope out of his pocket.

Here it goes, she thought.

She couldn't afford another rent increase so soon. She was paying too damn much already. Some months, she didn't take a cut from the profits. She was content as long as she had enough to pay her staff and the bills. But if Emilio put more on the rent, balancing the bills and keeping her team would be impossible. But she couldn't see a way not to have her people. Each one was vital to their role in the salon.

"You know I hate doing this."

Yeah, right, you greedy fucking snake.

"Times are tight, but I have overheads to meet, Nina."

"How much this time?" she snapped.

Emilio smiled and approached to hand over the envelope like he was enjoying the drama of fucking up her day. She tore it open and nearly choked seeing the figure.

"This can't be right." She blinked. "It's an extra fifteen hundred a month. I can't afford that."

"They are competitive rates, Nina. For this size property, you have one of my biggest stores."

"Competitive where? Harrods? This is Laketon, and that price is a fucking joke." She regretted showing her despair when Emilio only smiled wider, tucking both hands into the front pockets of his jeans.

"You could always find somewhere else. But I think you like this spot, *si*?"

"Yes," she answered through her teeth while her brain frantically worked through math that wouldn't math. There was no way to afford that much on top of everything else. "Is there a way to postpone? I'm not a problematic tenant, and you've never had to chase a payment."

Even the thought of telling her staff she'd be closing the salon made Nina feel sick. It wasn't only her business. Those people relied on her for their livelihood. Her shoulders felt heavy with burden.

"There are ways and means for everything, *bella*." He circled her as a shark would in the sea, scenting blood. She didn't like his suggestion or his fucking nearness, and she went to step back until Emilio dared put a hand on her by gripping her chin. "I like this little shop, Nina, it's very…" he skimmed her body before rising to her face where she saw unmasked lust in his eyes. "pretty. I do not want you to lose it. If you need help, you only have to ask me nicely, *bella*."

The implication was clear, and as Nina knocked his touch away, disgust sat deep in her stomach.

This fucking man, who knew he held something important over her head, had the guts to suggest she pay him in other ways. Nina's hands clenched into two tight balls at her side, and her blood burned beneath her skin as Emilio continued smiling.

Before she could tell him to get the fuck out, he turned on his heels.

"Give it some thought, *bella*. Business does not always have to be so tedious, hm? There are many pleasures between friends who only want to help."

Nina stood frozen, watching until he drove away.

"That fucking prick." She shrieked. "The absolute fucking balls on that prick."

He'd just sexually propositioned her. Pay the rent increase or put out to him.

She shuddered with revulsion.

Leaving the salon clean-up for the morning, Nina took off home after locking up. The journey took no longer than usual, but her head was whirling, so she arrived home within a blink. Pulling into the driveway, she parked next to Tomb's Harley.

Entering the kitchen through a small utility room, she felt a different burden on her shoulders, having left one difficult conversation to face another.

Nina didn't know if she had the strength to face Tomb. He wouldn't be here any other night, but she smelled the dinner. Walking into the long hallway, she hooked her jacket and purse on the coat pegs, kicking off her shoes, which came next.

That's when she felt his presence.

Her skin came alive with sensation as if he'd touched her.

No woman thinking about a separation should feel that way.

If based solely on lust, she was the happiest woman on earth.

Lust was never the problem.

"Hey, baby. Long day?"

Just hearing his resonating timber voice made hunger lash through her belly.

"Yeah, the longest. How was yours?" She asked mechanically as Tomb came up behind, placing his hands on her shoulders, and pressed a kiss to the top of her head.

There was nothing in her field of vision, only building tears, with the inexplicable urge to fall into Tomb's barrel chest and cry over her woes.

But more than half of those woes were about him.

She listened to his short answer about his day, then watched him plate up the dinner. He'd brought home her favorite Greek food. He scooped a little of everything onto a plate. "Do you wanna eat in here or in front of the TV?

"The TV." She answered automatically, knowing she couldn't take the silence if they ate in the kitchen. She could count on one hand the number of times they'd eaten dinner together this month, and the number was pitifully low.

"Get comfortable," he told her. "I'll bring it through."

"I can get it."

"You look tired, princess. Sit down."

Again, the tears threatened the back of her eyes, so she quickly did as he said, choosing the wide gray cuddle seat to curl up in.

The food was delicious, the right amount of spice she enjoyed, but it chewed like sand in her mouth as she ate on autopilot. Once finished, she leaned forward when her plate was half empty and let it rest on the matching ottoman. Having not taken a lick of notice of whatever was showing on TV.

Wordlessly, when Tomb had finished his plate, he rose and took the dishes to the kitchen, returning with a fresh beer and a glass of wine for her.

Each time, no exceptions, her pulse rollicked madly in her veins when she laid her eyes on Tomb. She was excited because the man she loved more than anything was nearby.

She was stupid.

Many would tell her so.

She had a man who provided for her better than anyone else.

Bills were taken care of.

She had a brand new car, which he ensured she never had to fill with gas. Ever. When it was time to switch out for winter tires, they were done without her having to think about it. Tomb was not greedy at all. If she wanted something, she got it without an argument.

But what she wanted most of all couldn't be bought.

And she was afraid it wasn't in her husband to give her.

Why rock the boat if she was going to lose?

Many women put up with less and were miserable with men who weren't good like Tomb.

How could she explain it when the gaping ache was in her heart?

It wasn't bruises.

It wasn't cheating.

Love, even one-sided, should be enough.

Incredible, leg-shaking sex should be more than enough.

What was to miss, anyway? His lack of appearance at the dinner table? Laughing at the TV together? Going on long walks and romantic dates? She couldn't miss what she didn't have. But she could miss his presence, which she missed a lot.

Even now, in the same room, she missed him.

Grabbing her hand, Tomb brought her to a stop before she could slip out of the room.

His eyes were so deep, and she fell into them effortlessly, pulled into his gravitational aura.

"You wanna tell me what's wrong?"

Nina's heart pumped hard, dragging dread around her bloodstream.

Did he know what she'd been thinking about for weeks?

Would he hate her if he did?

Could he sense her inner turmoil? What was the best for both of them? Because she reckoned if she wasn't happy, how could he be?

"Nothing is wrong," she smiled. "It's been a long day, a long week. Lots of new clients at the salon."

It wasn't altogether a big lie. The week had been long, compounded by the trouble brought by her landlord. Plus, her intern ran the salon's social media presence and gained much traction last month, bringing in new customers.

Tomb looked at her as though he could dig around in her brain. "You sure?"

"I'm just tired. A shower and bed will fix me."

There was another beat of silence while Tomb's eyes bore into her, then he smiled and tugged on her hand. "Give me a kiss before you shower."

She'd never been able to resist him.

That was part of her confusion. Intimacy clouded her feelings often because their sex life was *so* exuberant and *satisfying*. Leaning down, she tapped a long, closed-lipped kiss to his mouth, his beard tickling her chin. His hand stole underneath her hair and squeezed her neck, giving Nina delicious licks of pleasure over his rough handling.

"I could join you if you want company," he rasped, scratching her scalp. That timber once more stroked over her skin like a lover's tender touch. His meaning was clear.

Having a fantastic sex life, her body heated at his suggestion, she could easily fall into sex with Tomb, like the million other times before, and forget the problems weighing on her mind. Endure the loneliness for a while longer.

The temptation in his eyes as he caressed the back of her neck was like being offered the freedom to a shoe store. Something she thought she'd never turn down, but she dipped away from his hand and broke the electrical charge zipping between them.

"I'm only going to shower fast before I fall into bed. Another time."

She was miserable as she walked away from Tomb, unable to turn back to see if he was suspicious about her excuse. She'd intended to talk to him tonight, and lay it out on the table, but after the day she'd had, especially what occurred, she was emotionally drained.

Wrecking her life and breaking her heart would wait for another day, she supposed.

The shower took next to no time since it wasn't a hair-washing day. After going through the steps of her skincare routine, she pulled on one of Tomb's t-shirts, her preferred bed attire. The thing was like a sack, and Tomb always laughed when she wore his stuff, but she loved it.

The bed depressed sometime later, the TV in their spacious bedroom switched on, and the volume turned down almost immediately. Tomb enjoyed watching the nightly news, though she didn't know why, because it was always depressing. Someone was always getting murdered or going missing.

She regulated her breathing when she felt him leaning over her, and his hand slid under the covers to curl that massive paw around her hip. Couples didn't need to ask for sex. Or at least, they'd never needed to. There were clues when one of them was in the mood. Nina could tell Tomb she needed a good dicking just by glancing at him. Tomb's way was touching her, like now. Rolling over and opening her legs for him would be natural. She'd plunge into two orgasms and sleep like an angel after a sugar binge. But for once, she wasn't allowing her sex organs to rule over the entire ship.

So she feigned sleep, and Tomb, after a moment of touching her, tapped a kiss to the side of her head. She eventually fell asleep to the quiet sounds of the newscasters talking.

Unsure what woke her, the room was pitch black, and the blue light of the nightstand clock told Nina it was only 2 a.m. She stretched out her arm to curl into Tomb's bigger body; he was usually warm like a stove, but her fingers only encountered cold sheets. Confused, she raised her head from the pillow, expecting to see the shine from underneath the bathroom door. But the house was dark and still.

Huh. Sleep disappeared from her brain, and she sat in bed, flipping on the nightstand lamp. Where was he? It was then she noted the dresser top was empty. That was where Tomb dropped his wallet, phone, and spare change from his pockets. Slipping out of bed, Nina padded to the window where she could see the carport, and what she saw made her feel queasy.

Tomb's Harley was gone.

He'd actually left their bed to go out.

Oh, now she was mad.

It escalated from her toes until the top of her head felt like it might explode. Had he sneaked out of the house?

No prizes for guessing where he was, either.

Snatching up her charging phone, she thumbed out a message.

Nina: Where are you?

She didn't have to wait long before the dots danced on the screen, and Tomb's message came through.

Tomb: I'm at the clubhouse

Nina: Are you for real? Did you sneak out of bed to go to the club? It's after 2.

Tomb: Something came up. Will explain later, baby.

Yeah. Sure. *Right*.

She bet an emergency party needed his attention. Beers to drink, laughs to have. A wife to avoid.

Story of her fucking life.

She'd known about bikers and their nomadic, couldn't be tied down, lifestyle. She then observed it up close for herself during the years with Tomb before and after marriage. Nothing changed in between, not as she thought it would. She'd foolishly thought marriage would come first. Time and attention with each other. And though she enjoyed the biker way of living, to a point, she didn't want to be constantly locked into whatever shit they were into.

She was in her forties and no longer wanted to party every night. Those wild days were long in her past.

A husband who didn't leave their bed in the middle of the night to hang with his buddies, and women willing to fuck a married man, shouldn't be something Nina had to ask for.

But here she was.

And now she couldn't go back to sleep.

3 a.m. came and went. So did five and then six.

By that time, Nina was fit for nothing short of murder.

Tomb hadn't come home. She was so sure he'd ride home once he saw her text.

Why did being wrong hurt so much?

She loved her husband more than anything or anyone. But she'd had enough. The end of her tolerance had been reached. So when Nina dressed for the day, she did it patiently and without a rush. The task she underwent took some time, and emotion kicked up a fuss in her chest, but she refused to let it free, or she'd bawl her eyes out for days.

No, she *had* to do this.

If the neighbor across the street wondered why Nina was stuffing three bags into the trunk of her car that morning, she didn't pry. Nina waved to the older lady who walked her dog about fifteen times a day, and then she climbed in and headed away from the house.

Her mood was sour.

It was in the dumps. Her heart felt battered and bruised. But the overall feeling was she'd had enough of being an afterthought.

Marriage was more. Or it should be.

It shouldn't feel this empty in her chest.

And she was about to give Tomb the biggest wake-up of his life.

Tomb

Tomb might like to think he'd accumulated some intelligence in his forty years.

But nothing could have prepared him for what was barreling toward him.

He rested a hip against the corner of a tool-heavy workbench and sipped at the hot brew Scarlett had brought to the garage only moments ago. That chick might go toe-to-toe with her old man and make Axel react in unstable ways, but she sure knew how to make a decent cup of joe. He drained the cup and left it sitting on the bench. Thanks to the events of last night, he was running on fumes while he worked on car engines.

There was never a dull day being a Diablo.

The last year had been peaceful since Ruin eradicated his trouble-making brother with his revenge plan against the club, and the prospect who'd aligned himself with the wrong side.

Fresh trouble always came along, and like clockwork, it had appeared recently, and now the Diablos had shit to sort out before it escalated.

Tomb rubbed a hand over his tired face, wondering if there was time to duck inside to get some shut-eye for a few hours. His twenties were long gone, and he needed more than an hour of sleep. He was fucking tired.

"What'd you think Axel will do?" he caught Splice asking. The SGT. AT. ARMS was usually found touring their glut of legal businesses to ensure they were all running smoothly, but after the late-night call-out last night, the patched brothers had stuck close to the club to discuss tactics.

"Dunno yet."

"Ruin should just wipe him out."

Tomb chuckled and caught Bash's eye-roll. The guy was sitting with an iPad on his lap, doing some secretary shit. Tomb didn't know exactly what that meant, sitting on the boss's lap, maybe. Who the fuck knew? But Bash took his work seriously.

"We can't tag the enforcer in to go apeshit every time someone irritates us, Splice."

"Why not? Ruin loves it."

What Tomb knew for sure about their enforcer was he loved his old lady and his twin brother. And he suspected Ruin only did club shit, for Reno's sake. He was a master at his craft, though.

"We'll reassess when Denver's out of hospital." Luckily, the stab wound hadn't been life-threatening, and he'd been kept overnight for observation.

"You think that cute little nurse is looking after him?" asked Splice. Tomb bit his cheek because he knew what Splice was doing. Bash growled without looking up from the iPad. "You put Charlotte's name on your tongue, brother, and you'll be walking fucking funny the rest of the day."

Splice thought this was hilarious and winked at Tomb, intent on winding Bash up further about the nurse he was chasing.

"Why can't I say Lottie's name? You've had a year to stake a claim, brother. As far as I see it, that's enough time. Let someone else take over."

The idiot might as well have signed his broken legs decree.

Tomb shook his head and let Splice fight his boyish battles. After hearing a bike start-up, he shifted his butt off the bench and walked to the doorway. It was only Ruin, and he cocked his chin up to the enforcer, but then a car pulling into the gates caught his attention. Recognizing Nina's Escalade. He grinned, liking the surprise.

Behind him, he heard Bash threaten a cackling Splice. As much as the guy liked to make the brothers fly off the handle, Splice wouldn't step on a brother's toes over women they wanted to claim. It was why Tomb trusted Splice to be near Nina so much.

He had no insight his world was about to blow the fuck apart, though.

When his thorny rose jumped down from the Escalade, he expected one of her saucy smiles. The kind that turned his stomach inside out and his brain fucking feral to maul her on the floor. The heart in Tomb's chest gave a kick, sending the beat into free fall when his nasty gaze wandered over the tight jeans molding her ass. He knew precisely how that ass fitted into his palms and latched around his giving dick.

Nina's actions made him realize something was off. She went to the trunk and took out a large sports bag. Sending an angry-filled stare his way, she threw it down near his feet.

A confused scowl pulled down his brow. "The fuck, princess?" Tomb could only speculate she was pissed about him not waking her last night.

Half-amused and always turned on by her, Tomb stepped forward to grasp her around the waist but didn't get a chance when Nina pointed a finger. An emotionally quiet tone replaced her usually loud voice.

"You wanna be single? Tell the club sluts they have my blessing."

What the actual fuck? He thought it was a joke for a second and waited for the smile to cut across her face.

The smile never came.

The anger remained, but he saw deeper than that. He could read Nina's face like a well-used book, and she looked hurt.

He looked from the bag to Nina. "What's going on?" she was like a cat backed into a corner as he tried to approach, but two more bags came from the trunk and joined the other on the ground; she shot him another stare and climbed behind the wheel.

It happened in under a minute, and Tomb's jaw became slack. There wasn't even the time to round to the driver's side before his wife tore out of the compound without another word.

"Whoa. Did Nina dump your clothes here?" asked Splice, sidling up to Tomb. "What did you do?"

"You guys have the weirdest kind of foreplay, my brother." Chimed Bash. But Tomb was moving; he rushed into the garage to grab the key to his Harley from inside his leather jacket. Dressed only in his overalls, he hoofed it over to his parked bike and started it in moments.

What Bash didn't know was this shit wasn't one of their epic sex-instigated fights everyone had witnessed. This wasn't his Nina flirting to get him riled up, because there was no teasing when she tossed his shit on the floor.

And to mention the sweet bottoms like she thought he was fucking cheating on her? He only hoped her anger was talking, and she didn't believe that, or he swore to God she was about to feel how red his hand made her little ass.

A sexy fight he could handle; he loved her volatile temper, but knowing she was hurt made him feel physically sick, so he broke the speed record to get out of the gates. Fortunately, his Nina drove like she had Miss Daisy in the back, so it took no time for him to catch up to her on the long stretch of road. His focus locked onto the Escalade, his mind going in all directions, wondering how she'd ever think he'd cheat on her.

The actual fuck. He was already punching above his weight, landing a goddess like her. No way would another woman match up to

Nina. He hadn't looked at another woman since she first captivated his attention.

Increasing the Harley's speed, he came up alongside the Escalade. Nina's eyes widened, but then she scowled and turned away. Tomb went faster, passing her by, going up ahead; he cut her off, so she automatically had to slow to a stop. Once Tomb knocked down the stand with his foot, he swung his leg off the seat and strode to her.

The door was locked when he tried it. He tapped his knuckles on the window when she had no intention of opening it. "Open this door right now, Nina, or I'll rip it off its hinges."

"Ha, I'd like to see you try." She sassed. She had no idea the level of determination flowing through his blood.

"Don't test me."

She rolled her eyes, but the lock depressed, and he wrenched the door open. Nina sat like a regal queen, facing forward with her arms folded.

"You wanna explain what that little show was all about?"

"It was not a show. And you're such a man, if that's what you think."

"I am a man, sweetheart; don't make me remind you."

"Ha." She snorted. "Typical. You can't win an argument, so the dick threats come out."

Wanting to tear at his hair, he sighed. "Jesus Christ, Nina. Just tell me what made you dump my clothes at the club."

It was then she fired a stare his way, and again, he was hit in the chest by how hurt she looked. She flinched when he attempted to reach for her, and the move poured ice through his body. She always wanted his hands on her, even when they fought.

"Seriously, you ask me that, Rome?" she chewed on her lip, shaking her head. Right then, Tomb knew this stunt wasn't one of her detailed foreplay games. Whatever she was thinking, it was as severe as a heart attack.

He unhooked Nina from the seatbelt, pulled her legs out of the car, and barricaded her in. Dropping his head down, he looked directly into her eyes.

"Yeah, baby, I ask that because I don't know what's happening. Other than you're pissed at me, my clothes are on the compound floor, and you throw some shit at my face about being single." That made his back molars crunch together. Of all the shit she could have said in anger, that bothered him the most. "Do you think I'm cheating on you?"

"I don't know anymore." She said, decimating him. That meant he'd failed as her husband if she doubted where his loyalty was. "I know you're never away from the clubhouse, which makes me wonder what the attraction is. There's only one, as far as I can tell."

"Nina…"

"You left the house in the middle of the night, Rome!" she snapped. "I'm tired of it. I'm tired of all of it."

Resting a hand on top of the car roof, he caught the tone of her words. *I'm tired of all of it,* and Tomb knew he'd have to revisit that, but he needed to explain first. Should have taken the time last night.

"You were exhausted, and I didn't wanna wake you. I didn't go to the club for a party. Denver was in an altercation last night and ended up in hospital with a stab wound."

Nina gasped, snapping to attention.

"Is he okay?"

Her concern was evident. She cared about the club brothers and their families; it was one of the many things that made Nina who she was. He couldn't have conjured up a better woman to bring into his lifestyle.

"Yeah, they'll cut him loose to go home today; he spent the night bitching. But that's where I was, baby. We got the call, and we scrambled. You know how it is."

"Yeah, I know how it is. But you should have told me."

"I knew you were safer at home." Their home was wired better than Alcatraz, and his priority when any club mess went down was to ensure Nina was secure.

She shrugged, looking away. Tomb didn't fucking like that one bit. She constantly gave him her eyes. "That was last night. The excuses aren't always dire, though, are they? And you still prefer to be there than at home."

Fucking never.

Tomb was only now realizing how much he'd fucked up.

Unable to help himself, he had to touch her, so he cupped her cheek, turning her to face him. "Listen to me, princess."

"Don't princess me."

He smiled. "You're always my princess, you know this, even when you wanna kick my ass. You wanna kick my ass right now, don't you?"

"I've been thinking about it."

"I should have woken you. That's on me. But cheating on you? For fuck's sake, Nina, you know better than that."

He moved his torso lower to edge inside the car with her and saw how her eyes flashed from anger to warmth and vulnerability.

"Do I? You're still not answering, just dancing around it."

Tomb gritted his teeth but leaned closer until his lips almost brushed against hers. The fire in her eyes was like a siren to him, calling out to tame her wildness until she purred. Every instinct he'd masked came flooding to the forefront of his mind. In these unfettered times, Tomb wanted to dominate every inch of Nina's life. Then she'd understand how silly her cheating thoughts were because she'd *feel* how much he belonged to her.

"Woman," he growled, "I'm not fucking cheating on you now or fucking ever."

And then he crushed her lips in a bruising kiss.

It was the only thing he could think to do before he exploded and took her over his knee to deliver a few short spanks, leaving his handprint behind on her ass.

Ownership in its most sordid form.

"Open your mouth for me, princess." He growled low, biting gently on her bottom lip. When she gasped, Tomb slid inside with his tongue and tasted all her anger in long, lashing strokes.

He grabbed the back of Nina's neck, she resisted before giving in and kissing him back passionately. She inclined into his chest, winding her arms around his neck. Her fingers found the back of his hair, and she tugged. *So fucking good.*

"Wait, wait, *wait*," she protested weakly, still biting his mouth, when Tomb went for the zipper on her jeans. Nina's hand caught at his wrist, but she wasn't shoving him away, so he slid down the zipper and flicked the button open.

Every inch of Tomb, especially the hard inches pulsing between his legs, said to fuck the submission out of his wife here and now, but if he got his cock into her, he'd want to stay there for hours.

Tomb would give Nina anything she asked for within his power, but not freedom.

He didn't have that in him to give, even if he wanted to, which he didn't.

"We fought; now I get to make you feel good," He told her, roaming his mouth over her cheek before he dove for her mouth, greedy as ever to steal her taste. It was never enough. How much he glutted himself on Nina, he was still starved for more.

Sometimes, he wondered how he'd muted his greedy, over-the-top possessive side, letting it bubble beneath the surface. Because she made him unbalanced to control her like a madman with no plan, making her life his only project. His personal heaven. His only precious thing.

Only the fear she'd hate every second, turning her love for him sour, meant Tomb only allowed that side out when they were in bed.

In bed, Nina let him dominate, begged for it, trusting him to give her the pleasure she craved.

He experienced it now as she moaned into his mouth. She never suppressed how she wanted him and the sexy way she put her pleasure in his hands.

Nina kissed him deeply, and he touched her intimately despite the limited space her tight pants allowed. Still, he was a resourceful bastard when he had to be, and he shoved deeper until he palmed the heat of her covered pussy.

The patch of road they'd stopped on was quiet, but that didn't mean a vehicle couldn't drive by at any moment. To a do-gooder, they might see it as Tomb attacking her from the way he had Nina locked in. He'd hate to break someone's arm for interfering, but he wouldn't accept anyone getting between him and his wife.

"*Wait.* Not here, Tomb," she breathed, fisting her fingers in his hair, angling her body into his. A counter-protest to what her swollen lips were saying. "This doesn't fix anything."

Without a clue what needed fixing, putting an orgasm through Nina wouldn't hurt, and he was savage enough to do it there, in the only way he could dominate her.

"*Right now*, princess," he replied. Sucking his mark on her neck until she cried out when his fingers penetrated her panties, and he fondled the wetness along her slit. Whatever her lying tongue said, her body was *ready*. Attuned to every cue her body gave him, Tomb pounced when she relented before latching onto his mouth with a dick-breaking kiss.

Finger-fucking her on the side of the road wasn't ideal. But he worked with what he could, and Tomb pounded steadily. The flat of his palm hit her clit as his digits slipped deeper into the spongy part of her cunt that brought whimpers out of Nina.

Sounds he'd usually swallow and devour, to force more from her throat for hours on end until he could savagely fuck his wife into a blissful coma.

Time and all that. He gripped her around the back of the neck and wrung the pleasure out of her until he felt the first tremble against his fingers. Then she exploded with only a puff of air expelled from her lips to let him know how hard she enjoyed the orgasm.

With more room and time, he would have buried his face between her legs, licked her clean until she dragged handfuls of hair from his head, and begged for more.

His Nina was constantly greedy, and he was happy to supply the fix. He was frustrated, withdrawing his fingers free but consoled himself by licking them clean, one slow suck at a time. Her eyes were all dark and sultry, watching him.

He realized he'd had his oil-stained hands all over her like a dirty bastard, and Tomb grinned. *Satisfied.*

"You had no right," she stabbed a finger in his chest. All her lust from seconds ago washed away in a dirty little scowl.

"Do I need to play the husband card? Didn't you have fun, princess?"

"I didn't want fun. I wanted you to listen, but why change a habit of a lifetime, huh? Sex doesn't fix things."

That was the second time she'd said that. Tomb's eyes narrowed as he watched her lean back so she could fasten the jeans. She swung her legs back into the car.

"What needs fixing?"

Nina sighed and shook her head, putting a hand on her stomach as if to hold in whatever she wanted to say.

"Nina, tell me. How can I make it right when you don't tell me what *it* is? You made a show back there for my attention."

Her eyes flashed. "I made a show? You would think that. I stopped trying for your attention a long time ago, Rome, not that you ever noticed. You notice nothing, and nothing touches you, right? Our perfect little marriage where we do our own thing until it's time to fuck. Not everything can be solved with sex. But you just proved you think it can. Nina is in a snit, so finger-fuck her into submission to shut her up."

Each word came like a silent bullet, hitting the target in the middle of his chest. Had she been screaming at him, he would think she wanted his attention before a raucous round of sex. But she delivered her speech so fucking quietly he was hit all over with pain.

"Sweetheart, I didn't…" he trailed off when her following words brought a blow he hadn't expected.

"I can't keep doing this…" Nina stuttered, emotion in her voice as she met his eyes, and Tomb saw hers swimming with unshed tears. "I need to get to work. Can you let me close the door, please? And Rome?" she paused, chewed on her lip, and inhaled a shudder. "I think it's time we admit this isn't working. At least for me, it isn't. And how you assume our life is great only makes it worse. This isn't easy to say, but we should separate for a while."

Tomb prided himself on being one step ahead of any decision, anticipating what was needed, and striving to see it done.

But this took the fucking ground out from underneath him.

Those words ricocheted inside his ribcage like steel claws.

Standing there on I-15 as a heavy goods truck approached from the distance, his ears rang with his wife telling him their marriage was over.

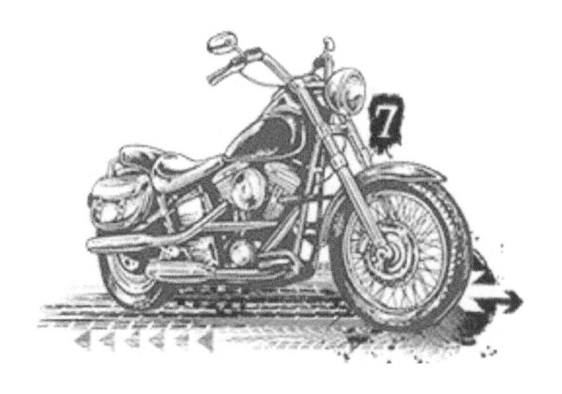

Tomb

O ver.
    His.
    Dead.

Body.

That would never happen.

Not while he had breath in his body.

Tomb's father left when he was eleven, bringing peace to their family for the first time and taking his alcohol-fueled harm with him. While he'd prayed for it every night, it still shocked him when it happened.

But nothing since then had broached that same feeling.

Until he glowered at an emotionally distraught Nina.

"You think I'm gonna let you drive off after you say that to me?"

"Please, Tomb. I'm already late."

"It's your salon, sweetheart. You don't need to show up if you don't want to." He tried to reason as his insides fucking charred to ashes. He reached into the car, and she flinched back from him like he was an abuser. She looked remorseful and said, "Sorry, I can't have you touching me. You know I succumb too easily."

Not touch his wife?

She might as well have shot him between the eyes.

But Tomb gritted his teeth and pulled his hand back. Nothing about his instincts said to leave her alone.

"Explain how you want to end our marriage."

Even saying those words made him feel violently sick.

Was he so short-sighted that he'd missed something all this time?

Obvious-fucking-ly.

Nina's confession left her looking resigned, and Tomb couldn't accept that it could happen, so he had to uncover the root cause.

"Not here. I shouldn't have said anything now."

Damn right. "But you did. You packed and dumped my stuff. That's not spontaneous, Nina."

She sighed, and all his instincts were to soothe her, to tell her everything would be okay, and he'd make her smile again. But he didn't know how to do that if he couldn't touch her.

A lot of their marriage was based around his hands being on her. It was the only time, he realized, when she was fully open to him.

If Nina thought he was stubborn, then his darling thorny rose was a locked box that opened only sparingly. And he'd lived for those moments like a drug addict, high on her.

"No, you're right. It wasn't spontaneous. It's been building inside me for a long time."

A long time. Where the fuck had he been?

"I really need to get to work. There's shit going on that I need to sort through."

Narrowing his eyes, he heard a worried tenor in her voice he didn't like.

"What shit?"

"Oh, just salon stuff, but I have to be there."

"You don't think telling me our marriage is done is worth a conversation?"

Nina's head reared up, and she *finally* looked at him. Goddamn, this woman undid him completely, turned him savage in the darkest ways until Tomb felt he could punch through the earth's center to find her again.

Something was happening with her, and he was determined to find out what she was hiding, even if it meant standing on the side of the road forever.

"Yeah, I do. But when are you ever home, Tomb? When do you sit around the house so I have time to talk to you? Do you know how shocked I was when you visited the salon yesterday? How surprised I was when you said you'd be home for dinner. You're somewhere else if you're not on the road running club errands. Unless I put myself in *your space*, I hardly see you until we're in bed."

All this time, Tomb thought he'd been holding himself in check, balancing his darker needs so they didn't boil over onto Nina until she hated him.

"I shouldn't have said anything yet. I'm sorry." Nina looked seconds away from crying, and he hated knowing why. In the distance, he caught sight of a truck heading their way. The noise trundled louder the closer it got, and he partially closed her door and stepped nearer to the Escalade so it didn't clip him.

He wished she'd said nothing at all. Wished she didn't feel the need to say anything.

"I really need to go." She repeated, and Tomb absently nodded, but he didn't think he could speak sense without exploding. He swallowed and met her eyes.

This woman who owned him could ask him to slaughter a village of innocent people, and he'd do it.

As devastated and angry as he was, Tomb had to clarify something to his rebellious wife. Once the truck passed them by, he opened her door. He watched how she tried to hold her recoil at bay when he leaned into the Escalade, but he wouldn't let her evade him this time when he fastened an oil-dried hand around the back of her neck.

Her eyelids flickered, and he felt her soften.

Little liar, his wife was.

He didn't discount her feelings and never would. Whatever Nina was thinking, that shit was real to her, and he'd get to that. But she didn't want their marriage to end any more than he wanted Venus to fall out of the solar system.

He'd gotten everything so fucking wrong, hadn't he?

Tomb had assumed he couldn't be himself because he wanted her so fucking badly, needed her, whatever he had to do.

What did he have to lose now if he unlocked every nasty padlock he'd ever used to harness his inner psyche?

He sure as shit wasn't losing the only precious thing he owned.

And there were no lies detected by saying he *owned* his Nina girl.

Now, she needed to feel his truth, too.

"You can go to work, princess, but if you think you can drop a bomb like that on me, and I'll meekly scuttle off with my tail tucked between my legs, you married the wrong man. And Nina? You married the *right fucking man*, you hearing me?" He leaned in closer, their mouths almost touching, and he watched her lips trembling, inhales increased. He recognized those cues because he'd studied her like she was the only important thing in this world.

Her mouth wanted kissing.

"We'll talk this out until we turn blue if necessary."

She tried to shake her head, but he clasped her neck, and she moaned, her eyes closing now. Her hand came to his chest, and whether she was aware of it, she held fast to the muscle tee.

Nothing in this life would make Tomb accept losing her.

Death would be the only thing that could separate them. And even then, he'd fight the devil with every ounce of cunning power to keep her for a minute longer.

So, throwing in the towel before he knew what needed fixing… never happening.

He smiled once Nina pinged her eyes open again, but the happiness was short-lived because Tomb understood he was in for the fight of his life.

Ding-fucking-ding, bring it on.

Nina was his wife.

The only wife he'd ever wanted.

"But ending our marriage?" he skimmed a kiss to her sweet-smelling cheek.

So fucking obsessed with her.

If only she knew she owned him right back in obsessive ways.

But she was about to.

He would toss all his cards on the table and reveal his hand if he was in trouble of losing everything that meant something to him.

"That isn't happening, *ever*, princess. You're my wife, and you *will* stay my wife."

"Tomb..." she shuddered, and he let her go reluctantly.

"I'm glad you said something to me, yeah? Now I know something is broken and needs repairing. But we'll talk about this later. I'll find you if you try to avoid me."

She snorted and fired her stubbornness at him with a scowl.

There she is. He bit the inside of his cheek to stop from smiling.

"It's not me who does the avoiding in this marriage."

"Fair point," he inclined his head. "Get to work safely." He shut her door and strode back to his bike, waiting until Nina finally pulled out in front of him. Their gazes sealed through the window.

She loved him.

He had to believe that, or he'd go nuclear.

She would have used it as a stake in his chest to escape their marriage if she didn't love him.

And for that, he had something to hold on to.

Tomb stayed braced on the bike seat long after Nina's car disappeared, his feet rooted to the road.

Plans were devised, which resulted in the same solution.

He wouldn't lose.

Nina

"He didn't!" Monroe gasped in Nina's ear.

"Oh, yeah. He told me I was his wife and was staying his wife."

Rubbing the side of her temple, she had a headache, which had increased over the morning and now was a full-blown annoyance. While on the call with Monroe, she rooted around her small office for a pain pill. She found three in the bottom of her purse and downed them dry.

"How did you react?"

"What could I do? We were on the side of the road. The maniac chased me down like he was Wyly Coyote, and he had to bring me an Acme anvil."

She heard Monroe chuckling. "I'm sorry, babe, but that's cute as hell."

Shaking her head, half-smiling, she sank into the pink leather chair and exhaled slowly. "Who's side are you on, friend?"

"I'm on team *I want your marriage to work*, you know that. I've been telling you for weeks to talk to him. Tomb is a man, and men are notoriously one-brained. They don't see it if it isn't put before them."

"Yeah, yeah. I'm a coward."

"You're far from that. Ending a marriage when you're wildly in love with your hubby can't be easy, but it's kicked him up the backside now, right?"

"Who knows? Tomb is good at giving the words I want to hear."

Nina didn't handle the situation well with Tomb this morning. She planned to talk to him more maturely but acted like a harpy by throwing his clothes in front of his boys. The shame settled in almost immediately. Thankfully, Monroe was at the clubhouse, and Nina had called to ask her friend to drop the bags off at home for her.

Unhinged love accurately demonstrated how her brain had been running on fumes, hurt, and inconsolable anger.

She'd wanted Tomb's attention; boy, had she gotten that.

Nina couldn't have conjured up that roadside scene in her wildest dreams. She left out the mention of the orgasm to Monroe because she didn't want to seem easy for letting him make her come right after trying to end their marriage. It was the very reason she couldn't have Tomb touching her. She fell apart so quickly under his hands. It was like her skin was hard-wired to fold under his superpower.

If only she could live on sex, she'd be the happiest woman on earth.

But she wanted more and deserved more.

If Tomb couldn't give her everything, then... then...

It was unbearable to think she could one day get it from a different man. Her entire existence was with him. He was the moon she rotated around, and pain stabbed Nina in every corner when she entertained the idea of someone meeting her needs that Tomb couldn't.

If it was sickening to imagine herself with a new partner in the future, then she'd be happy alone. She'd collect pets. Rory had a piglet. She could be a pet scorpion lady.

"Are you listening?"

Blinking, she put the phone back to her ear and apologized. "Sorry, I was miles away. What did you say?"

Monroe chuckled. "I was telling you it would be okay."

"Oh. Yeah. Maybe." Little hope was left, but her friend was deliriously happy in her marriage and wanted the same for everyone else.

"Are you going to give him the chance to talk it through? You only gave him the bare bones of your unhappiness, Nina."

"You sound like Tomb's PR team."

Another chuckle. "Sorry, you know I'm on your side. I love you, girl, but I'm not sorry for telling you that you're making a mistake if you walk away without attempting everything first. Be sure about decisions you can't take back."

It wasn't anything she hadn't told herself for months.

"I'm scared, Monroe."

"About what, babe?"

"Tomb will know why I'm unhappy, and nothing will change, or he'll say I'm too demanding in what I need."

"Then it's on him if he doesn't want to move the earth to make it right for you both. Can I stick my nose in for a minute?"

Amused, Nina moved her bangs out of the way to rub rhythmically at the pain in her skull. "Like you haven't already?"

"I married into that biker chaos, and you took me under your wing when I still hated Chains for forcing me into marriage."

"Darling, you never hated a hair on his mohawk head. You jumped his bones so fast." Laughed Nina, recalling the text from a newlywed Monroe telling her she'd fucked her husband. How phenomenal it had been, but she still hated his guts. Yeah, see how that worked out for them. Happy and in love with a husband whose whole being was about tending to Monroe's happiness.

Nina felt a pinch of envy but swallowed it down because she wasn't that woman to resent her friends' fortune.

"Yeah, well," chuckled Monroe, "he grew on me. And we're not talking about my marriage this time. So can I butt in?"

"Of course. Tell me your oh-so-wise words, my married little guru."

"You're resigned about it being a waste of time. To work at it, when nothing has changed in two years. But that's because you've held it in alone. Give it a chance when you *and* Tomb are working as a team. Try all avenues before you call it quits."

Resisting the urge to snap because that would be Nina's frustration speaking. Of course, she'd contemplated her relationship in many scenarios where everything worked perfectly.

But this wasn't a perfect world. Things rarely worked out. People settled for something they could tolerate.

But how fair was that to her or Tomb?

Maybe she wasn't the wife for him, after all.

A slice of pain ripped the breath out of her for even thinking about it.

No woman could ever love him in the same obsessive depths she loved him. That was a fact, if nothing else was true.

Monroe spoke when Nina's silence continued. "Do you love him still?"

"Of course, I love him," she replied quickly. "I wouldn't be here if I didn't."

"Then talk it out with him. Lay everything out there, Nina. Even if it makes you uncomfortable, or it might be something he doesn't want to hear. The good, the bad and the ugly. And then listen to him, too."

"You're wasted in accounting." She half-laughed, rising from her chair. Her break was over five minutes ago. Fortunately, she could lose herself in work, at least for the next few hours, before facing Tomb again. "You should try your hand at marriage counseling."

"Nah, I couldn't. I'd be a blunt bitch and would tell the man to spend more and for the woman to stop whining and take all that good dick."

Nina burst out laughing.

"It's sound advice."

"A good dicking can go a long way."

Hmmm… it could.

No man brought a better dick than Tomb brought to the table. Before Tomb, no man had ever spoken so graphically. She had no complaints about that side of their marriage.

Stop. She chastised; she couldn't fantasize about his prowess, or she'd crawl to him for a good round of fun and wicked games.

"My break is over, Mon. Thanks for listening."

"I'm always here for you. Will you be at the cookout later? It's for Denver's homecoming."

"Probably not. But is Casey going to let him out of the house?"

"You know the tough bikers and their ouchies. They never take them seriously. The cookout is planned anyway, even if Denver stays at home."

After their call ended, Nina returned to the salon floor and listened to her clients' stories while making them feel beautiful.

Tomb was rarely off her mind.

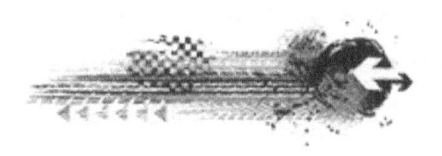

Tomb

Freshly showered and dressed in spare jeans and a shirt he kept at the clubhouse, Tomb strode to Axel's office. Remembering to thump his knuckles on the closed door at the last second. Or he might get *another* eyeful by striding in without announcement. No one needed to witness the club's First Lady horizontal across Axel's desk.

Axel had been pissed at Tomb like he'd made that shit happen on purpose.

Axel called to come in and found the prez alone in the office. "Tomb, brother." He was greeted. "Heard you had some drama this morning."

Tomb cursed the air blue. "From Splice, yeah? It was fucking Splice, that gossiping shithead."

Axel chuckled lightly, a palm wrapped around a mug of black coffee with a pile of papers in front of him. There was little envy for the boss and his leadership role within the MC. The man had to straddle lanes to keep the club in the black and evade the law. It wasn't easy, but bribed officials made the cogs turn easier.

At least Tomb had the vast open roads as part of his duties. Axel was trapped behind a desk making the deals and schmoozing people Tomb wouldn't piss on if they were on fire.

"He said Nina tossed your ass out of the house."

"I'm not tossed out." he smashed his teeth together.

"Good to hear it. Now, what's up?"

"I know you mentioned recently that you've squared time away at the lodge for you and Scar, but I wanna know if I can have it for a few days." Weeks if need be. There was no time limit on how he'd fight for his woman. "I'll pay for a hotel suite for you and Scar instead."

Axel looked at him in that reflective, evaluating way, as if he had seen every angle of a man without speaking a word.

"Why don't you stay in a hotel suite?"

Tomb went with the truth. He trusted Axel not to breathe a word to anyone.

"I need to take Nina somewhere remote, where she can't scream for help when I won't let her leave."

Axel nearly choked on a sip of coffee. "Fuck, Tomb. You considering kidnapping your wife?"

"If that's what it takes."

The smile fell from Axel's face. "So it's true then? Nina wants to end things?"

Sitting his ass down in the hardback chair in front of Axel's desk, Tomb scrubbed his knuckles against the roughness of his beard and half-shrugged. Unable to believe she'd said those words to him.

"I'm working on it."

"You need anything?"

"Yeah, you can stop everyone's gums flapping about it."

Partially smiling, Axel said, "It would be better asking to see Ruin belly dancing, brother."

He might have belly-laughed some other time. "So, about the lodge?"

"Sure, you take it."

"Just let me know where you book somewhere else, and I'll pay."

"There's no need. The lodge is club-owned for all of us to use."

"But you wanted it now."

"Your need is greater. My wildcat is happy to go anywhere; we'll ride through Colorado to see my grandbabies."

Tomb did snort then. "An unexpected visit to Roux and her old man. The Butcher will be pissed."

Axel answered scathingly. "My son-in-law can suck it up if it means he can take my daughter out while we babysit."

Those two butted heads like lame goats when really, Axel and Butcher had found a reason to get along, and that reason was the Diablos' princess, Roux, and her two kids.

"You mind if I give a piece of unsolicited advice?"

Tomb rolled a shoulder. "Go on."

"Women like to talk shit out. If they have a problem or something on their mind. You can solve a lot of things just by listening. Scarlett saw a TV show about healthy relationship communication. Now she likes to have a weekly family meeting, just her and me around the kitchen table." Axel half grinned. "It makes her happy to check everything is okay. I might think it's nonsense, but she doesn't, and that's what matters."

Tomb smiled, "does she have a little gavel, Prez?"

"Don't fucking mention it to her, or she'll be straight on Amazon to find one."

With his business arranged, he thanked Axel and lumbered out of the office, trekking his steps through the long hallways of the clubhouse. He'd always felt at home in the renovated old firehouse until today. Nothing held his attention. The blare of the 80-inch TV was showing nothing he wanted to see. The garage should be where he headed next, burying himself in work so he didn't stalk Nina at her salon to dig into her secretive thoughts. But work held no appeal either, so he carried a folded chair out of the storage shed and plopped his ass down with a can of soda. Wishing it was a scotch, but he needed to keep his head.

Fishing out his phone, he went to their text thread, scrolling back months, looking for clues about where he went wrong.

When he felt a presence come up by his side, Splice unfolded his chair and sat down, his legs in front of him.

There were no jokes, as Tomb expected.

But after a minute of silence, Splice asked. "You got a plan, brother?"

He was a man of extreme control. Of course, he had a plan.

And it had to work.

"Yes."

Splice nudged his arm. "That's good."

Tomb didn't move for the longest time. He was rooted to the earth to keep him from going nuclear and kidnapping his wife until this bullshit was no longer an issue.

He couldn't help himself when he fired off a text, not expecting her to reply, but he saw she'd read it immediately.

Tomb: Whatever I need to do to repair our marriage, I will do it, princess. We've always been endgame. I'll make you remember that.

My Princess: Will you?

Tomb: Yes. Trust your husband.

My Princess: I don't want to argue, Rome, but we need to talk about everything.

Tomb: We will.

My Princess: Monroe wants me to come to the clubhouse later for the cookout.

Tomb: We can do that if that's what you want.

Tomb: WE, Nina. There's no you or me.

My Princess: You're being dictatorial.

Tomb: You're about to know how much I can be.

My Princess: What does that even mean?

Tomb: When the cards are on our marriage table, you'll know.

Tomb: You're my life, Nina girl.

Tomb: I've fucked up somewhere along the way by not showing you that.

Tomb: You still love me?

My Princess: That isn't fair to ask, not after what I said earlier.

Tomb: I won't play fair.

My Princess: I'm not playing.

Tomb: I won't lose you, Nina. That's a non-negotiable for me.

My Princess: And what I want means nothing?

Tomb: What you want means everything to me.

My Princess: That's not what it sounds like.

Tomb: You're my wife.

My Princess: That isn't an answer.

Tomb: It is for me.

Nothing was truer.

Nina was *his wife*.

Nothing in this world meant more to him.

He had to prove it to her before it was too late.

Nina

Why was she anxious?

Her belly was full of flutters as she climbed into her car after shutting the salon. Tomb had wanted to collect her, she'd insisted on driving. It made sense, or her car would have been parked at the salon overnight. She also hadn't been ready to face Tomb yet.

Going to the clubhouse to see Denver only delayed the inevitable.

The talk would come.

And she was terrified of how it would go.

Though going by Tomb's texts earlier, his lane was pretty straightforward.

Could she believe him?

The words were good.

Actions were better.

On approaching the MC gates, Nina shut down her nervous thoughts as a prospect let her through. The younger guy waved a hand. She returned his greeting and turned into the courtyard to park.

Oh, boy, those nerves came rushing back when she saw a tall building of a man waiting in the doorway. Tomb was watching her park. Dressed in light-washed jeans, a blue plaid shirt over a white t-shirt, half tucked into the front of his jeans. The backward ball cap he wore made his rugged outfit 100% hotter.

Lord above, her husband was about the most attractive man on the planet. She'd easily pit him against Pedro Pascal, Henry Cavill, and The Momoa and know which man she'd go home with. His thumbs were tucked into the front pockets, and she caught sight of his black wedding band on his left hand. Seeing it gave her a strike of ownership deep in her belly.

That man was hers.

If only for right now, Tomb was hers.

And he wanted to stay being hers.

Even before the engine cut out, he opened her door and reached in to unlatch the seatbelt. "Hey, princess."

She felt like she had first-date jitters again as she swung her legs around to step out, but Tomb was there, spanning both hands around her waist to lift her down.

"You're being weird."

"I'm being your husband."

"Are you going to be my car valet everywhere I go?"

The smirk stretched his lips. "It doesn't sound like a terrible job to have."

"Grab the bag from the back seat for me, please."

An eyebrow shot up. "More of my clothes?"

She instantly turned red and shook her head. "No, I brought candy for the kids."

Tomb did as she asked and hooked a gift bag full to the brim with candy. She was the unofficial aunt to all the club kids, and they knew she always came bearing chocolate.

"Hey..." she stopped with a touch to his arm. "I'm sorry about the clothes, I was mad and reacted without thinking. I shouldn't have done that in front of everyone."

"Sweetheart, you do whatever you need to grab my attention." He sent a crooked smile her way, no sign of condemning resentment.

But that wasn't her Tomb.

He was as friendly as they come, and he'd never raised his voice to her meanly.

She was the quick-trigger hothead in their relationship. He might participate in their loud fights, but only because it led to his favorite activity, getting into her pants. *Her* favorite activity, too.

"I wish it happened in our kitchen, but we deal, huh?"

She nodded sadly.

She'd gotten his attention, and they'd deal. How they moved forward was still a mystery, which terrified her.

In the next moment, before Nina could even move, she was pinned to the side of her car, and her skyscraper man was holding her in place with only the use of his lower body. His belly pressed into her, and she nearly whimpered as flares of their intense chemistry rushed to life.

Nina would have found it funny if someone had told her she would be this obsessed with one person, and his smell would intoxicate her. Getting attached was never an issue. Even though her ex of two years turned out to be a jerk, Nina hadn't ever been unhinged by him. Dating was a sport in her teens and early twenties. She used to think it was absurd to be infatuated with one person and to prioritize their happiness.

Not when Tomb lowered his eyelids and stared in his tempting way to urge her to grab big handfuls of his gargantuan body until he moaned for her. She resisted only because he had her hands trapped against her car. And how would it look if she told him in one breath they should split up, but then she went full feral attack in the next?

"Why do you look like you need something, wife?"

Her compulsion shuddered. "I don't need anything. Are we going inside or not?"

"In a minute. First though…"

"First what?" she elevated her face and recognized her mistake when his crystal blue eyes glinted, and his mouth twitched a dirty-boy smirk beneath the trimmed beard.

Sooner than Nina could draw breath, his mouth descended and landed on hers.

After his little roadside stunt, she shouldn't have been surprised that this was the hand he intended to play. Using her body's rudimentary reaction to him for evil.

Keeping her lips pressed closed didn't deter Tomb, not when he licked a path over her bottom lip and then bit her. He bit her! Once she gasped in delicious shock, he slid into her mouth and kissed her with the skill of a husband who knew what triggered her lust.

How could she call it a kiss when she was devoured? His commanding hold around her nape sent her feelings into a sticky spiral. She couldn't get enough of his pursuing tongue dominating her mouth, letting her know without words how far to open for him.

Every conflicting thought and emotion fell under the spell of her addiction, and she accepted the kiss in the overpowering way Tomb delivered it.

Though only their mouths touched, she sensed him all over her in indecent ways. Tomb stole her lips and her breath, forcing her to succumb, and she crumbled so quickly.

When it stopped, it was because Tomb ended the kiss. Much to her embarrassment, she should have been the one to stop.

"You shouldn't have done that," she exhaled as he rolled a thumb over her wet lips. He'd always worshipped her body like he couldn't get enough of her, as if in those special, intimate moments, he revered her.

It was an intoxicating sensation to experience.

Nina struggled to catch a thought, ashamed she wanted more kissing.

But she shouldn't cloud her sexed-up brain any more than it was, so she pushed against his solid chest.

"Kissing you is a privilege. Also a fucking *need*, Nina."

He couldn't use her kryptonite against her, or she'd fall apart. He bent down to compensate for their height difference, something she loved to see him doing, like he was ready for round two. Her hands tried to hold him at bay.

"Sex isn't the issue. If you're going to make everything about sex, talking is a waste of time." Her traitorous heart galloped as his heart raced underneath her touch. The sharp inhalation stretched the t-shirt, and Tomb grunted, stepping back. But it wasn't very far because he hooked up her hand, still holding the gift bag in the other.

"Christ, you don't know how fucking badly I want to control you right now," he muttered in his deep, feral voice.

Nina was stunned into speechlessness. By then, he'd walked them to the entryway. The double doors were wide open, noise already at a high level, but her full attention was on the towering man leading her by the hand.

"Control me? What the hell does that mean?"

Sure, in bed, he was king. He was lord, master, and boss of her body. She happily gave up control there to Tomb for the devastating pleasure he brought in hot waves that lasted hours.

Attempting to tug Tomb's hand to urge his stride to slow was like trying to contact the mothership to request a ride home. Impossible, she lightly jogged after him until she came to a screeching halt inside the entryway when Tomb rounded on her, her hand still locked in his.

He looked fit for murder. Sexy murder.

"You're pushing me to my fucking limits, Nina, you wanna watch that mouth, or I'll..." he seemed to rein in his following words.

Stubborn as a mule in leather boots, Nina jerked her pointed chin in the air and squinted. "Or you'll, what?"

It wasn't alarm she felt, making her skin goosebump when she caught the look of a deranged animal in the blue depths. Tomb would never lay a finger on her in anger, of that she was sure.

His mother raised him well, and he would never cause her pain, even if it meant sacrificing his arm. It was why she always felt safe mouthing off to him.

In the same vein, he took it like a red rag to a rampaging bull, resulting in some of her funniest memories with him.

Again, Nina was trapped to the wall he'd walked her back into. Inhaling fast, she shut her lips when he pinched her chin between finger and thumb, tipping her head back. His eyes roamed over her face. The silence was palpable, energy zinging from his fingertips into her.

"My limits are reached, princess. I tried this your way and was happy to do that, but now, when this is all behind us, you'll have no one to blame but yourself for how we go forward. I tried to be respectable. For *you*. For *my wife*. Now you've unleashed the animal. Learn to live with it, or don't. But it's happening." Those emphasized words felt like the silkiest caress over her skin. Nina didn't know how to process what he was saying or why. Mute, she could only stare.

For once, her sassiness took a timeout.

"There's going to be no inch of your life I don't control from now on. I'll leave my fingerprints on every part of your existence to remind you of who you belong to."

The only way to describe how he appeared was predatory. *Determined*. The warning in his voice wasn't disguised, and she trembled, the fine hairs on her nape standing on end.

"We stay long enough so you can talk to Casey and Denver, then we're going home to hash this out." He restarted their journey into the clubhouse to see the main area filled with bikers and their families. Denver was stretched out in a chair, being fussed over by Casey.

Nina had to force a smile when people shouted their names in greeting. All she felt was shaken to the core, confused, unsure of what he meant, yet simultaneously intrigued by what he intended.

"Aunt Ninaaaa," she heard and watched a gaggle of little people dressed in adorable clothes heading her way, toothy smiles on display. Despite her chaotic thoughts, her smile this time was genuine as she waited on the spot for the gang to reach her.

Tomb handed over the gift bag of goodies.

"Enjoy playing the candy fairy, princess." He told her, pressing a kiss to her forehead. It was as though he'd morphed back into the Tomb she knew. The dominant predator from moments ago was gone. She watched his back as he strode off and straddled a bar stool.

As occupied as she was catching up with everyone and playing with the kids, Nina was aware of a pair of hot blue eyes on her. Wherever she moved, those eyes stalked alongside.

Sitting with the girls, Monroe nudged her in the ribs each time Tomb left his stool to deliver Nina another drink. His trips to their old ladies' table were wordless, but he didn't need to say anything when his eyes spoke for him. Sweeping over her, making her an absolute wreck inside. He ended his trip with a kiss on her forehead before he returned to his boys.

"Girl, whatever you said to him has put an erotic bomb under your man. I nearly combusted seeing how he looked at you," Whispered Scarlett.

Switching her head to the side, the breath swept out of her chest, finding Tomb watching her.

She'd have to change her panties if it went on much longer.

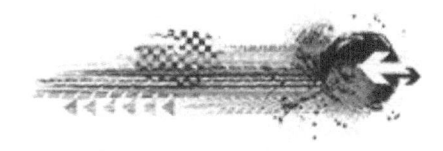

Tomb

"You eye-fuck her any harder, Tomb, and we're all gonna go home knocked up."

"Fuck off, Splice."

"Charming," the other man cackled, a bottle of beer to his mouth. If only he'd choke on it to keep his trap shut for an hour. "Is that how Batman talks to his Robin?"

Drawing his gaze away from Nina, he cocked a brow. "I'm Batman in this scenario? Control your fanboying, brother."

"I'd prefer to be Iron Man. I reckon the shit we've been doing deserved code names."

"Shut your mouth." He warned, drawing a beer bottle to his mouth, his eyes returning to the thing he couldn't look away from for long. She was laughing with her girls, and his chest hurt. "If she hears, I'll have to break your legs, and Nina likes you, which means I'll get yelled at."

"Protected by Mrs. Batman," he smirked. "I might need a new patch right here," Splice joked, slapping a hand over his club cut.

Splice rattled off into a new topic, but Tomb didn't hear a word when Nina's laugh drew his attention again. Irritation slithered down his spine. She should be on his lap so he could sip at her laughter, not given freely to others. Tomb wanted to punish her for assuming their marriage wasn't necessary to him, with his hand pushed down into the inside of her jeans, ripping cries out of her.

His wife needed a few home truths.

A lot of lessons.

And proof of his devotion.

All would come soon.

What he'd told her, he meant absolutely. She'd brought this on herself and would have to face the consequences. He'd pretended long enough. Pretended he was a decent, forward-thinking guy. Tomb was so goddamn prehistoric that he might as well be dragging a wooden club along the ground behind him.

Those first days spent getting to know Nina, she'd shared how exes had been too controlling, how much it had turned her off to serious relationships. By then, Tomb had known she was special, someone he wanted to keep. He didn't guess it would turn into marriage, but the infatuation grew uncontrollably fast. And knowing the man he was, he'd had to adjust or risk losing her.

But now he was losing her, anyway.

That's why he didn't feel guilty about what would come.

A drowning man would use any means to save his life.

Nina was *his life*.

When she turned her head for the tenth time in only minutes, he sent her a wink and watched her face bloom with color. She spun away, but like clockwork, as if she couldn't stop returning her eyes, she found him again only seconds later.

That's right, my wife, look at the man who is ready for a battle to keep what is his.

Nina

Anyone would stop to eavesdrop when hearing their name spoken privately.

Instinct told Nina to stop.

To listen.

To be *nosy*.

Her heart was wide open, begging to know what Tomb was thinking about her.

"There's been no issues with Nina lately?" she caught Tomb saying, and her brow folded down, confused. Issues? What issues?

"Nah, man, none. You know I got it in hand." The other voice belonged to Splice.

Nina was even more confused.

What were they talking about?

She hadn't asked Splice for a favor lately. The last time was months ago when her tire blew on the way to Colorado Springs for a day of shopping. Tomb had been out of town.

Some of what Tomb said next was eaten up under the sound of bike engines, but then she heard Splice say, "You know I don't want paying. I got your back."

His back with what?

"If anyone gets near Nina or even looks like they wanna put the moves on your old lady, I shut that down."

The what now?

Nina felt each hard hammer of her heart against her rib cage, the loud rattling she was sure they'd hear and discover her eavesdropping. She'd innocently tracked him down when he'd been gone too long, fetching more crates of beers. Now she was listening in like she was a secret spy.

"I'll repay the favor one day, brother, when some half-witted chick takes pity and tries to tame your ass."

Splice laughed. In any other circumstance, Nina would have found that funny because he was a dedicated bachelor, intent on sharing his passion with as many women as he could. Still, right then, she only heard how her husband had his buddy watching her.

"If I ever get as possessive as you are with Nina, going deranged if a man even looks at her for too long, shoot me in the fucking forehead because I would have lost my mind."

Her man replied with a grumble.

Possessive over her?

Since when?

It didn't make sense.

But then it did when she thought of the nights out with the girls, and somehow Splice was at the same bars by coincidence. Or at the movie with her work friends, and he was at the concession stand. It was how she'd become friendlier with Splice than any other of Tomb's buddies. Splice was the one she called if Tomb was out of town. It came about naturally.

But now she saw they'd orchestrated it that way. Little biker sneaks.

Unable to keep hidden any longer, she stepped around the corner.

Tomb spotted her first, as if he was wholly aware of her presence. His eyes came like tasers, holding her on the spot as Nina made her feet move. The clack of her heeled boots sounded like a warning on the cement floor.

Splice could guess what was up when he spotted her. He muttered "shit," side-eyeing Tomb.

Yeah, bros with their secrets were about to get their asses kicked.

"You need something, princess?" asked Tomb, advancing.

She was annoyed but couldn't deny how good he looked in his shirt. Chest hair crawled above the ribbing. Her man was a hairy bear. Not overly so, but she'd always loved how he wasn't manscaped to within an inch of his life. Especially that sexy line arrowed down to his groin.

She might have stroked her gaze over his body for a weak moment, but when she reached his face, he'd be an idiot not to recognize she was mad.

"Yes, I need something," she spoke in a frigid tone but did it smiling to confuse. "Which of your brothers gets the short straw if Splice is busy?"

"Come again?"

Ah, it was like that? She folded her arms. But not before his eyes dropped to her tits. Tomb was such a boob admirer, and she'd loved that about him, how dedicated he was to her chest. They'd had sex in this garage more than once. Sometimes, he'd stuff her inside the back of someone's car they were fixing, and he'd put her on his lap and tell her to ride him while he buried his face in her chest.

Tomb's co-conspirator rubbed the back of his neck, shifting on his biker boots. A total tell of guilt. What a little shit her friend was. She hoped he fell in horrible love and the woman made him miserable.

"Okay, I'll dumb it down for you boys. If I was going out tonight, and Splice, your little bitch boy…"

"Hey, what the fuck did I do?" Splice objected, but she was in a hate stare with her darling hubby.

"Was busy," she went on like Splice hadn't spoken. "Who would you have watching me? Because that's what you do, isn't it, Rome? You pay your boys to monitor me. Why is the question? Do you think I'm cheating?"

The realization hit her square in the chest.

But Rome wasn't the quiet type. If he had those suspicions, he would have confronted her.

Little made sense.

Splice whistled through his teeth. "I'm not being stuck in the middle of a marriage dispute. I'm heading back to the party," he announced, quickly backing out of the garage carrying the beer crates.

"You can run, Ryan, but we'll talk later." She warned.

"Nina girl." Tomb began, and despite her mood, she shivered at his regulated tone. Loving the hoarse rattle in his voice. It held a dominance that always appealed to her.

She raised her chin to meet his eyes as he advanced with measured steps.

"If I thought you'd cheat on me, you'd be locked up at home, and there'd be a bloodbath of dead bodies from one end of town to the other."

That slight shiver from a second ago turned into a whole shudder.

Why did that sound good? Why did the thrill of his possessiveness coat every kink she had?

"You wouldn't kill me?" she asked curiously.

He smirked from the left side of his lips, his eyes dark and sultry. All Nina heard was her heart thumps echoing under her skin. Feeling touched while his gaze raked over her face.

"Your punishment would be altogether more personal."

God help her, she believed that.

"Guess it's lucky I'm not cheating. Why are you having me watched, then?"

"Guarded, not watched."

Puzzled, she frowned, losing some of the tension knotting up her neck muscles.

"Guarded from who? The last time I checked, I wasn't in danger from anyone."

The MC recently had a disturbing time with Reno and Ruin's oldest brother. He'd been murdering prostitutes and dropping their bodies on Diablo properties to get the brotherhood in trouble. Fortunately, his wave of terror died with him. Any messy situation since had been few.

Nothing warranted being secretly supervised.

And she wanted answers from her tight-lipped spouse.

"Well?"

"If you drop the attitude, princess. I'll tell you," he dared say. He said that to her! Nina wasn't in the wrong here.

And then Tomb spoke. "You eavesdropped, baby. Shit you weren't meant to hear, then you burst in here giving me attitude and scaring Splice."

"I scared Splice?" she spluttered. Wild-eyed and unable to believe what she was hearing. "I should have kicked him in the balls! I still might for the crap he's pulled with me over the past months. Pretending to my friend when all along he's your little bitch boy."

Tomb chuckled. "Little bitch boy is gonna be his new name."

"Don't get cute with me, Rome King. I want to know what's going on." She nearly stomped her foot, which would give off brat energy, and she was too old.

"You wanna know why I have my boys watching you?"

"Yes." Her heart started fast again from the penetrating stare.

"Because you're mine, Nina girl, and I won't let anyone near you when I'm not there to protect what's mine."

Nina would later swear on a stack of newly printed Bibles how the ground swayed underneath her feet as he spoke those words.

Possessive.

Forceful.

Dangerous.

It was everything she'd always wanted.

So then, why did something feel off about it?

Why was his possessiveness such a secret?

Every wife wanted to be treated like a precious gemstone, protected and loved, knowing her man always had her back in every eventuality.

Why had Tomb acted aloof to their marriage if he felt so strongly about her safety and other men approaching her?

He'd always been a patient man, and she saw how he watched her, giving her the silence to think things through.

"How long have you been doing this?"

"Since we started living together."

Holy shit. That was years.

Years of going behind her back and having someone guarding her for reasons only he fully understood. Whether it was a husband protecting his wife or him not trusting her, it affected Nina unexpectedly.

She felt sucker punched with heat, like his admission had stuck a hot poker in parts of her psyche she hadn't known existed.

Any irritation and lingering anger melted away in an exhale, and Nina turned away from him on her heels to return to Denver's homecoming party.

"I'm still debating if I'll punch Splice in the balls." She said on her exit, knowing he was probably looking at her ass. He was an ass man, too.

Behind her, Tomb chuckled.

Maybe he'd expected a fight, but she couldn't face it.

She felt cared for. *Wanted*.

If he needed to watch her, that was fine. Nina had nothing to hide. Not really.

"That'll be a nice surprise for him, princess."

She thought so, too. And then she waited for Tomb to get in line with her steps, and they returned to the clubhouse together.

Nina

If the little ass-twitching tramp fluttered around Tomb once more, Nina would do jail time for the violence she'd put on the other woman.

Jealousy wasn't usually the color that made up who she was. The sweet bottoms gravitating to Tomb's area bothered her, especially since she'd become unmoored and uncertain.

"Are we about to start a brawl?" Monroe asked. "Should I take off my earrings and bangles?"

Hearing the seriousness in her friend's voice, Nina lost the shoulder tension. "Have you ever been in a fight before?"

"Hey, I might look corporate, but I can handle my own." She insisted, huffing and picking invisible lint from her pencil skirt.

"Keep thinking that, lady. Chains wouldn't even let you get close enough to a fight to smell the adrenalin, let alone stand by while you got bruised."

Monroe sighed dreamily. "I know. He's so cute."

Nina didn't know about cute, but the VP was a born protector. He'd taken Monroe's two remaining sisters under his wing and frequently had his family of women trailing him.

"Go find your cutie hubby and kiss him before you drool on my shoulder."

"Okay." Monroe jumped from her seat but checked first, "You won't start a fight? Tomb isn't even taking notice of the women."

"I'll be fine."

She was far from fine.

Nina was fit to strangle, maim, and put her wife's patch all over Tomb.

Their marriage might hang by a thin thread, but Tomb was still hers.

When she watched Lou-Lou make her way over to the boys, Nina had seen enough. She all but flew across the room and shoulder-checked Lou-Lou in a petty way, without regret, making the woman stumble. Nina didn't give a fuck, and shot her anger as only a pissed-off wife could. Lou-Lou would be fishing her head out of the toilet bowl if she dared try any of her slut tricks on Tomb.

Though sitting with his boys, Tomb wasn't taking much notice of their conversation. Their eyes locked as if they existed only in a world of two. And he looked so fucking impressed with her. So dark and dangerously sexy.

Where the hell was this Tomb two weeks ago? A year ago?

"I'm ready to leave." She told him and then whirled toward the door. "I'll be outside."

"Keys, baby." He said behind her. He'd followed her out to her car. "I'll drive us home."

"You're not taking the bike?"

"A prospect will bring it back for me."

Nina blinked in shock because Tomb was territorial over his Harley and wouldn't allow anyone to touch it much.

"Keys," he repeated. She handed them over, glad she didn't have to drive. He opened the door before she could.

The drive back to their house went by in relative silence. Nina was glad because her thoughts were too chaotic to make conversation.

The Talk was pending.

Tomb unlocked the house and proceeded inside ahead of her to shut off the alarm system. Hanging up her jacket and purse, she went around, flipping on lights. She loved their house. They'd gutted out entire rooms when she moved in. Tomb hadn't protested once, not even about the cost. Now, each day she came through the door, she was enveloped in how much she loved the place.

Would she live here much longer if they were incapable of fixing their marriage?

Her heart pinged as she sat on the hallway bench to pull off her boots. Tomb had moved to their bedroom, where she heard him hanging up his leather cut.

While waiting for Tomb, Nina carried the heaviest tension on her shoulders. Minutes later, he padded barefoot into the living room. The shirt was gone, and now he only wore jeans and a t-shirt.

"What do you want to drink, baby? You didn't eat a lot at the club. Do you want a snack?"

"No, I'm not hungry. You get something, though." They were painfully polite. "I'll take a wine, please."

He returned with a beer for himself and a glass of Chardonnay for her. Their fingers grazed when he handed it over.

Nina was grateful Tomb hadn't chosen to sit beside her on the couch. Unable to think clearly with him so near, his scent filled her nose. He took the armchair, his long legs sprawled before him, looking like the king of everything. Calm and controlled while her heart was bashing around her chest. Scared of the ensuing outcome.

"Do you want to start?" his rich voice startled Nina mid-sip of wine. "Tell me everything you're thinking, so I know what I'm working with."

So logical.

Unsure where to start, she had another sip of the dry wine, not tasting any of its usual gorgeous notes. It occurred to her that Tomb kept her favorite wine in stock. He did so many little things for her, she only realized now.

"Nina," he cut into her silence, his severe gaze unwavering. He'd yet to take a drink of the beer he had resting on his knee. "Is there someone else? Is that why you said you wanted to end our marriage?"

He might appear calm, but the hot rumble of Tomb's growl put shockwaves throughout the room.

Nina's head snapped up, and if not for the tight grip on the crystal glass, it would have toppled to the floor as her body went into trembling shock.

That's what he thought?

"God, no. How could you think that?"

"You told me we should split up. It's the natural to assume you want someone else."

"There's no one else. I'd never have a sleazy affair behind your back." She replied, offended he'd entertained the idea.

"I would kill anyone for looking at you, Nina." Again, he sounded calm, but his growled words begged to differ.

"You'd kill anyone for looking at me, but you hardly want to spend time with me."

"Explain that." He scowled.

Nina shook her head. "Are you happy?"

"Yes. Maybe not right this second." Another scowl. "You're every-fucking-thing I ever wanted, Nina. Don't question that. You insult me. But you're not happy?"

She felt like the lowest scum by replying, "No." but why else was this talk happening if not to speak her mind? To repair their marriage? She needed to be brutally honest and share her feelings.

"I thought getting married would feel different, that we'd be different. I slotted into your world, Rome, and we've been cruising ever since. It's like you have your life, and I have mine. We wear wedding bands, and the only part of us that works is sex. I feel alone most of the time. And knowing you'd prefer to be around your boys and those women at the clubhouse hurts a lot."

"I'm not around any fucking women, Nina. Christ. You can't think I'd fuck around on you."

"I don't. Not really, but the fear is always still in the back of my head. Men make mistakes, get drunk and *accidentally* fall into another pussy, and the old ladies never find out. It might sound ridiculous to you, but it's real for me. What job has women hanging around all day and night willing to stop, drop and suck at a moment's notice, huh?"

Tomb dared to chuckle like she'd told a joke, but then he sighed and rubbed a hand down his bearded face.

"See, I knew you wouldn't take this seriously if I told you my thoughts. This is a waste of time." She uncurled her legs from underneath her butt.

"Sit down, Nina." He issued in a growl, and her butt sat instinctively, something in her listening to the rough tenor of his command. "This has started now, and there's no putting it back in the closet."

"You wouldn't like it if I were around men all day just waiting for me to nod to go into a dark closet with them."

She saw him grip the arm of the chair until his knuckles turned white. His teeth bared, but then he became calm, like his flared anger had never happened. How good he was at that.

"But I'm supposed to accept that it's okay how you're around panting women. Women you've probably fucked." She'd never asked who he'd been with and didn't want to know. Truly, she'd never been a jealous woman, not until other insecurities crept in.

"What else should I assume, Rome, when you choose to be at the club instead of home with me? Instead of going on date nights with me, your wife? You're out of town more times than you're here. It makes me feel I don't interest you enough outside the bedroom. And that hurts. It's hurt me for a long time because I can't fix it, and God, I've tried. But I can only take so many rejections before I admit defeat. This is our marriage, and I shouldn't complain because this is how it's been from the beginning. You give me so much, so why should I want more? You're not a bad man, but I need more."

She drained the remaining wine in one gulp and placed the glass on the floor.

Her heart was going so fast. Her nerves were a jangled wreck.

She'd said things she thought she'd never say aloud because it made her sound selfish, entitled, and disrespectful.

To anyone else, she was probably whining over the most inconsequential things.

Maybe she was. Maybe she wanted the dream marriage.

Was she wrong about that?

It truly was too late to lock the stable door now.

Tomb

N eglect.
That's what his wife was saying. He'd neglected her.
From the beginning of their fucking marriage.
When nothing was further from the truth.
If she only knew.
Following suit when he'd watched her drain the glass of wine, Tomb took the bottle to his lips and didn't stop swallowing until he'd finished the beer in one. He leaned forward, letting it drop to the low-slung coffee table with a thud.
Neglect. Nina felt fucking neglected.
And that killed him down to the soul.
Sucking beer foam from his top lip, Tomb rubbed a hand over his mouth. He couldn't stop looking at her. So small, curled up on the

couch. He loved coming home and seeing how she'd tip her head up and smile, ready for his kiss.

Sexually, he knew he could overpower her and make her whimper with pleasure into his mouth. It would take moments to crawl between her legs, prying them apart and making her forget everything, including her name and this talk.

His urges screamed for him to overpower. To make her sweet and obedient underneath his tongue and hands, he swallowed them down until he was breathing through his teeth. She'd hate him even more if he did that now.

His balanced life had been shot to shit, assuming his wife was happy, and now learning how much she'd been lacking, punched a hole through his chest.

"What are you thinking?" she asked, her voice small. "I don't even know if you're mad. You're always so unreadable."

She was too far away, even a few feet across the family room, but Tomb didn't think Nina would appreciate having their serious talk with her planted in his lap.

"I'm not mad, sweetheart."

He was torn apart. Because he'd failed the one person who meant the fucking world to him. If he said anything now, he knew her sweet, vulnerable heart would interpret it the wrong way.

The possibility of her having a secret lover made Tomb feel like he was barely holding on to his sanity. Had there been a suggestion of someone else sniffing around his Nina, that man's life would have ended before the sun was up in the sky. He had no violent ceiling for what he'd do to keep what was his. But he'd always kept her satisfied in that department.

And as upset as she was, as much as he saw emotions clinging to her features, Nina would stay his wife.

Tomb was not a generous guy. He wouldn't let her go free so she could find happiness with someone else, *someone better.*

Nina had consumed him from the first moment he saw her, and nothing had changed in the time between. It wasn't the only attraction.

He was captivated by every aspect of his wife.

But she hadn't known it because he'd kept that demented part of himself hidden.

But no longer.

Not if it meant losing her.

That was unacceptable. Impossible to imagine.

When he rose to his feet, he startled Nina and watched her eyes widen as he advanced.

He needed a bottle of scotch, a timeout, or a calming toke of a blunt to rein in his actions. But he'd settle for putting his hands on Nina. She scowled as he reached down to clasp her hand, bringing her to her feet.

"Don't even think about sex now, Rome."

The *I can't believe you right now* tone made him smile.

"I'm not thinking about sex, Nina girl."

That was a partial lie. He couldn't look at Nina and not want sex. She was a cock-hardening dream come true. The term punching above his weight was made for him because he knew she was out of his league, but somehow, she'd chosen him, anyway.

"But if I were, you'd be flat on your back with my cock crammed into your little pussy, crying out my name, and all this shit wouldn't be happening." He growled through his clenched teeth.

Keeping her hand in his, he led her along the hallway.

"So, that's it, we're just not going to talk it through?" she huffed. "I don't even know why I bother."

Tomb stopped and rounded on her, dropping his head to look his mouthy brat in the eye. Her smaller height did things to him. Got him untamed to shelter, and to keep her locked against his chest, making her rely on him for every little thing she might need. How fucking happy that would make him.

Tomb fingered underneath her chin, forcing her to look up at him.

It wasn't news to him how stubborn she was, how globally independent his wife was. She'd rather get stuck in quicksand than admit she needed support, needed *his* help. And it drove him wild. But he'd respected her need for independence.

It had taken a lot of sex to make her submit when she tried to pay the bills. Tomb wasn't a progressive man and didn't give a fuck about equality if it meant he couldn't take care of her. If Nina wanted something, he got it for her.

He loved a strong-willed woman firing angry bullets from underneath her long, natural lashes. Any other time, he would have dry-humped her against the wall and made that scowl fall from her lips in minutes.

Sex he knew how to wield. It was his wheelhouse, his toy box, and his playground.

Feelings and emotions, he was a fucking prom night virgin.

Why did he need to emote when he grunted like a pro?

But for his Nina girl, he'd go to the ends of the earth. He'd talk himself goddamn hoarse if that's what she required from him.

But if that was the Pandora's box she wanted to open, she had to accept the consequences, too. And he didn't know if she could while she was raw and vulnerable.

"I'm putting you to bed, baby. How long have you had to stew on all these thoughts? Months?" she dared look guilty. Fuck, it had been *months*. "I need to process what you've shared with me because I'm torn the fuck up that I've made you so unhappy. I don't want to say something to make shit worse."

She frowned even deeper and tugged away from his hand.

"I shouldn't have said anything," she said, walking away from him. By the time Tomb caught up, she was in the bathroom.

Tomb had no sense of privacy, never had. He'd take a piss while she showered. Or sit on the edge of the toilet while she took a bath, watching her like she was putting on a private show for his deviant eyes. He enjoyed seeing her go through her beauty routines. Tomb didn't think Nina knew how captivating she was in everything she did. She'd skinned out of her clothes, now only in mismatched panties and a bra. She was fucking flawless, and his cock twitched, eager for her. He had to palm between his legs, making the bulge more comfortable because it wouldn't get used tonight. He could push the issue and make her scream for him. But how would that make her feel once she knew he'd used sex to bring her under his submission?

Tomb paused in the doorway and watched her while she brushed her teeth, trying to avoid him but occasionally glancing at him through the mirror.

"A little privacy." She snapped.

"Nope."

She scowled and finished washing up, tossing the towel into the hamper, but he thought she wanted to throw it in his face.

Pushing past him, Tomb caught Nina around the waist and pinned her against him. His hand snaked into the back of her hair, so she couldn't avoid his touch or gaze as he ate her up. His hold on the decency not to fuck her into compliance might be frayed at the edges, but he could still remind his wife of a few things before he tucked her into bed.

Even mad, his Nina girl's eyes fluttered when he tested her reaction by intensifying his fingers around her hair. So sure that she was holding in a moan, and he longed to rip it out of her throat. Those sexy little sounds belonged to him.

"You can be as mad at me as you want."

"Thanks for the permission, Daddy." Nina smart-mouthed.

She'd often told him how his touch drugged her. Tomb caressed her scalp and noticed her blushing cheeks as she struggled to open her eyes. She had so many tells, and Tomb lapped them up with a hungry, roaming glance.

"Let me go."

"Never." He replied evenly.

"I didn't mean… I meant so I can go to bed since you're avoiding the most important talk of our lives."

The little witch knew how to push knives into his chest, but Tomb wasn't mad. She could be as angry as long as she needed to be. It was in his hands to fix now.

"You've had longer to think about this than I have, princess. Our talk is far from done."

He needed Nina somewhere without distractions, unless he tried to lock her in the basement.

Which he was keeping as plan C.

"Yeah, says you." She sassed again, and he couldn't help but press his mouth to her forehead.

"You're testing my patience."

"And you're going to avoid this like everything else. Just forget it, Tomb, forget it all." She said, the emotion clear as the words stuttered from her lips. The pulse in her neck fluttered erratically, another sign she wasn't ready to give up. He brushed his thumb over that vein.

"Forget us?"

She couldn't answer, and he was grateful for that, at least.

It held Tomb's sanity in a holding cage.

But it was a fine line he was walking.

Again, he put his lips to her forehead. "I haven't shown you attention how you needed it, and that's put me in hell. So, I can't forget a word you said, baby, and this isn't over, just postponed. *We aren't over.*"

He entered the bedroom and watched Nina select sleep shorts and a shirt. She always looked so beautiful doing anything, but he loved these quiet moments with her when she was sleepy. It would only take minutes to fall asleep once she was tucked up in the covers; she was like a nesting possum.

"You don't have to watch me," she said.

"I like to watch you."

Her eyebrow shot up. "What are you doing, Tomb? What's this?"

"I'm putting my wife to bed."

"Since when?"

"Since now."

He prowled forward, noticing how she watched his movements. Locked in this tense bubble, Tomb had a solution for how he would make it right, but he still needed time to put his plan in place. But he couldn't bear his wife believing he didn't enjoy being around her, didn't enjoy the simple pleasures of watching her climbing into their bed.

He pulled the covers back. "In you get, princess."

She sighed but chose not to argue. Tomb might have preferred it because it would have given him a reason to pin her to the bed and his mouth to hers. But she silently slid in and curled up close to the edge, away from his side of the bed.

Tomb covered her right to the chin, brushing some of her wispy hair back from her beautiful face as she looked up at him.

He was delaying; he knew that.

Because once he put in place what he had in store for her, there was no putting it back in the box. No going back to how they were.

From what she'd said, Nina had never been happy with that way.

So, what did he have to lose?

A fucking lot.

He could lose her.

"Sleep tight, baby." He kissed her forehead.

"I guess you're going back to the clubhouse…"

"Nah, I'll be in our bed. Just gonna lock down the house, look around, like always."

Leaving Nina in bed, Tomb followed a path through the house and headed out to the backyard, where he pulled out a joint; he sat his ass on the deck and took a long toke, the smoke arrowing down to his lungs.

Even when he'd finished the joint, he didn't feel the calm as he might have yesterday or another day.

Sleep didn't come easy when he climbed into bed.

But the plan was set in his mind. And as Tomb gripped Nina's hip while she slept, unable not to touch her, he prayed to a God he didn't even believe existed that his wife would understand.

Nina

Breakfast was waiting for Nina the following morning.

A plate of cheesy eggs, crispy bacon, and a cup of steaming coffee.

Her feet came to a natural stop next to the kitchen island, and she ran her eyes over the hot plates of food.

She wasn't usually into breakfast unless that breakfast was four cups of coffee laced with creamer and natural sugar, none of that sweetener crap. If she wanted to taste sugar, she wanted the real deal. But seeing the food and her husband sitting at the table did soft things to her insides.

The chair beside Tomb skidded out; he'd used his foot to push it.

"Sit down, baby, eat before it gets cold."

She sat because her belly grumbled. "Since when do you make breakfast?"

"Since now." Tomb showed her a half-grin, using his fingers to pick up a crispy slice of bacon; he crunched half between his perfect white teeth.

"Is that going to be your answer from now on?"

He winked, and her fluttering heart betrayed her. She'd thought she'd locked that organ up tight, to avoid disappointment, yet Tomb knew the combination to get inside.

"It might be. I did a lot of thinking last night."

"When you weren't in bed…"

"I was only in the backyard, wife." He said. "I realized I haven't made you breakfast in a while."

Nina shrugged and sipped the coffee. Of course, it tasted perfect, so she swallowed again before spearing a piece of egg on the fork. The food was good, too.

"I haven't made you breakfast in a long time, either."

"I haven't been here, but that's about to change." Her eyes rose at his statement. Was he for real? Or would this new Tomb slowly drift back to his norm when he thought she was no longer mad at him? "Eat your food, baby, and we'll discuss it."

After a few moments of silent eating, Nina found Tomb watching her. There was no particular look on his face that she could guess his thoughts, but his eyes were territorial.

She thrived off that look, drowned in it.

Now, it seemed to have intensified overnight.

Swallowing, she said, "Thank you for breakfast. It's delicious."

Whatever she'd said cracked something in Tomb because that intense stare turned into a frown in a hot second, and he slammed the fork down next to his empty plate.

"I hate this polite bullshit, Nina. You shouldn't thank me for making food, for fuck's sake. You're my wife."

Nina's eyebrow hiked high on her forehead. "So you've reminded me several times over the past twenty-four hours."

"And as my wife," he gnashed his teeth together. "I get to do shit for you that you don't need to thank me for. Got it?"

Who knew her sweet, friendly guy knew how to throw a mood? Nina certainly hadn't.

Tension in her neck loosened while she sipped coffee and enjoyed him scowling like an angry bear. His shoulders were all hunched as he stared at her. Seeing him being grumpy diluted her inner turmoil.

"Whatever you say."

"Yes," he growled. "It's whatever I say. I'm glad you agree. And now I can tell you, you're not going into the salon today. You're coming on a ride with me."

Now, it was Nina who dropped her mouth open with shock. "I'm what now?"

"You heard me. I already called Esther; she'll watch the salon."

Nina just about pumped the brakes on her temper. "Rome, you can't do that. It's my goddamn salon, you don't have a say in *my* business. I'm going to work, not a bike ride with you."

"You laid it out for me yesterday. How do I make it right when we're always busy? It's only a few hours, Nina."

"You can't just expect me to skip work because you've decided."

The slapped hand on the table made her jump. Those crystal eyes were now like razor-sharp lasers, staring across at her. A tick worked on the side of his jaw.

"I'm fighting the fight here, Nina. Aren't you?"

Without speaking, Tomb cleaned up the dishes and left the kitchen.

Her eyes tracked his back until he was out of sight.

Only then did she breathe. Her heart frantically raced through the delirium, beat after beat.

Ugh. He was right. She reminded herself she wanted their relationship to work, which meant stepping out of her comfort zone to put in the effort.

After washing her hands, Nina changed into jeans and a Madonna concert t-shirt. Switching from her work heels, she found a pair of squared-heeled leather ankle boots in the closet. Next, she had to tie her hair in a ponytail if she was going on Tomb's bike. Before leaving the bedroom, she sprayed a little perfume on her neck.

Nina found Tomb standing by the back door, sliding his leather jacket over his beefy shoulders.

Just for a moment, she stared at the man she loved beyond all measure and reason and wondered, was she naïve to want more from him when he was already giving so much?

The breath caught in her throat, and that's when he turned around.

The surprise lit up his eyes when he skimmed down her body and back up again. Nina fought the urge to rub her thighs together to stop the ache between them.

Sex would not fix a thing, Nina.

"I'm ready. Where are we headed?"

"Princess." He breathed, stepping forward, and Nina prepared herself to have Tomb so close again. If he sensed her reluctance to be touched, it didn't give him pause when his hand glided around the back of her neck, clasping. "You look fucking gorgeous."

"I couldn't very well climb onto your bike in a pencil skirt, now could I?"

The devil winked. "Wouldn't be the first time." That was true. She'd been on the back of his Harley, dressed inappropriately for a biker's wife. Those rides usually ended with another particular kind of ride.

"We have more to talk through. It won't be easy. I have things I haven't discussed with you."

Frowning, she wanted to ask what things but only nodded.

"We're making a few drop-offs. Let me grab your jacket."

A while back, he'd had a replica of his jacket made for her birthday, but without the Diablos insignia on the back. It was midi and fitted across her chest perfectly. It even had a Road Captain's Old Lady patch. She loved it, but realized it had been ages since she'd worn it.

It felt like a homecoming as he helped her slip into the leather and then turned her around so he could zip her up.

"Thank you," she whispered nervously. Tomb was fraying her nerves at the end until she didn't know if she even had a problem.

"What did I say about that?" he smirked, using his thumb to knock her chin playfully.

"Yeah, yeah, I remember, bossy. Can you go back to the Tomb I know?"

Tipping his head down, he looked utterly masculine and so intimidating suddenly. Now, he pinched her chin and brought her face up.

"I thought you didn't like him?"

Frowning, Nina felt the weight of his resigned words. She wasn't cruel, and never to him, so she couldn't let him think that.

"Certain parts of our life aren't working for me, Tomb. I never said I didn't like you."

"You like me then?" he smirked cockily because he'd forever know that answer. It wasn't as though Nina could hide every reaction she had to his proximity. Even as mad as she'd been with him in the past, one squeezing hug and she could evaporate into calmness.

She swore Tomb's pheromones called out to hers. And she didn't mean only sexually. His presence was her elixir. It was why she craved more of him when he wasn't home.

"I like you fine." she rolled her eyes at his fishing, and he laughed, patting her on the butt to get her moving out the garage door so that he could lock up.

"Knew it, princess. Now, I gotta ask for something."

"Oh, asking now? I thought you'd move into your demanding era." She arched her eyebrow, hands on her hips.

"Do you wanna see how demanding your husband can be?"

A bolt of heat hit her straight down the middle, and Nina had to swallow a rock of lust before she answered.

"If it doesn't involve sex."

He chuckled. "You got it. Now you gotta give me the bike tax."

Confused, she frowned. "Bike tax? What's that?"

He dared tap a finger to his puckered lips, eyes like the devil, hot and tempting.

"Gotta pay the tax before you ride, princess. I don't make the rules."

"Ha. I think you make all the rules."

He was being ridiculous.

And cute.

Where had this cuteness come from?

Whatever the reason, she went up on her tiptoes. Tomb hunched down to help her, and she pressed a closed-lipped kiss to his mouth. Pulling away before it caught fire and turned into garage sex.

No one would believe how often that happened.

"You're ridiculous."

"Got a kiss from my wife, so I don't feel ridiculous," he smirked down and dirty, pleased with himself.

After helping her onto the seat behind him, she clutched his hips, bliss coating every inch of her body, content to be on his bike again.

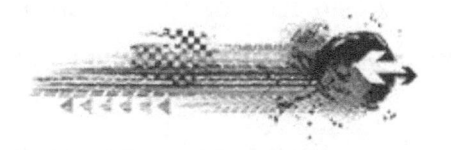

A drop-off meant delivering the merchandise.

Pharmaceutical medicines, to be precise.

She'd been told that it was a relatively new but lucrative endeavor. And one she was kind of proud of the boys for taking a risk with. Sure, it was against the law, and their aim was for profit, but it also helped many people who couldn't afford regular medicines without insurance.

Being a biker's wife meant not asking too many questions and trusting in your old man that he came home each night. Prison stints happened to the bikers. It was inevitable with the things they dabbled in. It wasn't as though they were selling candy to babies.

The Murphys, the Diablos' business partners, took most of the risks importing across the Canadian border. She supposed that's where they were headed, to meet with the elusive drug smugglers. Nina held onto Tomb while he rode to an undisclosed location.

They rode for at least fifty minutes outside Laketon until he pulled onto an abandoned lot. Nothing had been there in at least nine hundred years. But Tomb didn't park; he went around the back to a construction site. He pulled in at the side of a food truck.

Holding her hand, Tomb helped her down before he swung his leg over the seat.

"What is this place? Do you own it?"

Tomb put a hand on her lower back, steering her to the incredible-smelling food truck called *The Irish Spud*.

"No, baby. My construction days are behind me. I think they're building apartments on this plot. We're here to see this guy; he moves the truck around."

A blond man in a black apron, serving construction workers, gestured to the side door when he saw Tomb.

"I can wait here," she told him, but Tomb latched onto her hand, his nasty glower aimed behind her. When she glanced, she saw him staring at the men waiting to be served. Warmth spread through her middle at his protectiveness.

The food truck smelled heavenly. From the menu board, it seemed they sold every potato known to man. And she wanted to try them all.

"Brogan, good to see you, man. We won't stay long."

"You found the place, alright?" asked the man with the lyrical-sounding Irish accent. He didn't wait for an answer because he was grinning at her. "And who's me little darling, you've brought with you?" he offered Nina a hand. "I'm Brogan Murphy." But Tomb intercepted and knocked Brogan's hand away before she could shake it.

"She's not your little darling, don't start your Irish charm, you shit," warned her husband, making Brogan laugh.

"I'm Nina."

"My wife."

"Well then, hello, Tomb's darling wife." Brogan winked. "Anything you fancy to eat?"

She declined with a smile.

Tomb put his arm around her waist in a possessive style to keep her close in the small truck. She stayed there to avoid getting in the way.

"What did I say?"

"Hey, me mammy said to keep a lass sweet was to feed her."

"This lass doesn't need your feeding, Murphy."

Once the last customer was gone, Brogan retrieved wrapped packages from a drawer.

"Any problems?"

"Not this shipment. Me cousins had to change some dates around, fucking nosy officials sniffing around the docks."

The pickup lasted only minutes, and she wondered how Tomb would even get the packages into the saddlebags, but he managed it.

"Is this where you come all the time?"

"Brogan changes places every few days, his truck is popular on social media. He airdrops me his location when I get close."

"Smart," Nina remarked.

"It's not our first rodeo, baby." He half-smirked as he helped her onto the bike again, fastening the helmet strap underneath her chin. "Tax."

"Not this again. I already paid." She huffed.

"I don't make the rules, Nina girl."

"It appears you're making all the rules."

He waited. Cocky-like.

Huffing a breath, Nina grabbed Tomb by the jacket and yanked him forward, paying his damn tax again with another closed-lipped kiss. Even as he tried to use his tongue to pry hers open, she pulled back.

"That's not on my tax return. Nice try."

He laughed and grazed a fingertip on the tip of her nose, climbing on the bike.

"Where to next?"

"We'll drop this load off."

"Okay then, start this colossal beast up. Let's go."

"That's usually what you say to me when you're straddled over my lap, wanting my dick."

Flaming all over, she jabbed her fingers into his ribs. "That's enough of that."

"Just saying, baby."

"As you said to the cute Irishman, quit with the charm."

Craning his neck, Tomb blasted her with a low-lidded glare. "You thought he was cute? It's not too late to go back and strangle him."

Nina witnessed Tomb handling other men who flirted with her, and each time, she'd fallen more in love with him over his territorial dog display. With Tomb, she dropped feminism at the door to bask in his rugged machoness.

"No, I barely noticed the cute Irishman. You don't need to strangle him."

Tomb grunted and started up the engine. The heavy throttled vibrations traveled through her legs, making her instinctively clasp onto his waist.

Color Nina surprised when they stopped at a suburban house a few miles outside their town. The street was quiet. Every lawn was cut to the exact inches. The HOA had a tight authoritarian grip on the neighborhood because every house looked like a photocopy of each other. She cast a look toward the house with the four steps leading toward a wraparound porch decorated in hanging baskets of overspilling flowers.

"What are we doing here?"

She hadn't expected the club 'dealers' to be women in their sixties.

"Well, that was a surprise," she shared with Tomb. She'd let him go inside the suburban houses while she stayed outside with the Harley. She was leaning a hip on the seat as he stalked down the pathway away from the last drop-off. Each lady had greeted Tomb like an old friend. "I had no idea what I was expecting, but it wasn't that."

"When you think of a dealer, you picture a tweaked-out guy in a hoodie, doing deals in a back alley." He said. "No one looks twice at these bingo gals. It was Chains' idea. They get paid, plus all the necessary meds they need, and they know the right clients."

This gig was highly illegal, but it made sense. Now she knew the Diablos had retirees selling their products, she chuckled.

"I learn something new every day."

"I've enjoyed showing you one of my typical days, baby." Tomb shared as he cupped the side of her face. Each time he'd touched her today, she'd felt their connection, bright and alive. But she was still skeptical.

Rome wasn't built in a day. And Rome couldn't change in a day, either.

Assuming they were headed into Laketon, the bike took a different turn, and he eventually parked alongside a sedan on a cozy Main Street.

"You hungry?" He asked when Nina climbed down from the seat. As he'd done all morning, Tomb got there first to unclip her helmet before he did his own. Hanging them both on the handlebars. "Let's grab something." With a hand on her lower back, he guided her across the street before he shifted himself to the outside of the sidewalk.

It occurred to her he often did that, putting himself closer to the road. Then Tomb tagged her hand, locking it in his.

They walked in silence just a block to a chain bar/restaurant. Once seated in a window, and a server had taken their lunch order, he asked. "What do you think of this place?"

"It looks fine. Why?"

"The club is considering buying an empty lot on Phillips Way to become something similar. A coffee bar during the day and a bar/restaurant at night. Axel has me scouting when I'm out of town."

Their coffees arrived, and Nina thanked the younger girl.

"Who would oversee it?"

She waited for him to volunteer, putting more space and lost time between them. When he said Splice's name, she let out her breath, relieved.

"Splice manages the new start-ups." Tomb offered the info, sipping his black coffee across from her. "He does the hiring and firing."

"Would I get free coffee?"

"Of course, princess."

"Maybe he'd hire me if the salon folds."

His two eyebrows winged up. "That's not the first time you've mentioned something is going on with your salon. What's up?"

He was perceptive, and there was no point in lying.

"It's nothing major. There are always slow periods."

"That's what has had you worried? It's a slow period?"

"A rent increase. It's making things tight. I might have to let someone go, and I don't want to do that if it can be avoided."

Tomb frowned but said nothing while the server placed sandwiches before them.

"Why didn't you say anything?"

"Because it's not a big deal, it happens. Things will improve." She hoped, anyway.

"I could have helped."

Nina's lips twitched, amused at the image it formed in her head. "Are you good with coloring and cuts, Rome?"

He took a large bite from his beef rib sandwich. "If you want bald customers, sure. I meant with money. How much do you need to keep afloat?"

Everything in Nina froze, and she stared across at him.

"Absolutely not. No."

"It's no big deal, baby."

It was a considerable deal, and he didn't get it. "This isn't a discussion I'm having. It's my salon. If it succeeds or fails, it's because of me. I don't need you to swoop in."

His gorgeous eyes slit to accusing lines, and she noticed the tightness around his lips like he was offended.

Anger ignited in her veins.

"The salon is in trouble." His correct assumption made Nina feel sick for not confiding in him sooner. "And you haven't said a word to me about it. How long?"

"It doesn't matter."

"How fucking long, Nina?" he asked quietly. When she said nothing, he only stared harder, longer, until she wanted to confess every little sin she'd had in her lifetime. "How many more secrets are you keeping from me, my wife?"

"When you say *my wife* in that tone, you make me sound like I'm property."

"You *are* my property." He issued, and it sucked all the air out of her body.

"You did... You did not just say that."

"I said it and meant it. Eat your food, Nina."

"I'm no longer hungry."

Tomb pushed his plate aside and reached into his wallet to pay the check.

"Fine, let's go."

Nina followed because it was automatic, every muscle listening to his commanding voice. Once outside, he stepped around her again and put himself closest to the roadside of the sidewalk. He tagged her hand, and she let him.

They were both pissed, that was clear, and the walk across to his motorcycle was done in silence. The quiet treatment didn't stop Tomb from making sure she was clipped into the helmet and safely sitting on the bike.

"Your stubborn streak is making my teeth ache, baby." He growled when sitting in place, the engine yet to start. "I get you think I've been a shit husband, but I'd never see the salon go under. The money is right there. You could have drawn from our account."

"It's not salon money." She protested weakly. "I can handle it." She already felt like a failure.

"You don't need to handle shit. And you didn't tell me what was happening. It stops now." Before she could speak, he started the bike and powered off with force, she knew to hold on tight or be thrown off backward with the motion of speed.

Why hadn't she told him what was happening? If not two years ago, this week? Nina could have shared her worry at any point, and Tomb would have helped. He wouldn't have let a jerk get to where he'd propositioned her to pay the rent.

Sometimes, she hated how she couldn't easily ask for help without feeling sick.

She was exhausted most of the time.

Offloading her problems to someone else would be a massive weight off her shoulders. But she couldn't break the lifelong habit of refusing to be weak and unsuccessful.

She was the least likely to succeed at anything when she graduated high school and had to forgo college to find a job to help her mom pay the bills.

While her flaky mom bounced from boyfriend to boyfriend, it was Nina keeping the lights on and food in the pantry. And when her mom split for the last time, she was finally free. Nina then vowed never to rely on anyone as her mom had.

But Tomb wasn't any man.

He wasn't a deadbeat guy with nothing to offer.

She'd fallen deeply in love with him for a reason. He was addictive. Whatever Tomb was made of, she craved him.

Even when he made her mad, she'd always felt safe.

Even when pushed to the point, she didn't think she could stay married to him.

How she felt about him would never change.

"I don't want to argue." She shared that when the bike came to a rumbling stop outside their house, He rested his feet on the ground, not switching off the engine, when Nina squeezed Tomb around the middle.

"If you did as I said, we wouldn't argue." He stated in a flat voice. "You'd be happy, cared for, have everything you wanted."

Off the bike, she stared at him.

"It's not that easy."

"Yeah, Nina, it is. I wasn't lying or being cute when I said I wanted my fingerprints all over your life. It wasn't me teasing. I've wanted that since the moment we met, but I held back; I pushed that need in me so fucking deep so I didn't scare you. You say I neglect your needs, but you don't tell me what they are. And now all these secrets you're keeping from me are escaping. So maybe I don't know you either."

With his last fired words, Tomb walked toward the house. He left her there, stunned, unable to speak, with her heart cracking open.

He was right.

It was her fault for the lack of communication. She was too doggedly independent; she'd always known it.

Attention.

Affection.

What she needed most from her marriage. But Tomb needed things, too. For Nina to rely on him. His anger became apparent, and it was justified. She'd felt lonely, but some of it was her fault for not trusting him enough with her worries.

Sighing, she unglued her feet from the gravel driveway and followed Tomb into the house.

The last thing she expected to see were suitcases sitting in the hallway.

The angry man, with his arms folded, glared at her.

Every emotion in Nina raced to the surface, putting her in a state of shock and panic, of hurt and disillusionment.

Oh, God, no. The worst was happening.

Tomb was leaving her.

Tomb

T hat he might have hurt her should please Tomb because it meant something he'd said had reached inside her castle and moat.

But there was no joy when he saw her putting two and two together as she glanced at the cases, coming up with an unfathomable negative answer.

"I wanted to do this the easy way, but as I'm finding out, my wife doesn't do it easily." He stated.

"You're leaving?" she asked. Unable to disguise the quiver in her voice, another part of Tomb cracked open. There was no inch of Nina's life he didn't want to control, to make better, to predict her wishes, and to make the happiness spill out. From the moment they'd met, and he'd known she belonged to him, he'd nudged her along with marginal control to appease him without shaking her foundations apart. It seemed like a fair compromise.

A delicate fucking middle ground he'd accepted or risked losing his independently stubborn goddess.

Enough was enough.

Tomb was no longer playing by conventional standards.

She already considered him an unfeeling, unbothered jackass, immune to the wants she craved. When, in fact, Tomb made it his daily mission to feast on her desires.

His Nina girl was about to experience what his true obsession felt like. Whether she was ready for it was another story.

But Tomb was done waiting.

"I should have known," she scowled, her cheeks so lovely and pink with emotion. "Fine, do what you want."

"Thanks, sweetheart, I'm about to." He smiled, and she sent him a deeper scowl. Grabbing the bags, he stalked out the door, knowing she was watching him. He dumped them in the back of his truck and returned to find her unmoving. "You ready to go?"

She blinked, her face blank. "Go where? Aren't you the one leaving? Or... you're kicking me out?"

Jesus fucking Christ. Her low opinion of him needed to change.

If not for the lip captured it in her lower teeth, fighting against showing any emotion, he would have spanked her raw for that remark. Instead, Tomb engaged a little patience as he palmed the side of her face. His thumb worked slowly to free her trapped lip until he could stroke the warm skin inside. There would be the time for him to discover when her erosion of trust set in.

There was work to do, but having his hands on Nina was when he was most at peace because she succumbed to him so quickly. With his hands on her, she trusted him to give her everything.

"*We* are leaving," he shared. "Me and you need time to repair this, and we can't do it here where we're constantly pulled into other things."

"Where you're pulled into other things, you mean?" She stabbed, but the sweetest part was she never tried to move away from him.

"Yes," he growled. "When I'm always gone, princess, because I made it that way, so I wouldn't put you under lock and fucking key, so I wouldn't own you completely and make you hate me. But now, losing the thing I own is already threatened; I no longer have to play nice. We're going away."

"No, we are not." She scoffed, pushing his hand away, but he scooped an arm around her waist and dragged her back before she could even take two steps. "I can't go anywhere now. For God's sake, Tomb, I have the salon. You're being too drastic. It doesn't need a big gesture. I wanted attention and to see you gave a shit."

"The salon is fine. I've taken care of it."

"You had no right." She pushed his arm, but he locked it around her struggling frame. If she wriggled anymore, they'd end up fucking on the hallway floor. Dirty, angry fucking, his hardening cock was on board for those plans. But there was going to be time for a lot of sex. If he could reach inside her locked thoughts, he'd fuck every one of them out of her until Tomb owned her secrets, too.

"That's where you're wrong, wife. I have all the rights." He earned a cute little elbow to the gut, and Tomb laughed, capturing her arm so she couldn't throw another and hurt herself.

"Don't puke that patriarchy shit at me. You don't make the rules."

"I do. You've never seen it up close. Quit struggling, princess, or we'll end up on the floor with my mouth sucking an orgasm out of your pussy." He grunted, holding her ass tight to his groin to help her grasp his point. "Now, are we doing this the easy way or the Nina way?"

Of course, she struggled. He'd expect nothing less from his spitfire wife. She had enough temper in her to raise chaos in an empty room. The surge of heat went through Tomb's cock, and he considered derailing his thoroughly constructed plans to make her scream into his mouth while he hammered orgasms out of her.

"You're being absurd. Think about this, Rome."

"I have," he grunted and bent at the waist, putting his shoulder against her stomach, then hoisted her into the air to put his wife over his shoulder.

"Oh, my God." She squealed, thumping his back. "Put me down right now. I'm not going anywhere with you! Put me down!"

"The Nina way it is then," he grinned and strolled out the door, tapping her on the ass. "Quit moving. You're only hurting yourself."

Another harder smack on her ass, and Tomb heard her moan, but she quit squirming long enough so he could engage their house security.

"If you do this, Rome, I'll make your life hell. I swear it."

Chuckling, Tomb palmed her ass and gave it a nice squeeze. He was in-fucking-vigorated for the first time in a long time. Shedding his skin to be the deviant beneath felt fucking good. "Do you pinkie-swear, wife?"

"I will kill you." she wriggled, but he kept striding toward the truck.

"Let's do it with our clothes off." Once he wrangled the truck door open, he told her. "You stay where I put you," he warned, plopping her into the passenger seat. Though she glared at him as he shut the door and rounded the front of the vehicle, she didn't move.

"Where the hell are we supposed to be going?"

"Away."

"This is kidnapping. I don't consent to this, Tomb." Arms folded, a pissed-off scowl in place, she'd never looked hotter to him, and Tomb adjusted his jeans as he slipped into the truck.

"Did you hear me asking for consent?" the tightening in his chest loosening by the second.

Finally, he could be his authentic, totalitarian self, living in a world worshipping his wife, even when she scowled at him.

Reaching across the console, he placed a hand on her thigh while taking turns out of their quiet neighborhood. When he'd bought the one-story house with the sprawling backyard and two port garages, he'd never expected to have a wife living with him one day. He'd been happy rolling along as a lone wolf, picking up pleasure when he fancied it, but not being bound to anyone.

The idea Nina could untangle herself from him and walk away made the bile slosh from side to side in his gut. He wanted nothing more than to lock all her molecules to him.

He had to touch her.

Nina was his breath of fresh air after a smoke-choking existence.

She was the pulse in his chest.

Even resting furiously at his side, refusing to grant him the satisfaction of glaring at him, not acknowledging he existed, she had a tight grip on his soul. And for a man entirely demented over his wife, there was nothing Tomb wouldn't do to keep her.

What was a touch of spousal kidnapping to prove his love?

Nina

Her libido should not be lit up like a Christmas tree while she was being carted who-knew-where. But then, her body never listened to the warning signs, or she wouldn't have fallen for a wild biker.

With her range of thoughts from cluttered, confused, and a little turned on, she still gave Tomb access to hold her thigh as he drove silently with the other hand on the wheel. Her initial burst of anger had long since burned out. She could deal with her husband kidnapping her.

Whenever she looked at Tomb, memories of their past overwhelmed Nina and reminded her of what she might lose if she didn't take a chance. Agonizing, beautiful memories.

Not everything had been wrong.

But he'd organized this, hadn't he?

As dramatic as kidnapping was, though tame in a True Crime documentary sense.

He'd done this for *them*.

Because Nina could not latch onto one whirling thought at a time, she remained silent as Tomb drove, taking them out of Laketon and onto the highway.

The scenery whizzed by with speed. She was completely clueless about her whereabouts, losing her sense of direction miles back. They were somewhere remote, that much she knew. They'd hardly seen another car for ages. Now, they were on a long stretch of road with not much in the distance.

"Are you gonna give me the silent treatment all day, princess?"

Only when he'd needed to switch gears had Tomb moved his hand from her thigh. Even now, he rubbed her knee, sending warm waves of pleasure to her clenching core. She was hard-wired to be turned on by him. Especially when she was riled up, it was their foreplay, after all.

But this was his game show. She had to see how Tomb imagined this would play out.

Did he think he could kidnap her, and she'd go along docilely? If so, he didn't know her all that well.

Deep down, a part of her loved what was happening. Having him take any decision out of her hands tasted like freedom. Free from consideration, planning, and worrying.

Her husband had kidnapped her, but knowing Tomb would never put her in danger was a liberation.

Love wasn't linear.

It ebbed and flowed and raged at various times.

She loved Tomb. Maybe too much.

She felt that love in every atom of her body, in her brain, taking her over, making her illogical and unmoored.

But loving him had strengthened her, too.

It made her yearn and reach for things she'd thought impossible.

Love was impossible.

It couldn't only be words and platitudes. It had to be actions and motions and promises. Love had to be stronger than fear and mistrust. It had to be the biggest thing in the room, controlling the mood and stability.

For love, she had more fight left in her.

Fighting for a marriage, she wanted to keep more than anything else in the world.

Lifting her knees, she rested her bare feet on the dashboard, having kicked off her shoes long ago for comfort. A kidnapee deserved comfort, after all.

"I don't know the kidnapped rules, do I? This is my first foray into the dark romance arena. You didn't provide a guidebook, forgive me. I wasn't sure if I could talk." She answered, and a second later, she heard his rumbling growl as he speared a scowl across the truck.

"Get your feet down. If we're in an accident, your legs will be shattered in a thousand places." When she didn't comply right away, Tomb growled again. "Nina, *now*."

She planted her feet firmly in a dramatic act of rebellion as he abruptly stopped the truck and stormed out, pacing a few feet away. The restlessness came off him in thick waves.

He grabbed at his luscious locks and paced again.

Nina watched as if she were seeing Tomb for the first time.

How often had he lost his cool that she could remember? Hardly ever. If his football team lost that week, he might curse out the TV, but emotions weren't Tomb's weakness. He took most things in his stride.

When the club got hit by a bomb, and Ruin was injured for months, Tomb hadn't lost his head or gone off half-cocked for revenge. He ensured Nina was safe, driving her back and forth from work for weeks.

Huh. How hadn't she grasped what he was doing then? She'd taken it for granted and hardly acknowledged his behavior during those weeks. With her head rushing with insight, she wondered, what else was Tomb doing in the background that she didn't see?

Things to make her life, their life, better?

She was confused more than ever, but her heart split open with love.

Nina gawped. Watching, she whirred the window and stuck her head out, admiring her man with his hands on his hips, head to the sky, probably speaking to God or someone higher up.

"You should have asked Ruin for psycho tips if you can't hack the kidnapper's stress." She said, seeing how his eyes narrowed when he turned them on her. Within five steps, he'd yanked open her side of the door and loomed in, almost touching her all over with his sheer size alone.

"You don't know how badly I wanna spank your little ass, Nina. Keep that bratty tongue in check."

She gulped. Wetness pooled between her legs, soaking her panties. "It's hardly," she had to swallow before going on. "It's hardly little."

God, he wanted to spank her? *Yes, please.*

Even as frustrated as he appeared, there was something predatory about how he grasped her chin, urged it up, and quickly kissed her lips, leaving them tingling when he pulled back too soon.

Spending time with Tomb wasn't a chore. Far from it, it was what she dreamed of most days. Endless, clingy days together would be bliss.

The calm and orderly Tomb was back in business when he got behind the wheel again. Sliding a pair of shades over his eyes, he looked her way.

"We're almost there."

"Oh, goodie. My torture chamber awaits."

The tyrant chuckled gravel-like, and every inch of her body awakened to the noise. Her heart thumped with staccato drums. The carefree Tomb was loveable, but this domineering Tomb would be a problem.

An addictive problem.

They were cocooned in a calm bubble for the rest of the journey.

She wouldn't fight him with words, but Tomb wouldn't get her easily.

He'd made this happen and had to show her the winning move with more than words. She wanted actions to burst her heart open. She wanted to witness how he needed their marriage as profoundly and loyally as she did.

A thousand percent.

There was no accepting less.

Maybe before, but not now.

Make or break, they were in this lane now.

And she had to trust her kidnapper knew how to navigate.

"We're here," he rumbled twenty minutes later as he took a dirt track, still driving forever with no end in sight.

Here, where?

But then they came through the trees, and an incredible two-story lodge appeared.

How she missed it was a mystery, because it was a large house, standing on sprawling land as far as the eye could see. It boasted glass doors and a balcony with a glass railing. Sitting on a raised deck was a covered hot tub, and around the side of the lodge was a table big enough for a large family.

It was gorgeous as it was picturesque with a forestry backdrop, like something out of a romantic movie. And already, Nina felt a melting in her tension at the prospect of alone time with Tomb.

"You're doing kidnapping wrong if this is your idea of a dungeon. I'll Amazon Prime you a copy of Kidnapping for Dummies."

"You haven't seen anything yet, princess." He flashed her a panty-melting side stare and slid out of the truck. Rounding the hood, he came for her with a single-minded focus, which had her skin goosebumped with anticipation when he pulled open the door.

His stare grew effective as he slowly scanned across her body. As he visually devoured her inch by inch, Nina felt bathed in his attention, owned by a visual caress.

"Out you get," he rasped, but didn't allow her to move before he plucked her around the waist, depositing her feet to the ground.

"Shouldn't you put a bag over my head so I don't know the location of your torture chamber? Isn't that how it goes? Should I march like I'm going to the gallows?"

"You can use that wild imagination in bed," he suggested, hooking up her hand. "Come on, let me show you inside. I'll come back for our bags."

"Okay, kidnapper, let's get this show on the road. This shack better have Wi-Fi."

Tomb

Tomb couldn't peel his eyes off Nina as she walked around the lodge, waving her iPhone. He chewed the inside of his cheek, knowing what rampage was coming. When awareness set in, she sent him a furious glare; he counted to three in his head.

"I can't even get a signal. There's no internet here, Rome! Are we in the 1980s? How could you do this to me? How can a person live without the internet? It's fucking barbaric, *unforgivable*. It would be best if you took me home right now. I'm not even playing."

Entertained by her annoyance, his wife was addicted to having online shopping at her manicured fingertips. "I'm sure Amazon Prime will live a few days without you, princess."

"That's what you think. Those delivery drivers rely on my packages for their yearly bonuses."

He watched her track every inch of the lodge for another few minutes, looking for the elusive signal that would never come. Axel installed a blocker at the lodge when it was built to take the location off the grid. Fortunately, it also stopped Nina from using her phone for rage tweeting. He needed her entire focus. The lodge and the surrounding land were a dead area. No technology was getting in or out unless he turned off the blocker.

It was primarily the reason he brought her here. No interruptions.

"I'm gonna get some heat in here, but it'll take a while, so I'll grab some logs from out back and build a fire."

"Build me a Wi-Fi tower while you're at it."

He chuckled, leaving her to her inner fury. Tomb was back in minutes, his arms full of chopped logs. The probies had followed his instructions to a T getting the lodge ready. He set about building a fire in the four-foot-high brick fireplace.

Tomb didn't know he was smiling until he heard.

"How can you look so smug right now?" she stomped her foot, a hand on her curved hip. He was such a down-and-dirty animal for loving when she became fiery. He loved touching those curves, tasting them on the tip of his tongue. No one else on earth had a banging body like his Nina girl or a more reactive temper. Something compelled him to cradle her strength in his hands, to take care of her in ways no one else ever had.

He cocked his head to the side to catch her eyes on him. "I have my wife all to myself. What's not to be smug about?"

She rolled her pretty eyes, tossing the obsolete phone on the low coffee table in front of the unlit fireplace. That woman's temper did it for him in the worst way. His cock was threatening to split out of his jeans. The entire car ride, he'd wanted to pull over to fuck the mood out of her.

"Yeah, I'm sure you're thrilled about that. I'll give it twenty-four hours before you miss all your bros and biker time together. You'll rush me home faster than a speeding train."

His stomach took a rollercoaster dip at hearing the hurt.

How wrong she was.

And he was going to prove to her she was his goddamn priority.

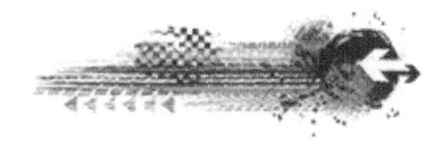

Nina

"How long are you gonna stew in the tub for?"

After observing Tomb building the fire, she'd explored the four-bedroom cabin from top to bottom. The kitchen and the sizeable hot tub outside on the deck were impressive. The fridge was stocked well. As soon as there was hot water, she'd taken herself away to soak in the bathtub adjacent to their bedroom. It was heaven, and she'd tried hard not to let her thoughts run away, but she wasn't holding much success in that area. She was a born overthinker.

She only wished she knew what Tomb was thinking.

Nina didn't bother looking up when he spoke, but sensed Tomb taking up all the space in the bathroom, and his nearness caused a riot of temper and tingles to align.

"Until this charade is over, and I can go home."

"You're home, princess." He spoke quietly, approaching on silent, bare feet. "I'm your home."

That was true, and he knew it, too.

When he was directly in front of the tub, hands lazily down in the front pockets of his jeans, he emanated nothing but relaxation.

"I took your control away from you, and you're pissed. I get that. But I told you we were doing things my way now. This was my way, princess. There are no distractions. Only you and me. You've had long enough to stew in your mood, plotting how to kill me. Tell me about it over food. You need to eat, so let's get you dried."

"I'm not pissed." Anymore. "I'm confused. You've explained exactly zero things. All I wanted was to talk to you, for you to hear where I was coming from."

"We're gonna do that. After you've eaten, I can hear your stomach from here."

"I get hungry when I'm kidnapped. It's all the adrenalin and danger."

He had the audacity to flash her a devastating grin, but when she rose out of the water, his smile fell, and his eyes turned greedy and dark with lust.

"Christ, baby."

His examination was downright lewd, and reverence all rolled into one. With water dripping off her body, she felt empowered by his stare. Not an inch of her was untouched by his eyes. Tomb looked at her like he hadn't seen her naked a million and ten times already; he looked at her like she was hotter than the sun. And for any woman with her heart unlocked and begging, it was a total ego high. Nina climbed over the lip of the bath. Tomb was there, already holding out a fluffy towel. He didn't let her take it; he wrapped it around her to do the drying. Dropping to his haunches, he ensured no water drip was left on her skin.

"Let me dress you," he rumbled thickly, leading her into the bedroom, where she found he'd unpacked the bags.

"I can do it."

"I want to."

Her pulse surged, heavy and thick in her veins as she remained unmoving as he drew the pale pink underwear up her legs.

"Did you rent this cabin?"

"No, it's club owned."

Weird, she didn't know that. Odder still, they'd never been here until now.

Maybe he'd brought others here.

"It's the first time I've been." He answered her unspoken thoughts.

"We've used it as a safe house, but the boys and their old ladies primarily use it as a weekend getaway."

"We've never been here."

"That'll change in the future, Nina. A lot of things will."

She was powerless to hold back the pour of hope filling her heart. Before he rose to drop a baggy sleep shirt over her head, she stroked her fingers through his hair and watched how Tomb's eyes burned as he glanced up at her.

He was the most beautiful man inside and out.

"I'm going to walk around, make sure everything is okay. Get comfortable downstairs, baby."

Nina frowned. "Is it safe?"

He winked over his shoulder as he walked out of the bedroom. "I'd let nothing happen to you."

She knew that one hundred percent.

Her husband might not emote as she wanted him to and might prefer the company of others to her, but he was a natural protector.

She took her sweet time going downstairs. Instead, she found he'd packed her practical clothes and stocked the bathroom with all her hygiene items.

This meant this trip was super planned. It wasn't a spontaneous kidnapping. He would have had to note her bathroom products to buy and bring them up beforehand. There was even all her hair care electronics, too.

Next to the bed was her sleep mask and noise machine.

He'd brought all the comforts of home to his kidnap site.

What a contrary guy Tomb was.

For better or for worse, this train had left the station, and she had to stay on board to reach the final destination.

Her nerves skittered when she walked barefoot down the open staircase, her heart arrested when she caught sight of Tomb, already watching her.

Slouched in the leather seat, legs spread out before him, his bare feet peeking from the end of his ratty-worn jeans. She took the seat furthest away from him. His mouth twitched as if he'd known her angle.

She didn't have internet, but there was a big TV and a stack of DVDs.

After a few minutes.

"We have all the time in the world, Nina. You might as well relax until you're ready to tell me what you're thinking."

"I thought this was your show? I don't know what's going on. You plucked me out of my life. I can't even make a call to check on the salon."

"The salon is fine. Forget everything but you and me."

Easier said than done when her life's work was teetering on collapse. Only held together by the grace of a fucking megalomaniac.

"Okay," she agreed and was rewarded by Tomb's slow-growing smile.

By now, the fire was crackling in the fireplace, casting a warm hue around the cabin downstairs area. In any other situation, this might have been romantic.

But this was their Camp David.

Not exactly a cozy retreat, but the most critical location of their lives.

"You wanna come sit with me, baby?"

Her eyes pinged across the room at him and saw how tempting he was. How he made a hot twinge go through her clit at the offer.

Yes. Was her answer. It was always yes. She never missed an opportunity to sit cuddled with Tomb.

But Nina shook her head. "It'll turn into sex if I do. And sex has never been our problem."

Tomb half smiled, kind of sad, and she felt the hit of it low in her stomach.

"I'm glad I don't fuck up in all areas." And then. "I need to hear it all, Nina, before I say what I gotta say."

Nerves skipped down her arms, and she clutched at her leg, curled underneath her butt to keep her fingers occupied. "Can I be honest?"

"Only honesty between us."

She agreed with that and wished it had been the case from the beginning, wishing she'd said it all long ago.

"I feel lonely most of the time."

"Fuck," he hissed, dropping his head over his hands.

"The whole point of marriage, or at least the big part, is our lives were supposed to change. We'd become partners in all aspects. But they haven't, Rome. You still do what you do, and we sometimes sleep in the same bed or go to your mom's together for Sunday dinner."

His head lowered, and she saw his knuckles turn white as he clasped his fists.

"I don't know if I went wrong somewhere if I wasn't doing something that made us this way, Rome. Couples fizzle out, don't they? Maybe we need a break. A temporary separation to work out what we each need from this marriage."

She felt her throat thicken with a brick of emotion, and every cell of her body, which loved Tomb, screamed in rejection of that suggestion.

Leaving him was the very last thing she wanted. The idea made her want to vomit all over the floor and to cry for a month.

Please give me an alternative suggestion, Rome. Please, baby.

His growl rippled through the room, echoing loudly. Then he lifted his head, and she caught his thunderous reaction.

"Don't ever let me hear you say those words to me again, Nina." He instructed between his clenched teeth. "Don't fucking think them. We are *never* separating."

Breathing, letting the anxiety out with each exhale. "You keep saying that, but nothing can back it up."

"My words not good enough?"

Deflated, she sighed, letting her feet land on the floor, ready to get the fuck out of there. Wherever there was. She fell quiet.

After a minute, "I knew this was a waste of time. You're not interested in a discussion; you're just throwing commands at me and expecting me to swallow them. I want to go home."

"No," he growled. Shooting to his feet, the sight of an angry-filled, vibrating Tomb dried up Nina's tongue until she had to unpeel it from the roof of her mouth. "Princess, you're working my last nerve with this idiotic notion that we're ending because you're having some female month-long bad mood. Keep going, and you'll be punished."

Everything came at Nina in a total wave rush.

Working *his* last nerve.

Idiotic notion.

Female bad mood.

Punishment.

Fucking punishment?

The words—Tombs words he'd said from his addictive fucking mouth. Words he'd never uttered to her before spun around her head like they were on one of those out-of-control fairground rides.

With so few words and so much to unpack, she was consumed by how her skin felt on fire.

She couldn't be turned on.

Not while being the most furious she'd ever been in her whole life.

"Punished?" she squeaked out through her tight throat. Suddenly, her nipples hurt beneath her thin cotton shirt, and she needed his fingers to pull them. Punish them.

Oh, shut up.

"You can go all the way to hell and then take the number eleven bus to fuck off from there." She screeched and spun around barefoot, heading for the staircase. "I'm going home."

"Good luck trying to get out of locked doors, princess." He provoked as she turned around to glower at him. Yet again, he'd shed the anger he wore only moments ago, but Nina was still bristling when he pointed a finger at her. "Sit your little ass down, or I'll cart you back."

"This is pointless."

"Nothing between us is pointless. But swear to fuck, Nina, I don't wanna hear one more word about you leaving me." his or else lay thick in the air between them as she watched him stride for the back door. "I need to grab some more wood." His last parting words.

Tomb didn't realize it wasn't her leaving the marriage.

It was him.

She sighed and parked her ass on the couch again, glaring at her useless phone. Fucking Wi-Fi-free zone. There wasn't even an excuse to avoid her life by staring at the screen for an hour or six.

Great.

Nina

She must have dozed off because a repetitive noise brought Nina from her light sleep. After rubbing her eyes and finding her bearings, she swung her feet to the floor.

"Tomb?" she called out, wondering where he was.

Outside the bank of windows, she caught sight of Tomb swinging an axe at sizeable logs.

"Jesus." She puffed air onto the glass pane. That man was stupendously sexy. His butt looked ridiculously good in jeans, and each swing highlighted his arm muscles until they bulged with sweaty strain. It was seeing masculinity in its raw form.

She noticed towels in the bathroom closet during her cabin tour. So, she grabbed one and went to her husband with a peace offering.

Without speaking, she put the towel on the outside seating and started picking up the pieces Tomb had broken in half, throwing them into a basket. He stopped in mid-swing when he saw her.

"You chop. I'll gather. You've made enough to last for five winters."

He only grunted and resumed swinging the axe like the sexiest lumber-snack. But then he paused.

"Wait, Nina, be careful of splinters. Here, put these on." He pulled work gloves out of his back pocket, laying the axe against the chopping block, he strolled over and held one out for her to slide a hand into and then the other.

When he resumed chopping, she stared at him. A lot went through her mind.

Not in a month of Sundays and a few Tuesdays would she ever stop desiring Rome King. He was made for her, or she was made for him. When they were together, they became a combustible matter.

He gave her slow and sweet.

Fast and hard.

No two fucks were ever the same in a row, and she'd loved that. Still loved it.

If Nina could be content with only the physical side of their relationship, she'd be the happiest woman alive because no man on earth could fuck as Rome could. Her goliath of a husband was composed of sin and sexual allure.

No man before Rome had spoken to her sex drive the way he did. He could make her shake, cry, beg, and burst out of her skin. He made her shudder with little effort, with a look from his savage eyes, a quirk of his lips, and a skim of his tongue.

After she filled two baskets and dragged them over to the pile where she carefully stocked them tall, she brought the towel over.

"I think we have enough logs unless we stay through winter."

She'd said it in an attempt at a joke to lighten the tension swirling around them, but Tomb only raised his eyebrow. "Maybe."

"Ha, ha, funny."

She handed him the towel, but Tomb didn't grab it. "Dry me off, princess." He rasped, and a shiver arrowed right through her. Obediently, she ditched the gloves and stroked the towel over his chest, stomach, neck, and back. She dabbed once more when she traveled around him, this time over his torso of tattoos. He was dry, but she couldn't stop touching him, even letting the towel fall through her fingers to get skin-on-skin contact.

It was like caressing forbidden fire.

That heat pounded Nina low in her stomach when she looked up and found Tomb's dark eyes trained on her. The towel fell to the floor, and neither noticed. Her fingertips were left on Tomb's chest.

"You don't need an excuse to touch me, princess."

She didn't try to deny it. Didn't remove her hands either; she couldn't, not while she was trembling with lust attacking her from all corners. Tomb was her favorite thing to touch; she'd even say she was obsessed with his sturdy body. All that golden skin decorated in ink and fine hair.

Tomb swiftly took hold of her hands and guided them to his neck. He then lifted her and carried her in his arms.

"Tomb," she whispered, her head and body at war.

Their bodies spoke volumes, and his was saying so much when he squeezed her ass cheeks. She wore only skimpy panties underneath the baggy t-shirt. Nina felt his hands pull her ass cheeks crudely apart in the way he did when he enjoyed looking at her pussy from behind.

Nina moaned, unable to tear her gaze from his eyes. So low-lidded and appealing.

"I thought we were arguing?"

"We're hitting the pause button because you need something from me."

"Wha—what is it you think I need?"

"The same thing as always when our hands are on each other. How much we want to fuck."

Oh, God, he wasn't wrong. She was vibrating, wanting him.

"But..."

"We've hit pause, Nina." He growled, and then Tomb crushed her mouth underneath his, kissing her with the horniest passion she'd ever tasted on his tongue. Moaning into Tomb's mouth, completely surrendered in the kiss, she wasn't aware of moving until she felt the warmth of the cabin interior on her skin.

She moaned again, digging her fingers into the back of his hair, anxious that Tomb might pull away. But he delved deeper, tasting her with aroused tongue strokes, taking her away one kiss at a time.

The sensations were euphoric, and she could scarcely breathe before a fresh kiss assaulted her. Tomb wasn't gentle, biting and licking her into a whimpering mess. His desire was contagious.

His mouth was wild even as he moved across the cabin, managing not to crash into any furniture while holding Nina by her ass. Tomb's beard left scratches on her face. She needed more of his mouth and aggression, so she sank her body softer into his and held on.

Until he lowered her to the wide brown leather couch and hovered over her, one knee braced on the cushion.

His eyes burned deep into her stomach, making hot, sticky waves of need vibrate in all directions. Her clit pulsed, and her nipples pebbled under his roaming scrutiny.

"Take the shirt off." He rasped, going for his belt buckle; he slid it free, and then, in the sexiest move she'd never seen before, he used one hand against the leather while he pulled it free in one whoosh with the other.

Nina shuddered and grabbed the t-shirt, yanking it ungracefully over her head before throwing it onto the floor.

Tomb didn't move other than undoing the jeans. Letting them gape open enough, she saw the thick crown of his cock because he was almost always commando.

She wondered how he could look at her like he saw her body for the first time. He was the man who'd seen her body the most in her lifetime, yet he gazed with fiery lust smoldering out of him.

Before Tomb descended, she had a tickle of doubt, but it vanished as quickly as it came.

Sex was forever powerful between them. It was like they'd put a match to a gas bottle and basked in the hedonistic flames.

Every inch of Nina wanted to be possessed by him. To be held down, taken roughly, pinning her underneath him while he forced orgasms until she blacked out.

"Rome, please." She begged, watching him kick his jeans away.

The weight of him when he brought it down on top of her was ecstasy, and she scraped her hands over his broad back, glorying in feeling his strength.

"Stop thinking," he growled before capturing her lips again. His thick fingers delved between her thighs until his touch brought her up in an arch. Tomb's forceful mouth swallowed the scream.

This mind-blowing euphoria was what she needed.

This overpowering presence he exuded, the many ways he could take her over and have her brain emptied of all worries and obligations. Just him. Only Tomb and the pleasure.

With his mouth slanted over hers, she couldn't even beg, but Tomb already knew from how she clawed, pleading without words for him to fuck her now. To fuck her hard, make her forget everything but the pleasure.

Nothing in the world compared to Tomb mastering her body.

When his fingers pawed her underwear, they were gone in a motion, slipped down her legs and discarded, and then he groaned as she watched him torment her hooded clit.

Pleasure, like pain and oh-so addictive, assaulted her senses, sending her mind reeling.

"My drenched princess. Even when you hate me, you still crave me."

She'd never hated him, not even a little. It might make things easier if she did. It might hurt less, that's for damn sure.

Being the one who loved more in the relationship wasn't fun.

She opened her legs for him on instinct, and his whole-ass bigger body dropped into the space. A perfect fit and a sigh whooshed out of

Nina as she felt the rounded tip of his cock notch to her entrance. Shivers racked her, causing her back to bow in the middle, seeking more, needing more of that good feeling only he brought out in her.

"No, princess, you don't get my big fucking hungry dick yet. I wanna tease you first. Make you sweat and swear and beg for it."

"That's not going to happen, Rome."

He smirked like the devil had taught him how and that devil rubbed along her clit, making stars burst behind her closed lids.

"Yeah, it is, Nina. You gotta learn to trust me, princess."

About to confess to every sin if it meant she got him inside of her. The breath was shredded from her lungs as Tomb put himself in place. Dragging the leaking crown against her equally dripping entrance, he shoved in a measured yet vigorous thrust.

There was no letting her walls relax around his girthy cock. He speared home and repeated it several times.

It felt brutal, unhinged, and *heavenly*. Alive and flying.

Nina moaned like a whore might in church in front of a sexy, off-limits priest.

"Oh, God, what's this?" she moaned, the noise strangled from her throat, unable to deal with the pleasure violating her.

Each downward punch of his hips brought on a cascading eruption of goodness threatening to break Nina in half. "It's a husband fucking his disobedient wife." As if there was nothing he enjoyed more than the sensual pleasure of dragging his cock along her swelled tissues, he grunted in her ear.

How was she disobedient? She loved him to distraction. She loved Tomb more than anyone and would follow him straight to Hell's waiting area.

"*Harder*," she issued and felt his hand curl underneath her chin, straining her head back, and his face came close. The thrusting never ceased. His pelvis rubbed deliciously up against her clit with each motion. Her body was trusted in his muscular arms as she was stretched to the limit.

"Not a word from you, my wilful wife. Now you get to take it and feel how fucking feral I get every single goddamn day about you."

Nina's mind emptied. The sex oozed out of him. She swore all the nuns in the Vatican heard how whore-like she moaned as she took Tomb's fucking. The pleasure increased after each aggressive thrust.

It only reaffirmed everything she knew. Sex with her husband was the ultimate high. She'd never need drugs when she had him.

And then he stopped.

Just like that.

The bastard stopped, pulled out of her pussy, and climbed to his feet. His wet cock bobbed like a damn missile against his stomach.

"Not a word, Nina." He issued in a tone hard enough that it licked gratification over her pleasure zones. Tomb picked her up like she weighed less than a grain of sand. Instinctually, she latched her legs around him, groaning when she felt him bump up against her vagina. It was about the sexiest thing in the world when he directed a hand between them and put his cock in place again, driving in high and fast.

Oh, Jesus. She rested her head on Tomb's shoulder as he prowled toward the stairs, intimately connected. Through her desire-heavy eyelids, ferocious passion looked back at her.

He didn't fuck her as he strolled casually, but Nina gave a little bump with her pelvis. Tomb groaned and smacked her ass, continuing on their way.

"Stay on my cock, or you'll be punished, my disobedient wife." How silky rough he said it, and she was shocked at how hard her clit pulsed at the threat. A swell of pleasure gathered in Nina's stomach at his gravelly, masculine chuckle.

She loved being on pause.

She needed this. They needed this.

Tomb's gravitational pull was too enormous for her to ignore.

Even if it was a façade, sex never lied when it was between them. It roared and screamed. It vibrated and brought happiness, even for a fleeting time. She needed it so badly, so when she wrapped both arms around Tomb's shoulders as he started his ascent on the staircase, she nuzzled his beard with her lips.

"If I were allowed to talk, I'd ask what kind of punishment, but I've been told to shut it."

He growled and smacked her ass again.

Holy shit, did the smack have a direct line to her clit? She pulsed so hard down there that it swept all the breath from her lungs. Dropping her forehead to Tomb's shoulder, she held on until they reached the bedroom, where he unceremoniously dumped her on the bed.

It was an ordinary bedroom with all wood furniture. But nothing held her attention, not like her man did while he gripped his turgid cock and stroked himself.

The lust in his eyes let her know she was in for it.

And she couldn't freaking wait.

Nina comfortably positioned herself on the bed, reaching for the pillows. She could count on two things in her marriage: how efficiently Tomb provided for her and how obsessed with her body he was, even when she grew a little heavier.

He'd worshipped her body from day one like a man who'd newly discovered religion.

The ability to zero in on her and how his blue eyes would heat her all over. The filth he spoke in low, husked ways when they had sex. Even out of bed, his way of turning her on with only a few words was magic, and she needed that worship.

She was reminded of his uncensored tongue when she slipped a hand between her legs, and he warned her. "You touch my pussy, and there will be consequences. Hook your fingers around the headboard."

No amount of control could stop Nina's hips from jerking upward into nothing at the roughly spoken command. First, a punishment threat and now consequences; she was eager to discover what they were.

But she followed his orders and reached behind her to hold on to the wooden slat headboard. If he was giving the orders, she could tease and let her legs fall open. She watched how Tomb's eyes flared and followed a path down her body.

"Jesus," he cursed, and that's when he moved. She thought he would climb onto the bed and get to the fucking, but he opened the nightstand, pulling out a length of red ribbon.

Momentarily stunned. While they'd had sex in every position imaginable—using toys included—they'd never gone down the BDSM route. She gaped when her wrists were manacled to the bedpost. Tight enough that she was not getting out of those knots unless Tomb set her free.

"Now you've tied me up, what do you plan to do with me, kinky biker?"

"Try to leave me now." He smirked, climbing onto the bed with her. He pulled her legs wider and kneeled in between.

"I'm not trying to leave you." Nina was overwhelmed with pleasure as he caressed her thighs.

"Aren't you? If I knew what madness was on your mind, I would have tied you up the second my ring was on your finger."

The bad feelings crept in to dampen the lust. Nina attempted to close her legs, but the mammoth man kneeling between them kept her thighs hinged open. "You said we paused that."

His thumb pad pressed to her exposed clit. A whole lot of thick nine inches from him was needed ASAP.

Using sex as a distraction was a bad idea, but she couldn't think clearly while he edged her closer to a climax. Lust won every time. They wanted each other wildly.

"Please."

"What are you begging for, princess?"

She'd known she could turn Tomb on, but this felt like something new, some untapped level of him he'd unchained. To see how passionately he was staring, even as his hands tormented her, was breathtaking.

Tomb's sinful mouth sucked on a nipple, causing a mix of pleasure and a slight twinge of pain.

"For you." She exhaled, curving up, seeking what only he could give her. "I'm begging *for you*."

"Right answer." He sucked again and then popped her nipple free.

She would die of overexposure to sin if he didn't get on with it. Before Nina voiced her horny frustration, Tomb crawled into place, putting the generous crown of his cock at her entrance. Then he pushed in slow enough that the moan emitted from Nina's throat was guttural in tempo.

"Oh, God, right there, yesssss." He felt incredible once he was as deep as he could go.

"I should've put a gag in these lips so I don't hear your garbage about leaving me," he grumbled, forcefully running his thumb over her lip. Tomb gave a leisurely thrust and then another.

Her shoulders ached as she bent upward to touch him, only remembering she was anchored to the headboard and couldn't reach him.

"But I wanna hear the moans I rip out of you, Nina." Another hard thrust rendered her speechless as Tomb bowed inches from her face with his hand braced up by her head. Their lips were within touching distance. "I want you to know who makes you feel this good."

"I already know that." She went for Tomb's mouth, and the devil pulled back, smirking at her. "Rome. Kiss me."

"Are you asking me, princess?"

His hard body churned, burying himself in her slick pussy. The wet sound was indecent, building her arousal higher than ever. The orgasm was fast approaching, becoming ferocious as his cock hit her bliss regions.

"Yes." she whimpered, close to begging for her kryptonite.

Tomb lowered his dark head and brushed her lips with his. Even when her mouth sprang open, inviting his tongue to come inside, he teased her with those silky beard brushes.

His thrusts increased as he told her. "Knowing you exist turns me on." By adjusting his knee, Tomb could penetrate deeper, causing her to let out a strangled cry as colors popped behind her closed eyelids. She was a prone body tied beneath him, and she'd never felt so wanton before as his churning flatlined her. All Nina could do was take his indescribable fucking.

"Knowing you belong *to me* fucking undoes me, Nina. I wanna bite you all over, mark you as mine." He growled and thrust, her eyes flying open automatically. "*Mine.*" His gaze was predatorial and so damn hot.

Those words did something to Nina. The orgasm overwhelmed, slamming through her while Tomb used her body to get himself there. Her mind emptied as she accepted the throbbing pleasure, undergoing pure euphoria. It stole everything from her, shaking her foundations, zapping her energy, leaving her encased in his scent, causing her to moan with relief.

"Fuck, yeah," he grunted, pushing and pushing while she felt his orgasm spurt out of him. "Soak my cock. Show me how much this pussy wants me around, even when you hate me." He pumped *harder* than ever, twice more, before rolling to a groaning stop. With her wrists tied, Nina could only hollow her back slightly from the bed. Despite the constraint, she wanted to share in his pleasure and his trembling breath against her lips. It was when Nina was coming down off the highest high that Tomb slanted his lips over hers and kissed her. His possessive tongue entered forcefully, causing chaos.

"Suck my tongue, Nina." He ordered her, and she eagerly complied, tasting his groans until he ended their passionate kiss.

His fingertip traced along her eyebrow, descending her nose and across her wet lips. The gesture was gentle and romantic. "I love the way you burn for me."

That rust-soaked voice sexed her up harder than anything else could.

Tomb knew how he affected her when his smirk turned sexier, and he rolled a warm palm up between her breasts, stopping only as he rounded the front of her throat. His fingers gripped firmer, and every inch of Nina relaxed into that hold.

Holding her by the throat, he kissed her in their language, chemistry speaking loudly. His kiss danced along her nerve endings. Each swipe of Tomb's tongue dominating hers sent reels of satisfaction all over her again, renewing what she thought was already sated.

Sated didn't mean a thing where Tomb was concerned.

Nina tugged at the ribbon, and it was immovable.

Climbing from between her legs, Tomb threw himself at her side, and Nina turned her head to watch him. His hand returned to her body, stoking her fires. Once more, he cuffed her throat, and a sense of peace settled deep into her bones.

"You don't know how fucking sexy you look right now." He said, trailing his hand down again, and her thighs opened for him like he'd spoken magical words. "Tied up and glazed eyes. You need more from me, baby?"

Her moan was answer enough.

Tomb's long fingers played around her entrance, pushing his come back into her obscenely. He got her wetter before he fingered inside her in gradual strokes that made her back bend in response. Drugged with pleasure, her eyelids fluttered, and what she saw caused her desire to quadruple. His irises were darkened to a dense navy, and the want staring back at her was instantly recognizable. She couldn't help herself when she lifted halfway to meet his mouth, and that mouth was so responsive when they collided. He tasted of needy desire as she accepted his pursuing tongue. Everything in that kiss was about domineering intention. He was stating who she belonged to.

"You're not finished," he said, shoving another finger deep inside her pussy until she thought she might split open from pleasure.

"I can't. I'm done," she panted, trying to pull her hips back, but Tomb wouldn't allow it.

"This pussy wants me."

The white burn of another orgasm tore through her at speed. Her toes curled as she cried into Tomb's shoulder, biting down hard with her teeth.

It was intoxicating, addictive, something she wanted every single day.

If that made her a gluttonous bitch, then so be it.

Not knowing it was possible until he straddled Nina over his lap, she realized he'd made the ribbons long enough to maneuver her around. Resourcefully kinky.

The sense of powerlessness was freeing. Nina whimpered when she watched him handle his rock-hard cock. Wet at the tip, so red and swollen, he stroked it along her slit, and she had to grip the headboard as sharp spasms made her squirm.

"You want this again?"

"You know I do."

It was torturous, the way Tomb wouldn't just slam in to feed her screaming craving.

Instead, he slowly inched his cock in.

Agonizingly slow until the root of him felt a part of her.

"Say your husband's fucking name when you come."

Nina

Once he'd notched himself in place, he'd taken hold of her hips, controlling the depth despite how much she tried to push down on him.

With little effort, he let her know who was in charge, and when she grasped that, the air in her lungs evaporated, and she surrendered to the feeling.

"How does that feel, huh? You're goddamn extra tight after your orgasms, aren't you? All those little muscles clamping down on my cock, needing to keep me inside you. When you can, I want you to come crying my name, baby. Tell your man, with the sexiest fucking moans I ever heard, how good it feels." Tomb gathered her closer, almost cradling her like a baby as he fucked up into her. His voice raked over her hearing like liquid seduction, and she detonated on a stuttered exhale.

It was indescribable how full she was. She felt lost and found all at once. Like he was using the sheer girth of his cock to save their relationship, one hard slam at a time.

The need for him pulsed, shaking her fucking foundations.

Desire. Passion. *Screaming lust*.

Their physical bond was unbreakable in these moments, which was crazy since they were at the lodge for marriage crisis repair.

The release came in a roaring wave of sensations attacking every inch of her body, decimating her without sound. Every muscle clamped up tight as the gorgeous wave continued. Tomb anchored her as he churned, grunting after each resounding slam, working into her until she felt too sensitive to take more.

"You are mine, wife. *Mine*, do you get that? Tell me you get it."

"Yes," she sobbed, needing to cling to him, but was suspended against his chest with Tomb elevating her to take his last, more profound than ever, slam before he stilled in place. "I know. *I know*."

"If sex is how I keep you, then get ready to be sore every fucking day, princess." His lips were at her ear, his rough voice seducing her as always.

Sex wasn't a fix, but it was a damn good band-aid.

She'd realized so early in her marriage that love was a weakness.

But it also could be the most vital connection, too.

Love was built like a brick wall, bonding a relationship into an impenetrable strength.

Until one brick crumbled the foundations.

She'd tried to reason for years that she had enough bricks to hold their marriage together by sheer determination because of the enormity of her love for him. Until recently, she admitted it took more than one person doing all the loving and sacrificing.

Despite her uncertainty about the future, Nina loved Tomb more than ever and wanted to maintain her strength, to keep their marriage, whatever she had to do.

"I'll always make it better," he promised, kissing her head. "Lick all that soreness, won't I, baby? I'll kiss every part I hurt."

His groan was so low it shuddered along her skin, and she chanted his name until she was out of air and the orgasm had run its course.

High on the feel-good chemistry they generated, she was useless other than the pleasure trickling out of her and onto him. She didn't care. Nina couldn't move even if aliens landed in the hallway and demanded to have purple beach waves. Those little aliens would have to wait to look pretty because Nina was boneless.

Their heavy breaths synched. Unaware that Tomb was freeing her wrists until her arms dropped to his shoulders, she groaned when he rubbed them all over.

"Do they hurt?"

"Just a little achy, you kinky bastard."

He chuckled, and she lifted her head. Tomb looked pleased.

"Where did that come from?"

"From my cock." He smirked, misinterpreting on purpose. "Oh, you mean the ribbons? I've wanted to tie you down for a long time."

Nina frowned. She thought they had a healthy sex life where they could share every fantasy.

"Don't look like that." he rubbed her forehead until the creases disappeared. "Let me clean you up first, then I'll tell you. Though I'd prefer you wet and sticky, you're leaking my come all over my lap." He winked saucily, and she blushed like a virgin on her wedding night.

"I can do it."

"Stay right there." He demanded when he'd slid off the bed, giving her the commanding tone again.

Nina's stomach tumbled with love when he emerged from the bathroom, the sound of running water behind him.

"Change into something nice, princess. We're going out."

Her eyebrows shot up in surprise. "Where to?"

"You'll find out. I got the shower warmed for you." He kissed her neck. After all the sex, that small piece of affection felt good.

Since she was a kidnap victim, she didn't feel rushed and took a long shower.

She heard pipes rushing water somewhere else and presumed he was showering in a different bathroom. She went to find her husband with her hair styled in waves and wearing a frayed denim skirt, a t-shirt, and ankle boots. The downstairs was empty, and she popped her head out of the front door.

Air seized in her chest, seeing him sitting on a wooden chair looking out into the great distance. The area was spectacular as the sun lowered from the sky. But the man, with his spread feet and hands crossed over his stomach, was an even better sight.

Hearing her exit, Tomb switched his gaze to her and smiled slowly.

"You look beautiful."

Nina rolled a shoulder casually, all the while basking in his compliment. He rose to his sizeable height, and that's when she noticed he wasn't wearing anything to do with the club. Nothing that would tell others who he belonged to. Light wash jeans, a pale blue t-shirt, and a plaid shirt over that. His hair was still wet and combed back from his face with his fingers. He had her cotton jacket in his hand, holding it out for her to slide both arms into it.

"A kidnappee has to look her best." He chuckled like he was having the best time. "I suppose I have to come along without asking questions? Isn't that how it works in the movies?"

"Baby," he smiled, turning her around so he could zip her jacket, "you're doing so well. I'm proud of you. Let's head out." He grabbed her hand and walked down the few steps to the truck.

"Funny man, you know I won't keep quiet."

"I wouldn't want you to be. I have all the answers you need when we get food."

"You said once we showered, you'd tell me. You're stalling, Rome." Why couldn't he give her something tangible to hold on to, to show her they had something worth fighting for? Battles couldn't be won alone.

The shove came unexpectedly, but Tomb wasn't pushing her away. His body came up in her space like he had boundary issues. His eyes were focused like a missile when he dropped his head lower.

"I have plenty to say, wife. You want to know why I tied you to the bed? Because it's been in my head from the moment I saw you. I've imagined you in rope and silk ribbons, bound and at my mercy, so I could wring pleasure out of you until you passed out."

"Why didn't you say something sooner? We don't have boring sex; I would have tried things for you."

"I know you would, my sexy little nymph. It wasn't only that. I wanted to glue you to me so I'd always know where you were at, what you were doing, who you were with. It's been an unhealthy fucking obsession since day one."

Tomb stepped back and pulled open the door. He lifted Nina in and buckled the safety belt.

She turned to him once he climbed in and started the engine to switch on the heat.

"You're always out of town and prefer spending time at the club with the boys when you are at home. Your actions paint a very different story than what you just said."

Confusion rained down over her.

The more answers he gave, the less she understood.

She just wanted things to make sense and to have something to give her hope.

"That was my way of harnessing myself, so I didn't frighten you or make you leave. But that happened anyway, so plans change, and we do things my way."

He said it like he was announcing a new meal plan for the week.

Nina didn't know what to think, honestly.

But it wasn't anger.

What was he saying, exactly? That he wanted to be her dominant and play kinky games?

"I'm not submissive." She mumbled, halfway down the long driveway from the lit cabin.

"I'd never want you to be anything other than the feisty princess I married."

"But yet you want to control everything from now on?"

"I'm going to." He smirked in the dark interior, and something loosened in Nina's stomach, making her lighter.

What was it?

Relief?

Every inch of her independent feminism shut down as her excited heart leaped. No woman should crave a man to be obsessively crazy about her to the point he wanted to control every inch of her. Unless that woman was Nina and that man was Tomb.

Shit. She didn't know what that made her, but she couldn't argue with something that filled her with hope.

"Put your hand on my leg, princess. I need you touching me."

Tomb emitted a rumbling hum that could only mean he was pleased as he switched on the radio and Billie Joel's 'My Life' played.

Eventually, the seclusion merged into suburbia and then a bustling city.

"Are we still in Utah?"

"Now we are."

So, the cabin wasn't in Utah. Good to know if she ever escaped her Hell-cation. Not that she'd tried very much yet. What with the hot bath and then the sex. She might try to run for the woods later. After food. But what if Tomb hadn't packed comfortable running shoes? Her plans were thwarted by inappropriate footwear. Eh, she hadn't given this kidnap situation proper consideration.

Nina giggled at the spiraling thoughts.

"Something funny?"

She shared her thought process.

"If you run into the woods, you want me to chase you. I'm good with that. But you'll deal with the consequences when I catch you, princess."

Damn. She was inept at being a prisoner because her captor turned her on so fucking badly. "I'll decide later." She aimed for a sassy retort, but it came out breathily.

"Do you know why I was reluctant to leave you the day we met? Why I fucked you hours later? Why I couldn't go an hour without calling you that week?"

"Because I was a hot piece of ass."

Tomb chuckled, hot and smoky. "Then and now. I knew you were going to be mine. I was so fucking hungry for you, Nina. It scared the shit out of me, the things I wanted to do. The things I wanted from you, but nothing on earth would keep me away."

"Except you." She accused, "*You* kept you away from me for something I still don't understand."

"When a man fears losing the one thing that's brought him purpose, he'll do anything to keep her. Even if that meant locking away his baser instincts. I couldn't risk showing you who the fuck I want to be with you, Nina. You didn't love me then; you would have convinced yourself I was like that bossy fucker in your past." The last part he grated through his teeth.

"Neil only wished he could be like you."

"*Don't* say his name, Nina. I still wanna kill him."

She knew it. Grinning, she squeezed his thigh.

The place he took her to was called *Franks Building*. Tomb asked the hostess for a booth. An energetic blonde server came over as soon as they were seated.

What Nina loved best about him, for as much attention as he gained, was that he never flirted with women. So, when giving their order, he did it with a respectful smile and while stroking a thumb against Nina's wedding band.

"What are you thinking?" He asked once they were alone.

She opened up, no point avoiding sharing her thoughts, not when this felt like they could put their marriage back on track.

"For a while, I've thought we might be over, and I was scared to challenge it because I didn't want to lose you, even as fractured as it's been. I've loved you honestly, and you couldn't give the same back to me. It's made me feel like an idiot, Rome. I wish you'd told me your needs right from the start instead of hiding them from me. I would have done anything for you."

Tomb squeezed her fingers and then brought them up to his lips. "I wish the same, too, baby. If I thought you weren't happy, I would have done something much sooner. You gotta believe nothing is more important than you."

"My entire existence shouldn't hinge on your happiness. But it has. *It does*. And I don't know what that makes me. Who I am without you as my center."

"You think it's any less for me? We've lacked communication, Nina, but it's not unfixable. Do you get me?"

Her stomach muscles relaxed. Now, she understood a little. Nina wanted more than anything to make them work. To do whatever was needed.

The server came and dropped off their drinks, and not long after, she returned with a tray of food.

"Try your food, baby. I won't have you going hungry."

Popping a salty fry in her mouth, she arched her eyebrow at him, curious about this updated version of Tomb. "Oh, yeah? And what will you do?"

"I'll put you on my lap and feed you."

The fry which had started its journey to her mouth suddenly stopped. The air grew thick, and Nina couldn't help squirming a little in her seat, squeezing her thighs together.

Tomb hissed. "Fuck. Look at you, baby. All hot and bothered by that, aren't you? I wanna put you on my cock and feel how slick it's made you."

Swallowing, she felt the heat rising on her cheeks, across her chest, and lower between her legs. "I guess I better eat before I trigger Tomb 2.0."

"Pity, I was hoping to dole out the consequences for your disobedience."

The simmering heat intensified, and Nina had to spear a fry with her fork and jam it into her mouth, or she would have whore moaned.

When she felt seminally in control of her barking hormones, she asked. "Is that what you need from me? To be in charge?"

Without hesitation, he answered. "Yes."

"What do you get out of that?"

"More than you'd realize, princess. I get to be the one who takes the burdens off your mind. I'll be the one who sees you happy. To know I had a hand in it. To be the only man to provide whatever you need, to know what those needs are. Protecting you. Providing and making you content is everything I want. However fucking selfish that makes me." when she didn't answer right away, she saw his forehead furrowing. "I won't lose you. That's non-negotiable. You think I'm overbearing now? It's nothing to how I'll become if we go home, and this is still in your head."

More of her tension melted away.

Biting the inside of her cheek to hold her smile at bay, she tipped her head to the side.

"Does that mean I'd be kidnapped indefinitely?"

Another deep-etched scowl crossed his beautiful face. "I'll do what I have to."

"Is that so?" every tight knot she'd felt for the past months edged away into the background, replaced with relief and love.

"Ever since you walked into my life, I've been addicted to you. Our connection is priceless, Nina. I'll punch through to the center of the earth to keep it. Show me what I neglected so I know where to love the most."

Was she insane to hope her husband loved her in the same debilitating way she loved him?

"Nina?" he cut into her thoughts; his hand sneaked underneath her hair and gripped her nape. "Do I need to spank the answers out of you?"

Her stomach took a whirly dip, and she almost blurted out *yes, please*.

Tomb smirked and pressed his mouth to her ear. "Got it. We'll be home soon."

Nina tried to push aside her desire for him, reminding herself that sex wasn't the answer to their issues.

"Dates. Affection that has nothing to do with sex. I want you to be at home because you want to be there, not because I've asked for it. I want you to be in this marriage with me, Rome. And now you've told me what you've been keeping to yourself; I want full honesty. And I know we touched on this back when, but that was before this latest version of you entered the chat. I'll be clear that if you want to experiment by bringing other people into our bed, that's a definite fuck no. I will be out of that door so fast, Rome."

His chuckle and possessive grip caught her off guard.

"Woman, I'm goddamn infatuated with you and *only you*. If you and your ten other personalities all wanna attack me in bed, I'm down for that. You're the only one I need in our bed. And you just added a spank to your growing tally for thinking I'd want anyone else."

Well aware he toted a powerful sexual presence, maybe because their chemistry was intertwined. Still, if this latest version of Tomb showed things to come from now on, she was open to it.

About to challenge him on the spanking, she noticed Tomb was glaring at something over her shoulder. Nina twisted around to see a man propped by his elbow at the bar. And he was staring at them.

"Who's that? Do you know him?"

"Look at me, Nina." Tomb instructed, and she did instantly, "It's no one. No other man exists for you."

Well, duh. But she smiled anyway at the blatant show of jealousy.

Tomb kissed her shoulder and put the fork back in her hand. She'd lost it somewhere in their conversation. "Finish your dinner, princess. You'll need all the energy you can get."

Lust ran rampant across her skin as she stuffed five salted fries, dripping heavy with ranch dressing, into her mouth. "You keep throwing out these threats."

Watching her, Tomb traced his thumb across her lip, catching a dribble of sauce her tongue had missed; he sucked it away leisurely. "You're gonna learn I keep my promises."

Eating silently, she finished her food and trusted he'd keep those promises.

Tomb

"If you don't move, I'll just pee here."

His Nina said it like she thought it was the worst thing she could ever say to him. Piss wasn't his kink, but he'd never be disgusted by anything she did. So, he smirked and tapped his lips.

"If you want me to move, you know what to do."

"I'm not paying your outrageous tax to go to the bathroom."

"Guess you better get to pissing then."

He waited, and then Nina huffed, poking him in his ribs.

"Fine, you giant ass. I'll pay."

She might act like it was a big chore to kiss him, but Tomb knew differently as her eyes dilated when she leaned into him and bussed an innocent kiss to his mouth. There was no chance he was letting her get away with that. Cuffing her around the neck, Tomb coaxed her lips open and sought her tongue, making her moan.

That was better.

She was glassy-eyed and a little breathless when he broke the kiss, remembering they were in public before he slid a hand down into her pants and made her come to a symphony of his name.

True to his word, he hauled himself up and pulled Nina up after him.

"Don't take long." He said, and she shot him a look so heated he got half hard.

Once she disappeared, his smile vanished, and he turned his head, searching for the man who'd been observing them since they entered. He only had a few minutes at most, so he had to make this shit quick. His feet ate up the distance as he crossed to the bar where the twenty-something guy was propping an elbow as he drank a beer.

While he was used to Nina gaining attention, Tomb wouldn't tolerate brazen disrespect. Not only that, but he knew of this guy, which only made it worse on many fucking levels.

Of all places, he'd see one of Harvey's men, and it was eighty fucking miles outside of Utah.

Was it a coincidence? Especially after what had happened with Denver recently?

"Something I can help you with, my guy?" Tomb phrased the question with enough warning the other man wouldn't mistake it for friendliness.

"What do you mean?"

"You've had your eyes all over my woman since we walked in. You either think she's famous or want her."

The guy dared smirk like he was cock of the roost, and he arched a brow at Tomb.

"You offering?"

He chose the wrong thing to say, which was Tomb's first thought.

The second was how he could kill him in a busy bar and not get dragged away by the cops. While his blood raged with savage violence, he didn't give a single damn about what came after the murder. His defensive nature over his wife held no logical parameters.

Tomb wasn't wearing his club cut. Did the guy recognize him? Was he taunting Tomb by eye-fucking his wife? Hoping to antagonize Tomb into an ambush? Anything was possible.

"Not even if you begged," informed Tomb. His stare was deadly. "You keep staring at my woman, and one of two things will happen."

The guy snorted, attempting to act big and challenging, but worry leached out of him like sewage, and his eyes skittered nervously for the exit.

"You got a name?"

"What's it to you?"

"Way I see it, if I'm gonna snap off all your fingers and shove them up your ass, or my preferred option, run over your head with my F350, I should know your name first. My mama drummed manners into me, you understand?"

Ralf. This tool was called Ralf. It came back to him now. He was low on Harvey's roster of goons.

"No? No matter. Now you've heard the choices that will happen if I look over this way and see your vile eyes on my woman again."

"You're fucking loopy, dude."

Tomb smirked. "You'd be a wise kid to keep thinking that."

He sensed her returning from the bathroom because he was always aware of Nina. Tomb met her halfway before leading her back to their table.

"Who were you talking to?" he let her slide into the booth first, and then he followed until their thighs touched.

"Some drippy fucker."

"That drippy fucker is staring at you like you stole his lollipop." She snickered.

"Has Casey ever mentioned how she came to be with Denver?"

"Not much. Why?"

"She was young. Her brother ran with the Riot Brothers, a local gang of petty criminals back then, into low-level shit, making peacock noises mostly."

Nina sipped her drink and lifted her eyebrow. "Are they another MC? I've never heard of them."

"Nah, baby. We've had some try to become hangarounds over the years. They were a small operation back then when Casey got with Denver. Then they disappeared for a while. Axel thought they'd died or their operation fizzled out. But this past year, we've heard talk about a return. We got confirmation of it when Denver was stabbed."

Her eyes rounded, and Nina's sweet lips paused on the tip of the black straw poking out of the vodka glass. "That was them?"

"Yup. Casey's brother threatened to get back at him for taking her, as he saw it, even though she was escaping from fucking lunatics. That's why Denver's always had a tight grasp on security for Casey and the kids. We suspected something might happen, but it's been years."

"And the boy at the bar?"

"He's one of the Riot Brothers gang."

Tomb kept Nina in the loop if any danger lurked around the club. He'd never have her blindsided. He might have restrained himself emotionally, but not when it concerned her safety. She knew all about lockdowns; they'd been through a few over the years. She knew of their enemies and was aware some cops were as crooked as a paperclip and wanted the Diablos' asses in jail. Nina understood what to do if she were ever to be pulled over by one of them.

"Does it mean anything bad that he's here with us right now?"

Fuck, his woman's smarts turned him the fuck on. Tomb latched his mouth to the side of her neck, urged to leave behind a tiny mark.

"Not sure. Probably not." Tomb attempted to convince himself that it was by chance he spotted a Riot Brothers member near their safe house so soon after Denver's incident.

The conversation drifted into other things when Nina's fingers caught at Tomb's belt, his mind emptied and filled like a bucket of filth as she tugged at the leather.

"I'm ready to leave if you are?"

The petite size of her, Nina was a lightweight with alcohol. Three drinks, and she became goofy. Four, and she was all hands and needy demands. "Sure, baby, let's get your tipsy ass home."

"I'm so not tipsy. I could drive if I wanted to. That's how *not* tipsy I am."

Chuckling, he helped her out of the booth and locked her hand inside his. "Sure, whatever you say." She was smashed, and he enjoyed seeing the lightness in her eyes again. None of that heavy shit she'd been carrying secretly.

"Are you gonna give me a boost, love?" she asked him once they were across the street next to his truck.

Love. He was love again.

"Or should I drive us back to the torture cabin?" she poked her skinny fingers into his ribs.

"Woman, you'd wrap us around a tree, get your ass up there." He lifted her into the passenger seat, leaning in, and he snapped the safety belt in place.

"I thought you'd make me pay that stupid tax again." She pouted, looking adorable. His Nina was a tough-ass most of the time. She was feisty as all get out; it was her default setting, and Tomb got off on it.

But his stomach warmed when she was softer, poutier, and all sweet. It made his primitive side roar to life.

It was fucked up, but that's who he was underneath.

Smiling across at him, Nina roamed her hand up and down his thigh, driving him mad as he got them on the road to the lodge.

"You sleepy, princess? You can catch a nap. I'll wake you when we get there."

"Hardly," she scoffed, stroking him again, closer to his dick this time, and, of course, he hardened. Tomb would have to be dead in his grave a thousand years before he stopped reacting to her touch. "I could stay away for days, probably weeks."

"Do you mean awake?"

"That's what I said."

Tomb chuckled at his tough-talking girl. Full of shit because in the next breath, she was yawning loudly. Her wandering hands wrenched a pained hiss out of him when she grazed over his crotch again.

He knew what his needy Nina wanted, and lust inflated his chest.

Taking his gaze from the road, he asked. "Do you need cuddles, baby?"

Another squeeze of his dick nearly sent his eyes rolling into the back of his skull. If she kept that up, he might plow into a wall.

She purred. "Mmm, yes."

"Get over here then." He said once he'd stopped at traffic lights. She unbuckled quickly and crawled across the console, her bony knees and elbows digging into him as she got into his lap. She was like a hamster trying to get its bed just right. But while she wriggled, Nina was heating his temperature. Taking a hand from the wheel, he palmed her ass. "Settle down, baby."

"What if we crash?"

"We won't crash."

A growl gurgled out of his throat, almost blinded by lust, as he kept his gaze on the road ahead. Wishing like hell they weren't far from the lodge so that he could fuck her. Tomb squeezed Nina's hip and held onto his composure.

Five torturous seconds later, his tether snapped.

"Get on my dick, princess." He growled, and Nina's head reared up from his shoulder. Big, pouty lips and aroused eyes. Tapping her ass, he hurried her along. "Get me out and into your horny pussy."

Even as she yanked at his belt and jeans, tugging up the skirt until it was a useless belt around her waist, exposing the sheer underwear, she panted in Tomb's face.

"There's not enough room for sex," she exclaimed breathlessly. As Tomb drove, she spread her legs open and pulled her panties aside to form an entry for his bulging cock.

Putting herself in place, he felt the first suction of her soaked entrance, and the groan ricocheted up his throat. Taking a hand from the wheel, he palmed Nina's hip as she pushed down, holding his cock with one hand, the other balanced on his shoulder, encasing him in so much fucking wet heat. He could die a happy man.

"We're not fucking, baby. You're keeping my cock warm until we're home."

The purr she pumped out as she struggled to settle on his cock was crafted of depravity and made Tomb ache.

Turning to the private road, he was minutes from the cabin. Nina strained to take his inches, wriggling her gorgeous little hips and driving him wild as he grunted and pinned her in place.

"Just take what you can, princess."

"I want it all," she whined, lifting her head she came for his mouth. Giving her a fast kiss, in no danger of going into a wall now they were on a long stretch of road. He lashed his tongue around hers, tasting her sweetness. Tomb pulled back first to concentrate on getting them home safely, but he angled his head to invite Nina's teeth to his neck.

His horny savage didn't hold back either as she bit and licked him, popping her hips like she wanted the fucking of a lifetime. His cock was in heaven, keeping warm in her snug cunt, all wet and hot and held in the tightest vise.

And she'd wanted to walk away from this because he was less than a perfect husband? He could still spit nails at the thoughts she must have been having for months. For fucking months about leaving him! Tomb ground his teeth against the onslaught of pleasure tingling down to the base of his back. The warmth in his gut was more than he could stand, but he slid his hand up Nina's spine and held her by the back of her neck.

If lessons were given to his wilful wife, it would be never to give up on anything that felt this incredible.

"It feels good." She whimpered.

She tried to ride him more than once before they finally arrived at the lodge. Tomb needed the medal of honor to resist her insatiable advances.

"Climb off, baby." He grunted once the truck was in park.

"Nooooo," she whined, circling her hips.

"You'll get what you need," he assured, pressing his lips to Nina's, tasting her sexual heat in the air like the sun. "But I gotta get us inside the house first, so be a good girl."

Tomb grunted when she scooted off his lap. He told her to stay in her seat, and he climbed down, only adjusting his dick, leaving his jeans open as he rounded the front and opened her door. Goddamn, she was fucking beautiful, all clingy and needy as she vined her limbs around him again.

Tomb was no saint. And it wouldn't be the first time they'd gotten frisky outdoors. So when he pushed her up against the truck grill, he took seconds to fish out his dick again and bury himself inside her inviting sex.

They groaned together.

There was no warming his cock this time. Tomb gave her three deep shoves, and Nina cried into his mouth.

He could have quickly brought her off in no time and listened to her scream into the night if he hadn't seen something moving in the shadows up by the lodge entrance.

He was so infatuated with his woman that he hadn't noticed the parked motorcycle until now, realizing someone from the Diablos was there.

"Fuck." He ground out between clenched teeth, bringing his thrusts to a callous stop.

"Tomb," Nina whined, her fingers in his hair.

"Someone is here. Settle down." He told her, lips against lips.

But his horny, drunk wife had only one thought, and it wasn't about stopping until he squeezed both hands on her gyrating ass to hold her still.

"Whoever the fuck is there, you better have your goddamn eyes shut, or I'll scoop them out with a fucking spoon." He yelled.

Nina giggled into his shoulder.

"Fuck's sake." He heard a masculine voice say up ahead as he walked toward the lodge, still buried in Nina, while she savaged the side of his neck. "Between walking in on Axel and Scar, god knows how many times, and Ruin growling at anyone who dares talk to his old lady, I might as well be fucking blind over here. It's me, Boss." Mouse announced.

As Tomb got closer, he saw the younger probie had his back turned, with a hand slapped over his eyes.

"Keep your trap shut until I take Nina inside."

"Hey, Mouse." She called out like she was hosting a goddamn dinner party. Tomb playfully spanked her, and she moaned in pleasure, clamping down on his cock involuntarily.

"You mind if we don't talk, Nina?" asked Mouse. "Tomb seems like he might strangle me if I do, and I gotta get home so the babysitter can leave, and I need to make my kids' lunches for tomorrow."

She giggled again. "Sure thing, Mouse."

"Keep your sob story for the Lifetime special, probie." He strode by the man and into the lodge. He didn't turn on the lights but deposited Nina's exposed butt on the edge of the couch. She locked her legs around his waist like she couldn't bear the idea of him sliding out of her. Feeling the satisfaction pour like rain over him, he gripped her by the neck and brought her to his mouth.

"Look at you. Straining to keep my cock nice and warm, aren't you, princess?"

"I listen to instructions…" She quirked her lips a little, and light entered her eyes. "Sometimes."

The chokehold this woman had on him, and the lengths he would go to keep her forever, was frightening. Tipping forward, he smashed his mouth hungrily against hers, tasting the hot sweeps of her tongue as she fought to take more.

"Don't ever forget you are every-fucking-thing to me, Nina." He rasped, breaking the kiss. He wanted to fuck her into a coma, so she kept that horny, glazed look. And he would.

Just as soon as he found out why the probie had turned up.

Reluctantly, he tucked himself away, and his jeans buttoned again. Tomb carried her around to sit on the couch. Hunching down, he slid her panties down her legs, tossing them aside. He followed this with the rest of her clothes.

"You know it's cruel to undress me and leave me here, right?" she asked. And he loved she understood he'd have to deal with Mouse first.

"I'm a cruel husband," he smirked, kissing her again. Her nails found the opening in his shirt and dug into his skin. *That's right, princess, mark me up*. Tomb palmed her knees and drew them open until he could see the wet pink between them. His cock ached, having been robbed of fucking her silly. But that would come. And so would she. Making her sob was one of his favorite things, so Tomb plucked one of her puckered nipples and was rewarded with the sexy sound.

"Stay like this, and don't even think about touching yourself. I'll know, baby. This won't take long."

The disobedient fire sparked in her eyes. "It better not." She pouted adorably. Slowly blinking, he knew he risked her falling asleep, and then he would have to kill the prospect.

Nina

Nina was well-versed in living in a world of noise.

Music. Chatter. The pull of the internet. Always a sports show on TV because Tomb was a sports head for all things football and baseball. The stillness was a blessed change.

She listened to the crackling fireplace while Tomb attended to whatever Mouse had delivered to the lodge. Feeling so relaxed that maybe being kidnapped to a remote cabin wasn't so bad. Her eyelids drifted open when she heard Tomb's heavy footsteps returning.

"I thought you'd be zonked out," he remarked, dropping into the chair opposite her. Before she could answer, she saw Tomb's eyes lowered to her knees. In her dosing state, she'd closed her legs.

Like he had an invisible magnet attached to his hard stare, she widened them once more until she was in full view. His rumbling growl pushed heat through her stomach, and she felt his praise even without him having to say a word.

"Did Mouse leave?"

"He's stationed at the edge of the property. He'll patrol the perimeter."

Confused, she frowned. "Why?"

"I told Axel about the Riot Brothers being in the area. He sent Mouse."

Nina snorted. "That little boy isn't saving us, love. What's he going to do? Throw crayons at the gang?"

Tomb chuckled and reached behind him to hold the back of the chair. The move elongated his torso and made Nina's eyes dart to the gap of skin peeking out of his shirt.

"I'll be the one to save you. Mouse is only here as an alarm if anyone gets on the property. Just a precaution, nothing to worry about."

"Maybe we should head home."

He growled and shook his head.

"We're here for as long as it takes."

"You said you'd take me home after one night."

"I lied."

"You lied?"

"Desperate men lie."

A warm flutter traveled between her legs at his candid admission, and Nina ached to rub them. Of their own accord, her knees drifted together.

"If you close your legs, princess, this conversation will stop. And you're too curious not to hear the rest."

They returned to their original spread position, and she saw Tomb's nostrils flare.

"Why are you doing this?"

"Because I want to look at your pretty pussy while we discuss saving our marriage."

Nina arched her eyebrow, feeling light with a sense of the unknown, yet comforted by the look in his eyes. "Does that mean we're un-paused?"

Tomb grunted. "Who are you to me?"

"I'm your wife."

"And?"

She recalled what he had said not an hour before and felt her heart give a hopeful thump as her lips twitched. "I'm your everything."

He answered with a devastating smile.

The silence built between them, zipping from one side of the room to the other. Tomb seemed content to sit and look at her, but his gaze made her squirm with itchy lust.

"You're a liar, do you know that?" he asked, smiling.

Of all the things he could have said, it was the one thing that could levitate Nina's temper the fastest. Her legs snapped closed, and she dropped her clasped hands into her lap. Glaring at him.

"What the hell does that mean?"

"Open your legs, princess."

"Not a chance. Explain what you just said before I rip your head off." The audacity of her man, she thought, as she gave the death stare all wives kept in their arsenal for times like these when she wanted to go to war all over his face. "You can call me many things," Nina grated, "a hothead."

"You are," Tomb interrupted with a grin, only further cementing his untimely death.

"Impatient."

"So much."

Oh, he was a funny guy.

She pointed a finger. "I am *not* a liar, Rome King."

"Oh, but you are, Nina King. Want to know how I know?"

"Oh, please enlighten me. I like to have all the facts before I kill a man." Nina was ready to attack every hair in his beard. Poised like a God sitting on his throne, he confounded her equilibrium by doing nothing.

"You were pissed at me. But you would never have left me."

All her muscles relaxed, and she let herself sink into the cushions again.

"Don't be so sure, husband. This is only day one of the kidnapping. I'm still considering running into the woods, you know?"

"I hope you do." He rumbled a throaty noise, his eyes firing off lust-filled signals she'd have to be blind not to see. "It'll allow me to chase you, catch you and fuck you like an animal while screaming at the moon."

Well then.

Nina had to take a big breath to compose her riotous excitement.

Again, the silence swirled in the room. Tomb's eyes were all over her, but he seemed to give her the space to speak when she wanted to.

"If I had left. What would you have done?"

"It would be the same consequences as now, but I would have done it much angrier. I see you, every inch of you. I understand your moods and emotions better than a man should. Come over here, Nina, sit on my lap."

"Said the kinky Santa," she tittered, but did as he asked, unable to resist obeying.

Maybe she'd caught Stockholm Syndrome for her bearded kidnapper hubby.

Once saddled onto his lap, he pulled her in closer with a meaty hand resting on her ass cheek, the other laid over her closed thighs. He wasn't attempting to touch her intimately, but her body didn't know that and was practically purring like a well-oiled engine at his nearness.

It wasn't only that.

Affection between them, outside of sex, was few and far, so she felt high as a kite as he stroked her and held her close. Maybe it made her brittle to need those things, to crave his attention as though she couldn't cope without it.

But Nina was woman enough to admit her faults and her needs.

She was far from perfect.

Neither of them were. She would have known he'd hidden things if she'd been a top-notch wife. Blame could be laid, but it was taking them both to repair a crack.

As if reading her mind, he kissed her shoulder and looked her in the eye.

"When I pull into the driveway, I know I'm the luckiest sonuvabitch, Nina, because I'm coming home to you."

Her heart stalled and then restarted again. Nina slid a hand into Tomb's hair and held on.

"I was dim to assume you saw my utter fucking obsession with you, that you'd understand how I'd break the world in half to give you a sip of water if you were thirsty. I thought you'd understand my devotion without having to say anything. That wrong is on my head, Nina. It's going to be different now."

Tomb pressed his lips to the side of her neck, and she was soaked with deep warmth.

"It's not all on you, you know? Two make a marriage work, and I fell down on that, too. We've been together long enough to know I should have been able to talk to you about how I was feeling long before this." Nina repeated his last words back to Tomb. "It's gonna be different now."

His teeth sank gently into her exposed shoulder. "Yes, wife, it will be."

She took it as a promise and a threat. Nina was good with both.

The gasp came quick when he rose to his feet in a lithe giant way, her caught in his arms like a wedding night bride, and he strode for the staircase. Grinning like a lightheaded idiot, Nina looped her arms around his neck, nuzzling Tomb's soft beard.

"We've talked enough. We're going to bed," he growled, stopping on the first stair to kiss her stupidly.

They went to bed, but Tomb didn't have rest in mind.

Hours later, Nina fell asleep on top of his chest. Tomb held her possessively, like he thought she might abscond in the night. He'd fucked her brains out, made her beg and plead, withholding orgasms until she apologized for ever thinking of leaving him. Nina had no energy to rouse an eyelid, let alone a fantastical escape plan.

Maybe tomorrow, she thought drowsily as she smiled and dropped into unconsciousness for a few hours.

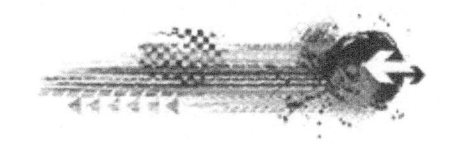

Tomb

Walking into the kitchen, Nina hadn't seen him yet, but he heard her muttering. "He just had to kidnap me away to a remote cabin. Not a beach in sight. No, he wouldn't think of that, would he?"

Tomb announced his presence by sliding a hand around Nina's waist, avoiding being elbowed in the ribs when he latched her in. "That's 'cause if we were at a beach, you'd be in one of those tiny fucking bikinis that show off your fantastic tits and ass, baby. That means I'd be fighting guys every minute of the day for looking at you instead of spending that time worshipping you."

Burying his face in the side of her neck, he inhaled hard enough it elongated his chest. She always smelled damn good. He'd gotten her out of bed early for five days running to go for a walk. His pampered princess protested daily, but her eyes flared excitedly when he crouched to put on her walking sneakers.

"I don't know how you're in a lousy mood today. I let you sleep in. Do you need a pussy-licking, princess?"

The wriggle aroused him. Tomb kept her hostage against the sink. Nina was his narcotic of choice. The thing he'd go to hell for.

"You *let me* sleep in?" she huffed, "you kept me awake until nearly four, and my pussy is out of commission. You wrecked it."

Wearing the smuggest bastard smirk, Tomb hummed against her neck, tightening his hold on Nina's waist. How did he not realize they'd needed this alone time to reconnect? She'd laughed more in the past week than he'd seen her laugh all year.

"You're only turning me on by saying that." It earned him another elbow jab. This time, she hugged him around the waist, laying her head on his chest.

Fuck. How quickly she could derail his mind.

How could he have been her man for this long and not known his wife was a kitten for affection? Last night, she'd chosen a movie to watch, and he'd pulled her legs across his lap to rub her feet while she gorged on a bucket of homemade popcorn. By the end of the flick, Nina sprawled across his lap, her legs tucked against his thighs and her face in his neck. If his body had been made with an engine, he would have been purring like a motherfucker. The contentment was unreal.

"Sit down, you randy biker. Your breakfast is warming in the oven."

As she rested her face in the middle of his pecs, he palmed the back of her head, feeling as though he held heaven in his hands.

Grabbing the plate of warm food, he poured Nina a freshly brewed coffee before sitting at the kitchen island. "Did you eat?"

"I'm not hungry yet, but I want the internet, Rome. I need to make calls and check in with the salon. It's probably gone bankrupt by now."

He chuckled at her dramatics. "The salon is fine, baby. I talked to Esther last night."

Tomb watched as Nina scrunched up her forehead, her eyes slit to accusing lines. "I can't have my phone, but you can? This isn't the land Tomb built, you know? Give me my phone."

Raising a brow, he smiled as he filled his mouth with a spicy sausage omelet. Damn, his woman could cook. Once he'd swallowed, he asked. "What do you have to do to get it?"

Her little foot stomp did things to his dick, and the urge to maul her was no longer a need he had to hide. He could unleash his fucking monster on his wife and drown her in his dark worship.

"I swear to God, Rome, if you mention paying a tax once more, I'll string you up a tree."

"Not with those puny arms, you won't."

The punch she gave to the top of his arm made Tomb laugh, and he dropped the fork and brought her across his lap.

"You're wearing my patience thin."

"Making your little pussy all sore and wearing down your patience, I'm talented." He smirked and felt her fingers tangle in the back of his hair.

"Rome."

"Nina."

She made a frustrated sound, but then changed her tactics. He saw it happening as light and warmth entered her eyes. Then, it was a straight-hot seduction. Fuck him. He was in for a helluva ride and couldn't wait.

The hands in his hair turned soft, stroking his scalp until tingles erupted all over his skin. Nina trailed her lips across his beard, over his mouth.

"Please, can I have my phone back, love? I won't try to Uber my escape. I'll be a good little hostage for my captor."

If only she realized how easily she could play him, she'd wield her power for evil. His saucy little wife continued waging seduction against him, kissing all over the face. The kisses lasted longer when they reached his mouth, and he enjoyed her minty taste until she tugged down hard on his bottom lip.

"C'mon, love, where's the harm in one phone call? It's not like I can sign into my social media and post that a biker-snack has kidnapped me, is it?"

Tomb laughed and palmed the back of her head so she'd look at him.

It was then his mean little wife returned when Tomb remained silent. He knew it wouldn't take long. She had about as much patience as he had ballet dancing training.

His abdomen muscles fisted with dark longing when she raked her nails over his scalp. But he wanted to play a little longer, so he only asked, "What do you wanna barter me for the phone?"

"You're mean." She growled and sighed, gusting the minty air over his face as she rested their foreheads together. "I'll do whatever you say today without complaint."

She'd already been doing that for the last few days, and he'd loved it like the fucking Neanderthal he was.

"Deal."

She grinned and made to get off his lap, but Tomb's hands gripped her hips. "Where's my phone?"

"Pay the tax first."

Another growl, but she smashed his lips hard and kissed the fuck out of him, using all her tongue and some biting. "You're so fucking unreasonable." She grumbled, but his Nina couldn't mask the lightness in her eyes when their lips parted.

Smacking her on the ass until she climbed down from his lap, Tomb strode across the large kitchen and pulled open a cabinet. On the very top shelf, he brought out her phone.

Oh, if eyes could snarl. "It was in there this whole time?"

"I knew my pintsize wife wouldn't be able to reach it."

"I refer you back to how mean you are." She cradled the phone to her tits like he'd given her diamonds. Tomb could do without technology altogether. He always fancied going off the grid and living a nomad lifestyle. Nina, though, would rather sit in dog shit than ever give up her phone. So fucking cute.

The smile dropped off his face, and a gurgled growl rose from his throat when she followed it. "I'm thinking about div—"

Tomb was across the kitchen, pinning Nina to the island with his hand covering her mouth. His chest expanded with rushing air as he looked down at the woman who owned him wholly. "Don't ever fucking say that word again, Nina. Not even as a joke. Divorce doesn't exist for me and you."

Understanding crossed over her features, and she mumbled something behind his hand. Dropping it, Nina immediately put her face in his chest, moving it from side to side in that nuzzling way he loved.

"I'm sorry, love. I know it's still raw for you."

"Talking about divorce will always be fucking raw for me," he admitted, stroking around her neck. He held his palm there in a noose shape.

Another chest nuzzle. Her affection took away all his anger.

"If I wasn't so *sore*," she started, looking up at him with devilment in her gorgeous eyes. "I'd say sorry properly, but hard luck, Tomb. Now go chop wood or tromp through the forest like a grizzly bear."

Neither moved, though, and Tomb dropped his cheek to the top of Nina's head, inhaling her scent until his heart settled.

When she announced, "Men don't like independent women." It didn't surprise Tomb. He'd been waiting days for her to speak what was on her mind. "Oh, they say they do in the beginning, until we say or do something that bumps up against their orders, and then we're not so shiny anymore."

"I'm not men. I'm Rome King, *your husband*, and I want every independent inch of you. Your strength and determination to succeed were among the first things I found attractive about you."

She looked up at him with serious eyes. Finally, they were in an open place, able to discuss shit.

"You need to take care of me, though. You need me to need you."

"Don't you?"

She blinked. "I need you because I love you and don't want to lose you. But I don't need you to dress me or choose food at a restaurant. Or to decide what you think is best for me."

She was so wound up inside, he vowed he'd work tirelessly until she trusted him with everything. Running a fingertip along her curved eyebrow, he asked. "Don't you?" he'd like to take care of her in every fucking way if he could. If that meant sliding her sexy little lacy things on her body each morning, he'd probably be late to work because he'd need to fuck her first.

They'd figure it out. He knew that now. They'd find their balance.

He felt the shudder go through her as he rolled a palm down her narrow back, soothing his worried wife. He could practically hold her in one hand, his delicately made princess with the mouth and temper of a sailor.

"Don't you want me to shoulder the loads, baby? Don't you think I haven't noticed signs over the years? But you won't take that extra step and tell me what you need. Nothing should make you worry. Try it my way. See how you like it."

"What do you get out of it?"

"My reward has always been you, sweetheart. I didn't trample through the dirt of my life and not get something fan-fucking-tastic like you at the end. You're stuck with me now."

He thought he heard her murmur 'good,' which was good enough for him.

It wasn't as though Nina could ever get rid of him, even if she wanted to.

If that day ever came, there were a lot of dirtier tricks up his sleeve.

His delicious wife patted him on the ass and sashayed hers out of the room to contact the real world.

Nina

The fucking nerve of her landlord to not only leave her a wall of text messages but now calling her.

Nina answered with a curt. "Hello?"

"*Bella*. You've been hard to reach lately. Your staff claimed not to know where you are."

She hated the familiarity he gave her with a stupid nickname.

"Mr. Conti, it's not a convenient time. Can this wait? I'm out of town at the moment and—"

"Did I interrupt you?"

"I'm out of town with my husband." She stretched the last words because, as familiar as he tried to push it between them, he seemed to forget she was married and who that man was. Likely, he thought he was above the Diablos.

"Ah, I see. Then I shall not keep you long. I wanted to remind you of our delicate chat recently."

Nina recoiled. The urge to tell him to go fuck himself was strong, and she bit back the words threatening to fall out of her compressed lips. She barely tolerated him as a landlord, and if she had any other choice, she'd sever that business connection right now.

Sometimes, dealing with the Devil was the only avenue available.

"I haven't forgotten. There's no choice but to pay the increase, Mr. Conti, unless I want to look for new premises."

"No need for such drastic measures, *Bella*. There are always alternative means, *sí*? Friends help each other out." He chuckled. "Inflation is a beast we must all ride. And many would snap up that supreme location. You are fortunate I keep the rent low for you."

Bull-fucking-shit. He was conning her and all his other tenants.

And then the bastard went in for the kill.

He stopped playing subtle games.

"We could have a lot of pleasant times together, you and I. I think you already know it." God, vomit. She'd rather screw a bullfrog. "I care for my friends, *Bella*, and you could be an exceptional friend. What do you say? I have plenty of money to spoil you with anything your heart desires. I have houses and yachts. Say the word, and we'll go to exotic places. All I want in return is your body."

The bile in Nina's stomach threatened to flood her mouth. The very suggestion made her feel violated, triggering violent thoughts as she held onto the den doorframe.

"I'm fucking married, you asshole. We have nothing more to say, Conti. Lose my fucking number, and I would appreciate it if you have your assistant contact me from now on."

Raging inside, Nina disconnected the call and switched her phone off. She could have avoided that creep if she hadn't begged Tomb to have the thing back. As he'd said, Esther was having fun looking after the salon and urged Nina to stay away for as long as she liked.

Outside the line of windows, she saw Tomb casually striding across the decking. He was still wearing his comfy clothes. Slut gray sweats hanging off his thick hips and a tight t-shirt clinging for dear life to his chest. His hair hadn't been combed, so it was all over his head in sexy tufts. Watching how he straddled a lounge chair, crossed his feet, and looked out into the great outdoors went a long way to soothe her temper.

If Tomb knew about Conti, he'd rip the man into a million pieces and piss on his chalky bones.

To make weak excuses, while Conti was a disgusting nuisance, he hadn't ranked high enough on her priority list to even mention him to anyone. She thought if she ignored it long enough, the man would get bored and move on. But it didn't alter the fact she was keeping it a secret from her husband. Something he needed, he'd already told her that. Give him her burdens, let him handle them.

Composing herself, she brushed her hands through her hair, sweeping it over her shoulders.

Out on the deck, her heart increased at a speedier pace.

He looked relaxed. And damn good.

It was impossible not to see the thick outline stretching the front of his gray sweatpants, like a loaded gun pointed at her.

His dark head cranked around when he heard the door opening, and his welcoming smile made every thought she harbored fall out of her head.

"Quit spying on me, wife, and get over here. Climb on my lap."

That right there was the most crucial issue in her life.

The vital part of her.

Nina would deal with idiot landlords and their foul offers.

"What if I'm too sore?" she inched out the door, gravitating toward Tomb.

"You can be sore later. I'll lick it all better."

"That dick is not normal, Rome. You stood in line twice when they were making penises."

His laugh was a rough sound that made something churn inside her sternum. "You flatter me."

Things had been so good between them for the past few days. It was like starting over on day one.

"You look in a better mood," Tomb remarked. "You must have called everyone in your phonebook, hm?"

Nina didn't hesitate, climbing onto Tomb's lap. She straddled his legs and sat across his knees. Instantly, his calloused hands came to hold her thighs.

"I called Esther. You're lucky my salon is still standing."

He smirked. "I told you it was. You need to trust your husband more."

She would trust him to run into a burning building and save all her shoes if she asked it of him. She'd trust Tomb with her life and her passwords.

But her salon was her baby.

Something she'd built from scratch, squirreling away meager savings for years until she could afford all the equipment.

And that was part of her problem. Letting go of control was hard.

It could be now she was a little pouty, knowing the salon could run perfectly fine without her.

"Your evil plan paid off this time," she said, her lips twitching to let him see she wasn't mad anymore. "Do you have any more up that sleeve of yours?"

"You gotta wait and see."

She pinched the chest hair peeking out of his undershirt. "Let me guess. It's not a dominant biker who'll emerge next. Is it the Devil?"

Tomb winked, and her belly warmed as he rubbed her outer thighs.

"Is that what you want? I can go Devil for you."

All this time, if only she'd opened up to him, she could have had this version of Tomb. She whittled her lower lip between her teeth, unable to stop the pang of regret.

It wasn't only Tomb who needed to change, to open up. Nina had to do the same.

Nowhere in the marriage rules said she had to take on responsibilities alone. She'd made that rule herself somewhere along the way. She'd been in a marriage of one, and she realized she had to own some of that blame, too.

The truth felt like bricks in her stomach.

By not telling Tomb what had been happening, she'd created a Molotov brew of errors that went on for miles. Not only by believing he didn't care, but she'd inadvertently denied who he was at his core.

These past few days gave her a clarity she hadn't been able to see for her stupidity.

Trust meant sharing everything.

As hard as it might be for someone hampered by raising herself for most of her life, standing on her own two feet had been all Nina had known. It was a tough habit to escape, but she was determined to do better with this fresh chance between them.

"You're already the Devil disguised in a lumber-snack biker package. That boyish smile doesn't fool me, love." She tugged a little on his beard.

Some loves came in waves.

Nina's love for Tomb was a constant tsunami, threatening to drag her under the current and never release her. But it was a drowning she'd happily submit to because loving him was natural. For all the rawness and hurts, she couldn't ever imagine living without him coloring all her pages.

As he'd told her, if she was his reward, he was her end game. And she wouldn't stop putting in the work with their relationship. Never.

Nina dropped her gaze, watching his mouth tug up at the sides. And her thoughts fell straight into the filthy pit and wallowed there as her stomach tumbled and her sex clenched.

"Princess, you're staring at my mouth." He knew why. "Is there something you want?"

"I'm thinking about sitting on it."

"*Fuck*." He hissed, and his hands flexed around her hips, pulling her deeper into his lap, directly over his thick bulge. "You feel what you've done to me?"

"It's hard to miss." She pushed down, and the tingling pleasure groan tore through her lower body. Nina folded down across his chest with her hands spanning his thick neck. She watched his pupils expand to pure black disks.

He was as turned on as she was.

And that was a good thing.

A wonderful thing.

She'd never recoiled from his command over her body. Why would she? Tomb played with her libido, gauging her sexual wants long before she could ask for them. But it felt different now when she asked. "Tell me what to do, Rome."

Those blue eyes dilated as he set her on her feet and made the chair recline back.

Even flat on his back, Tomb was entirely in command. It surged out of his pores like hot lava, and Nina trembled, tender all over for his dominance.

"Slide those panties off, baby, and climb up onto my chest."

She only wore one of his t-shirts, which swamped her like a dinner dress. She lifted it to waist height, giving him a full view as she pulled down the underwear, kicking it off her left foot.

His eyes trailed hungrily between her legs. Could he see how wet she was? She was practically shaking when she scrambled onto him again, shimmying over his hardness on her climb to his face.

"You remember the rule, don't you?"

Nodding doll-like, her breathing was erratic, so impatient to get to her seat like she was late for the opera. Nina moaned as Tomb brushed a hand over his silky beard. He was so sweet by warning her seat.

"Yeah." She wheezed as he took hold of her waist but let her fix in place directly over his face. But she hadn't lowered herself yet.

"Tell me."

"I don't give a shit if I suffocate you, and I don't move off your face until I've come in your mouth." They were long practiced in him giving her head. That first night, he'd told her to suffocate the life out of him. She'd laughed, but he'd meant it. Never since had Nina hesitated to sit on that beard. She was generous enough to let him breathe every few minutes, to give him the hope he might live if he kept stabbing his tongue into her pussy. And Tomb, even with the threat of death, loved eating her.

"Good princess," he smiled, and then he switched his gaze to her needy sex hovering only inches from his eyebrows. Tomb slid his hands from her hips down to her ass, giving both globes a hard squeeze, encouraging her without having to tell her to get a move on.

Nina felt pure bliss as his tongue stimulated her most sensitive spot. Her clit was tender already and so swollen.

She grabbed the back of the chair, hoping it would be steady enough because she became a bucking bronco on the back of that thought. Grinding on Tomb's mouth as he kissed and slurped and ate her alive.

The pleasure was magnificent. *Incredible*.

She wanted to die right there, and she stuttered a cry, telling him so.

"Grind for it," she heard his muffled growl as he swept his tongue deep inside her before lashing right up at her pulsing clit again. From behind, she felt Tomb's fingers stroke between her cheeks, angling down until he found her entrance, so wet, contracting to be filled.

She was born to be filled wall-to-wall by his thick cock. She knew that now. Nothing was as blissful as that, but she settled on his expert fingers. All three crowded in, causing Nina to see exploding stars and planets. She chanted his name as she reached climax until the shudders stopped.

Tomb wasn't done with his suffocating, though, far from it.

He made her go on two more rides, giving her three intense orgasms, leaving her weak and struggling to breathe. Every muscle, from her pinky toe up to her forehead, was locked up with tingling pleasure.

"Oh, God, am I dead?" she moaned, sliding down from him. She sagged against his chest, just about aware he'd brought the lounger to a higher position once more.

"I hope not. Otherwise, I'm about to skull fuck your corpse. I'll ask for forgiveness when we meet in hell, baby." His stomach moved with a chuckle underneath her cheek, and Nina gave him a sardonic yet amused look.

"You're filthy."

"For you. Now open wide. Let your husband do all the work."

He was already reaching into his pants to bring out the superhuman cock, stroking it until he squeezed a drop of pre-come from the engorged tip.

Incapable of looking anywhere else, her mouth flooded with moisture in preparation, just like her pussy did when they were about to fuck.

If she said no, would he force it between her lips, anyway? God, why did that concept make her pussy clench up hard? She wanted it. The force, the rough play.

But it wasn't necessary today. Not when she gave Tomb's cock a little hello kiss before she stretched her lips open, and he fed her every inch until he hit the back of her throat.

It was no easy feat; it never was. But oh, wow, Nina loved his hips moving in a speedy rhythm to make her take all of him. Unbothered if she gagged.

Shifting herself, she fell into the space his spread knees made. All Nina had to do was hold on to his legs, and Tomb did the rest. Pistoning into her mouth, she gave him licks and sucks, but most of the blowjob was done by him.

His sexy grunts were a fuel she never wanted to run out of. He groaned like she was torturing him, and he loved the pain.

"My hot, dick-sucking wife, that's it, you swallow me so fucking good. Christ, the back of your throat is so tight." He rasped with praise, lighting her up inside. She chased for more with keen sucks. Tomb rewarded her with defiled words of encouragement until he roared to the morning sky and poured his pleasure down her throat with fast pumping thrusts.

It was a wonderful thing to breathe again, and Nina, free of Tomb's shaft, collapsed on top of him, gulping in much-needed air. He cradled the side of her face and brushed a thumb underneath her eyes where the blowjob-giving tears had spilled over her lashes. Tomb looked pleased, arrogant even as he brought that thumb to his lips and sucked the tears dry. He did the same to her lips where she hadn't been able to swallow all of him, and some of his spent pleasure was on the corner of her lips. She watched him tasting himself, and she nearly fell into a fresh orgasm, but her body was too spent even to clench down on her pleasure zones.

With her face nuzzled into Tomb's neck, his hand idling on her naked butt, she asked, "How was your first corpse skull fuck, then?"

He laughed. "fan-fucking-tastic. I'm gonna do it again just as soon as I've restocked. I need to make you sore all over."

"You're an animal," Nina replied, finding his lobe with her eyes shut. She tugged at it with affection.

A hand that had been on her butt moved to lock around Nina's throat, and any slumbering pleasure pinged off signals in all directions as she whimpered with need.

"Naughty little wives who try to run away need punishing, and this is yours."

"I've never gone faster than a speedy walk and don't intend to start now. I'd rather get sweaty suffocating you again, though."

There went his husky laugh again as Tomb circled her throat, soothing the ache within that he'd caused by shoving something so big down it.

They touched with loving hands, unable to break any connection.
They talked and laughed, teasing each other.
Until it was time to play again.
They didn't return to the lodge until it was well past lunchtime.
Nina's sore throat and aching thighs were worth it.

Tomb

Climbing out of bed three nights later, Tomb padded across the room so he didn't wake Nina as he pulled on his discarded jeans. He never thought he'd have to go gentle on his dick when he tucked himself into the material, but the impossible had happened, and his shaft was well-used and tender. He smirked like a smug motherfucker, striding out of the bedroom on bare feet. Nina had fallen asleep after the third round of thirsty sex. He thanked God because Tomb didn't know if he had another go in him. As it was, he wasn't sure how his forty-year-old balls were refueling so fucking fast.

In the kitchen, he gulped down an entire bottle of spring water from the fridge, wiping his wet mouth on the back of his hand. He could eat a complete cow, hooves included, but it wasn't food he reached for first. He went for his phone, and though it was nearing the witching hour, Axel picked up the call after only two rings.

"Hey, Tomb, give me a second to go downstairs so I don't wake Scarlett," Axel told him in a hushed tone. "What's going on?" he asked once he was there.

"I was gonna ask you the same thing. It's why I'm checking in. Is there anything new with the Riot Brothers? Mouse got nothing when he was up this way. He nosed around the bars, but he got nothing."

"We've had some developments, none are good. Casey's brother sent a message to Denver's house the other night. A note was taped to their front door. All it said was, 'Hello, sister. I'll see you soon.' she was pretty shaken up." For years, the asshole had kept his sister as a virtual recluse until she took her opportunity to escape and ran into Denver. "Denver's moved her and the kids into the clubhouse for now; he's in no healthy state to protect his family alone."

"You think they'll make a move to snatch Casey back? Maybe her kids, too?"

"It's a possibility," Axel replied. "We don't take chances with family. Better they're on lockdown for the time being until we fish the fucker out. We received reports that local businesses are being threatened for protection money."

"The fuck." Answered Tomb. The Diablos owned Utah, and one thing they didn't do was shit on their doorstep. They were hired muscle if businesses needed it. They sure as shit didn't shake anyone down for protection money. That was a cowardly racket Axel had shut down fast after taking over from the last president.

"My sentiments exactly, brother. After Chains inquired and looked at the CCTV footage, he recognized a few faces. They were Riot

Brothers. As we've suspected for months, Harvey is trying to move his operation here by starting in on the locals."

"Fucking cowards," remarked Tomb. Bullying the weak was for spineless cunts. "What's the plan?"

"Look, I know you got issues there, my brother, but we need all hands on deck back here."

"Prez, it's fine. Nina and me were heading home tomorrow, anyway. If I keep her from her salon, I risk becoming a eunuch."

Axel chuckled on the other end of the call. "I'm not gonna pry, but you guys good now?"

"Yeah, we're good."

That was all that was said about Tomb's private life. There wasn't a chance he'd divulge the gritty details that would always be private between him and his wife. He was part of the club. He felt ingrained in the Diablos down to his fucking marrow and would kill for any of his brothers. But as his beating heart told him, his priority was to Nina.

Axel briefed him on their strategies to prevent the Riot Brothers from encroaching on Diablo ground. When Tomb got off the phone, he did a once around the lodge to double-check the place was locked down securely. He padded along to the bedroom again.

"Where did you go?" a sleepy Nina asked as he curled around her body once back in the bed. Her warmth seeped down to his bones, and Tomb exhaled as he relaxed into her.

"I had to talk to Axel."

"About that Ralf guy?"

"Yeah, baby. Are you ready to go home tomorrow?"

He thought she'd jump at the chance. His Nina was a city girl through and through and needed the hustle and bustle of that lifestyle to make her come alive. She needed coffee shops and traffic jams. He hadn't figured she'd enjoy the quietness of the lodge as much as he'd seen. And now he was reluctant to leave.

Tomb thought she'd fallen back asleep. But she turned and cuddled into his arms, finding her favorite spot on his neck. As she hooked her leg around his thighs, he cradled the back of her head.

"Things will be different when we go home, won't they, though, Rome?"

Understanding what she was asking, the guilt locked heavily in his throat, hearing the uncertainty in her sleep-heavy voice. She wasn't sure he'd be able to change once they were back in their routine.

"I've told you everything I was holding back, princess. You've got my full and deranged, overbearing attention from now on. You got it?"

A breath she'd been holding swept against his neck, and she giggled lightly as she squeezed his waist. "Yeah. Tomb will be bossy from now on. As long as you know, we'll probably fight more because I won't simply comply if you're *too* overbearing."

Tomb grinned in the dark, rubbing his lips over her silky hair. "We fight just so we can fuck hard, baby."

She hummed her agreement. "Go to sleep now." She prompted. "I'll make a last breakfast in the morning before we leave. My send-off as a kidnap victim."

Tomb kissed her head and held her as close as he could.

He loved the fuck out of his wife, and nothing in this world would ever change that.

They didn't need any more reassurances at that moment. Their bodies were pressed together, allowing their harmony to create an unbreakable bond.

Nothing would separate them.

Not while he had blood flowing in his veins.

Not while his wife looked at him with burning love in her eyes.

Nina

Returning to their ordinary life felt peculiar.

Nothing suddenly felt the same, like they'd been through a metamorphosis at the lodge.

Not bad. Not that at all. Quite the opposite.

For the first time in a long time, Nina was lighter. Freedom from her erratic thoughts and fears and aerated with hope.

On the way from the lodge, they'd stopped at Tomb's mom's place for an hour. Nina loved her mother-in-law and vice versa, but she'd never confided in the woman about their marital struggles. She hadn't needed to because when Lori had hugged Nina in the doorway while Tomb warmed up the truck, she'd whispered in her ear. "I'm so happy, girl, that you both look much happier."

She didn't know what Lori had seen in them for however long because they never argued around her. The visits to Lori's house were always spent happily, but who was Nina to disagree with her mother-in-law's sixth sense?

"We're great," she said, much to Lori's relief.

After changing clothes and kissing Nina, Tomb rode off on his motorcycle, leaving her with an irresistible wink. Now, she was busy in the thick of it at the salon.

Her happy place.

Where she felt most comfortable.

But she found her mind wandering throughout the day while she worked on clients' hair.

Tomb.

Her heart throbbed to be closer to him, as though she'd caught a kidnappee attachment to her mountain of a man.

Esther noticed. So did Ross, and they teased her mercifully throughout the afternoon for her lack of concentration and dreamy eyes, as Ross put it.

She was a tough bitch. Tough bitches didn't have dreamy eyes. Did she?

On a break, while waiting for her next customer to have her hair washed for a blow-out, she sneaked into the back office and picked up her phone to text Tomb.

She smiled a mile wide when she noticed he'd already messaged her.

Of course, it was a dirty text.

She'd expect nothing less from her savage man.

Tomb: How good did it feel to have me sliding your panties on you this morning, princess?

Tomb: I felt how you trembled.

Tomb: Fuck. I wanna be back at the lodge with you, making you scream and cling to me.

Every inch of air vacated the building as Nina caught sight of herself in the overhead mirror. She blinked at what she saw.

And then she smiled.

She had dreamy fucking eyes.

Nina: I was weakened by all the sex. That's why I let you dress me. Don't get excited, husband. It won't happen again.

A response pinged almost instantly, as if he'd been waiting for her reply.

Tomb: I love a challenge, my stubborn wife.

Nina: There is something you can do for me. Something I need.

She thought of passing the problem to Tomb and never dealing with her landlord again.

Tomb: Name it.

The way it came up on screen, she could almost hear the tone from Tomb, how commanding he'd say it as if he'd give her anything.

She had to force herself to relax or die from the swirl of love that was embedded deep in her belly.

Would she love this side of him as much as the man she thought she knew?

Yes. Absolutely.

It wouldn't be plain sailing, but she didn't want that, anyway.

Sparks, an unbreachable connection, fiery passion, and honesty.

She needed that in her relationship, and he'd offered it on a plate for Nina to slurp the juices clean. If she turned her nose up at it, she'd be a fool in expensive heels.

Nina: My car was chugging on the way to the salon earlier. Can you look at it, please?

A minute passed with Nina staring at her phone screen like a love-slapped teen, eager to see his new message.

Tomb: Dillion is coming with the tow truck to bring it into the shop. Give him the keys, princess. I'll come pick you up tonight.

Nina: Thank you, love. See you later. XOXO

Not twenty minutes later, the Diablo prospect swaggered into the salon. Making Ross clutch his pearls, almost drooling on the floor over the six-foot man in raggedy denim clinging to his ass and wearing the leather PROSPECT vest.

She'd noticed a change in the younger man this past year. He didn't scowl as much as he once did. It was almost like he'd made it his vocation to carry an attitude. After handing over her car keys, he hooked her car to the tow truck to take it into the garage. The rest of the afternoon was spent being hit with a barrage of questions from Ross, who was now fresh into a new crush.

But her mind didn't wander far from her husband.

Excited for quitting time so she could see him again.

Tomb

The church table in the back room of the Diablos clubhouse sat a mix of eclectic bastards, some meaner than others. He meant Ruin.

Tomb had been the last to arrive, having spent an hour fixing the fault in Nina's car. He then had Dillion drive it home to leave in their carport.

Voices rose above each other.

Ruin was, as ever, silent as a slayer. They were used to seeing him with his head over his phone now, having hour-long text conversations with his wife. It was no longer weird to see that towering lunatic in love. And if anyone dared say shit to him about it, as Tomb had once made the mistake of doing, they wouldn't do it a second time. Tomb sent Ruin a wink to mess with him when the enforcer looked over. Ruin scowled. He still wasn't forgiven then. But if Ruin hated him, Tomb wouldn't exist, so there was that.

Sitting on the other side of the enforcer was his twin brother. Reno was the opposite in every way but eerily similar in looks.

Next to Tomb, Denver groaned and tried to change positions on the durable plastic chair. He made another pained sound, holding his side.

"You good, brother? Why don't you sit this one out?"

"Suck my dick, Tomb." He barked, trying to find a position to sit at ease so it didn't aggravate his healing wound. He'd been jumped late at night as he exited a liquor store. Initially, they believed it was a random attack. Further investigation proved the involvement of Denver's brother-in-law, as confirmed by an informant.

Tomb knocked his knuckles on the scuffed wood. "Not even if the state of the world rested on it, my brother. You want me to grab you a cushion?"

With another frustrated growl, Denver sent pissed-off eyes at Tomb. "I already have Casey fussing 'round me like she thinks I'm gonna keel over at any second. Don't need it from you or anyone else. I'm fine. It's only a fucking scratch."

A scratch that nearly lost him a kidney.

"Fine, you sour-faced douchebag. Be uncomfortable." Smirked Tomb, giving Denver a thump on the back. His brother-in-arms groaned in pain.

On the other side of Denver, Bash craned forward, his ringed fingers lassoed together on the table. "Don't bother talking to this moody bastard, Tomb. You'd think he was the only one who ever got stabbed before. He's whining like he wants his comfort blankie and his mommy's tit."

Denver pinned a severe stare at his best buddy. "I will rip your head off and shit down your neck if you keep working me, asshole."

It caused a riot of laughs around the table as Scarlett knocked, carrying a tray of goodies. She barely got them set down before hands descended on the plates and coffee like a pack of wild dogs.

"Denver, I made you a hot citrus drink with lots of honey and ginger. It wards off infections. Make sure you drink it all." She beamed as she slid the cup in front of him. The thing smelled like steaming piss. Better him than Tomb.

He saw it happening as Denver opened his trap to tell their bartender and Axel's queen where she could stick the healing drink but caught the warning growl from their Prez.

"Thank you, sweetheart," Denver said wisely. Axel would have pitched Denver out the window for giving lip to Scar. Wound or no wound.

After Scar kissed Axel, she left the church, and the meeting began.

"As we know, the Riot Brothers gang is trying to put a foothold in Utah. I talked to Rider over at the Renegade Souls this morning."

"Fun for you, Prez," chortled Splice. His blond hair looked bed-fucked.

The two MCs had forged an amicable relationship because of a connection between Axel's daughter, Roux, and her old man from the Renegade Souls. If they needed help, the Diablos would give it, and vice versa. Information was also shared when it was beneficial to the cause. They had disputes with the Riot Brothers gang in the last few years when they attempted to set up shop in Colorado. They were soon shown the error of their ways. Everyone thought Harvey had moved his operation out of state.

The Diablos wouldn't give them a comfortable ride either, that much Tomb knew.

Not only because of the connection to Denver's old lady and how badly she'd been mistreated. It was a case of respect. Don't step on another man's plate. Utah was Diablos' eatery.

"Rider has crossed paths with Harvey before. They're big on pushing dope and bringing arms into the country, and word on the underground is an Italian is funding Harvey; he's buying up real estate."

"Laundering purposes." Piped in Chains.

"We already have enough dirty money going through Utah." Added Devil, the club Treasurer. He should know because he cleaned the money through the many legal channels. He was smart as a whip, that one. The IRS would love to get something on the Diablos, but Devil could cook the books like a five-star chef. That was why he was coined with his road name. He was like the King of the Underworld. No one saw what he did until it was too late.

Splice posed a question they all wanted an answer to. "Do we know who the Italian is?"

"Rider said all he got from his source at the time was Conti. Once the Souls removed The Riot Brothers' drug dealing, he stopped looking into them." Axel went on, reserved as ever, sitting at the head of the table. "The spate of petty crime, car thefts, burglaries, left town when they did."

"Funny how crime has increased here, huh?" noted Bash.

It was fortunate that Diablos paid a corrupt cop for info. Sofia Fielding was in close contact with Axel, not only about the crime sprees in Utah lately but also to let him know her side of the law had eyes on the Riot Brothers.

"Now that Primo has access to his hacking tools in prison..." started Axel, talking about their IT expert brother, who was incarcerated.

"Thank you, corrupt Judge Snow. So fucking easy to bribe and blackmail idiots these days." Smiled the VP.

"He did some backdoor hacking and discovered Conti's bought several hundred domestic properties to rent and has Harvey's boys running a protection racket."

"So the asswipe rents you a property and then jacks on a protection price, too? Swell, dude." Remarked Bash. "I don't care, but this is our patch."

"You're a bleeding heart, Bash," replied Reno across the table. He earned a fired middle finger.

"That's the gist of it. There's several ways we can play it." Informed Axel, "But I'm more inclined to go in heavy. The Riot Brothers tried to kill one of us. Denver wants his brother-in-law out of Casey's life for good. So we focus on that end first."

"It's been a long time coming." Snarled Denver.

Each male voice roused as they banged on the table in a collective agreement.

Once they knew where the guy was, Ruin would be tagged in to do his enforcer magic. No one could kill a man and make it look like it never happened, like Ruin. He was their silent assassin, a master of his trade. The soulless wonder who could kill without guilt gnawing at his sternum.

"Chains has a list of things that need looking into. I want every Riot Brother accounted for and monitored. He'll divvy it out. You know what to do." Said the Prez. "Any other shit we need to talk about today?"

There was no response.

"Good." he rose to his feet and looked down at Tomb. "You wanna head out with me, Tomb? I gotta see a man about an Italian."

Tomb grinned and climbed to his feet. "Yep."

Tomb

Days passed.

And then a week.

Who the fuck knew two years into his marriage that he and Nina would like playing house in wedded fucking bliss?

It wasn't even six a.m., and he was getting the ride of his life. His hands held up high behind his head, gripping the headboard with a death clasp as he gritted his teeth and groaned like a gigolo.

She was fucking *incredible*.

All creamy skin and little caramel sweet nipples grazing his cheek as she bounced her way into a second orgasm. The gush of it soaked his pent-up dick. He'd forced off his climax more than once, and his dick hated him for it. All Tomb could think about was pounding his come into her, watching how it trickled down her trembling thighs.

But Tomb refused to finish until Nina had enough.

"Don't let go." She warned when she saw his hands loosen. He wanted to grab her, own her, dominate her. But this was her show this morning. Nina had been the one to wake him by sucking the soul from his dick. Then she'd climbed on and impaled herself.

"Never letting go," Tomb grated, watching her rise and fall like a sweat-shined goddess. He meant more than just the headboard.

Tomb would pursue Nina to the ends of the earth and beyond if she got a wild thought in her head again.

When she came, she did it with her mouth crushed against Tomb's, sucking his tongue and moaning down his throat. Fuck him, he was done. The moment he felt the warm spasm of her orgasm around his cock, he dropped his hands to her hips and powered thrust after violent thrust up into her until he found his bliss. Only slowing when he felt less feral. But he continued to move his shaft through their shared wetness. Her gaze lowered to see how her pleasure glistened on his length.

Fucking perfect.

"Who's turn is it to make breakfast?" she asked once she'd stopped panting. Nina smiled at him in her gorgeous, manipulative way when she wanted him to make food.

"You use and abuse my body before I'm awake."

"Your dick was poking me in the back, practically begging for it, the slut."

"Now you expect me to make food, too?"

She dropped little kisses all over his lips, tempting him like a she-devil, and Tomb would happily fall into her ploys.

"Your eggs always taste so much better than mine, Rome. Pretty please with your princess on top."

This woman was his undoing, his reckoning, and his end-of-life paradise.

And she had him wound around her little finger. *Happily*.

"Is that so? I better make you eggs then, my sexy, manipulative wife." They shared a smile, lip-to-lip. Underneath his hand, where he'd lassoed her wrist, her pulse fluttered.

Tomb loved every side of Nina.

The tough and the mouthy.

The sweet and the soft.

Her heart was a fucking treasure, as sappy as it made him sound.

Bikers were not without feelings.

A five-foot-nothing blonde she-devil princess owned his feelings.

Nina triggered all his baser urges to the surface, making them roar, demand, and ask the impossible of her. Because of this Denver and Casey shit they had going on, Tomb had been extra vigilant with Nina's security since coming back from the lodge. He'd stationed Forger across the street from her salon, sitting most of the day in the café, ensuring she was safe and not harassed by anyone from the Riot Brothers.

He would be as feral as he needed to be.

The dark truth was he yearned to put a tracking device on her and was considering how and when. He knew folks who could inject the tiniest thing underneath the skin, and no one would know it was there.

Did it make him a bit unhinged? Overkill for her safety? Who fucking cared. He wouldn't let anyone lay a hand on his wife.

Nina brought his attention out of his warped thoughts by tugging his hair.

"Breakfast then?"

"After a shower fuck. My turn to be in control, wife." He rasped, rolling them off the bed. Nina squealed with delight as he carted her off to the bathroom, where he followed through with his sexed-up plan.

Then he made them breakfast. Nina sat on his lap, letting him feed her bites of toast laden with eggs while she went through her work diary.

Of fucking course, she grumbled about it even as she opened her mouth for another bite, trying to salvage her bad girl rep, but her need for affection and attention would win now he recognized her kryptonite.

"I don't need you to feed me, Rome."

"It pleases me."

Her eyes warmed. Tomb tasted victory when she opened her mouth for the next fork coming toward her lips.

"Are you leaving the salon at all today?"

"Not that I know of. But I will wave to Forger across the street if I do."

Amused, he kissed the side of her neck. Smart wife.

"Was he easy to spot?" he'd have to kick the probies ass for allowing himself to be seen.

"Ross mentioned Forger was always at the corner window seat every afternoon when he went to pick up the coffee order. I put two and two together and came up with a Rome King scheme."

He waited for the incoming protest, but none came. She was busy writing herself notes in her overstuffed work diary.

When she'd finished eating, he tapped her ass to lift from his lap while he took out the trash. Nina was filling the dishwasher when he came in, then wiped down the island.

Domestic shit.

And he loved it.

He needed to go out of town on another pickup run in a few days but intended to take Nina with him again. He'd leave that surprise announcement for another time.

"What's on your plate today, love?" she asked absently while she packed her suitcase-size purse. "I might drop into the clubhouse for lunch if you have time. One of my regular clients canceled."

He shared most of the details about the club with Nina, except for a few. She didn't have to deal with the grim side they encountered, but he was open about his work. He'd seen club brother's marriages get fucked up because of lies.

"I'm following an Italian, seeing what their movements are."

"Oh, yeah?" she quirked an amused eyebrow at him. "Should I be jealous?"

"No," he half-smiled, swinging into his leather jacket and pocketing keys. "It's a shitty guy. Conti is the lowlife who's funding the Riot Brothers."

If he hadn't been facing Nina, he never would have detected how she immediately turned ashen and her mouth dropped open.

"Emilio Conti?"

His brow fell over his eyes. "Yeah, that's him. How do you know his name?"

"Oh, shit. Oh, fuck. *Shit*." She repeated.

Now Tomb was really on red fucking alert. His hackles rose from his skin, and he dropped the cell phone he'd been holding onto the island, striding across to her. "Nina, baby. The fuck? What's going on?"

"First, I need you to stay calm, okay?"

Like Hell, he would.

He didn't need details at this point because he sensed something was fucked if it got his Nina looking like she was ready to throw up carrots.

When he took hold of the top of her arms, she latched her hands beneath his jacket on his waist, putting them toe-to-toe. She looked up.

"Nina, tell me how you know him."

"You and me are so solid now, right?" her eyes were pleading, like she had some dark secret that would split them apart.

The violent, heavy growl came from the soles of his feet, and Nina pushed closer to him. His soothing stone. But it didn't work, and every fucking instinct told him shit was about to fall.

"Rome, please."

"Of fucking course we are. Now tell me."

"Well, Conti is my landlord. He's owned the salon lease for years. And he's a bit of a dickhead. Actually, no, that's being generous to dickheads. He's an asshole through and through. He's vile."

Oh yeah, now he surged within to rip the guy's head off and piss on his grave.

A pour of anger ripped through Tomb's expanded muscles, embedding fuel in his brain, burning fire down his bloodstream.

Nina knew Conti. Conti knew his Nina. And she thought he was vile. That could only mean…

"Has that fucker hurt you?" he rasped through his clenched teeth, barely holding onto decency. He wasn't mad at her, *never*. "Tell me right now how hard I'm killing this motherfucker, Nina."

"No, don't say that. Please, Rome." She begged, squeezing his waist. "Look, let me call the salon and tell them to change my appointments. I think I should come to the club with you to tell you everything with Axel around."

Tomb narrowed his eyes as she slipped out of his arms, and he watched her search for her phone. "The fuck does that mean, Nina? *Has he hurt you*?"

"No, love, I swear. But I should say what I know with Axel there. With the others around. You can't go apeshit."

He was going to lose it.

But his intractable wife wouldn't budge. As pissed as he became, she wouldn't tell him the connection with Conti.

"You can't do anything," she implored to his reason. Little did she know he had zero.

"If my wife has a problem, I'm gonna sort it out. If that makes me bastard of the year, then hand me a fucking award to display on the fireplace."

The entire ride to the clubhouse with Nina clinging to his body, he thought of ways to slaughter that Italian, for as yet, an unknown crime, until there was nothing but dirt underneath his thick-soled boots.

He was living on borrowed time if he'd laid one fingertip on Nina.

Nina

Shit.

All her baggage and bad decisions were about to come home to roost for all to see.

And those poor decisions were saying Nina hadn't been able to deal with one lone sleazebag without getting her husband to fight her battles.

The truth was, Nina wanted Tomb to make it go away.

She would have shared much sooner if she had been aware of Conti's connection to the Diablos' enemy.

"Nina!" smiled Scarlett as she and Tomb walked hand-in-hand into the clubhouse twenty minutes later. "We don't usually see you this early." Most of the boys were around or still arriving. The club girls, as well. Cleaning and whatever else they chipped in with around the place. She didn't like to think about it too closely. In the last year,

Scarlett had started a club-funded cleaning business and employed those women.

Years back, when her relationship was still new, Axel's ex fabricated a gigantic lie about sleeping with Tomb, claiming he'd cheated on Nina. It caused a big stink in the clubhouse, especially between her and Tomb, for a minute, but those club girls went to bat for Selena. Though they'd half-heartedly tried to apologize once the truth was uncovered, revealing Selena as the lying tramp she was. Nina held grudges and would never forget it. So, when they glanced at her and Tomb, she glared back.

"Yeah, I won't be here long, babe. It's a busy day at the salon."

"Prez, you got a minute?" Her big scowling bear asked. Axel was seated at the bar with Scarlett, drinking coffee.

"Sure." He eyed them both. "Do we need privacy?"

Tomb angled his head down, his brow so furrowed and angry looking. "Do we?"

Nina shook her head. "No, I guess not. Just…" she spied Splice and waved him over. Hearing Tomb mutter, "the fuck." Once Tomb's friend came across, she looked toward Axel.

. But what she had to say was all for Tomb's sake.

"What I'm about to say will set a bomb underneath my man, so I need you both to be a wall in front of him, okay?"

"What?" laughed Splice, not getting what was happening yet. But he would. And Splice, being the one who'd spied on her the most, would understand how unhinged her words would send her man.

"Jesus fucking Christ, Nina." Tomb growled. She could practically feel him vibrating, standing so near like he wanted to cage her and never let her go. She wanted nothing more, but wouldn't see her man explode and do something that would get him taken away from her.

"What's going on, Nina?" asked the calmer Axel.

"Conti is her salon landlord." Spat Tomb.

"Yeah, what Tomb said. But he's a dickbag, as landlords go. He plays fast and loose with the rent. He's a bully. And I thought if I ignored it, it would go away, and I wouldn't have to bother Tomb with it."

"Bother me with what?" his voice was like glass now. Brittle, ready to shatter, she glided her hand into his. Nina's gaze remained only on Axel. "He puts pressure on his tenants. I've heard it from others. Most of their stores have collapsed because of it. They can't pay what he's demanding. The salon is looking to go the same way."

"Fucking hell it is." Roared Tomb. Dropping her hand, he raked both of his through his hair, his eyes so thunderous as he paced.

Ugh, she hated being the gasoline to his mood.

She needed her loveable man back, not one who looked like he could rip off limbs and stir a cup of coffee with it.

"Love, I don't want you to get mad. Nothing happened, okay? *Nothing*. I swear it. But it's not only money he's been pressuring me about. He's stated that if I have an affair with him—and I'm putting that in the best decent terms I can—then he would forget about the increased rent."

"Holy shit," she heard Splice exclaim from behind her.

"No freaking way. That creepy sicko." Said Scarlett.

If Axel reacted, Nina took no notice because she focused entirely on Tomb.

And it took less time for her to inhale than for him to respond.

It started in waves, like slow motion.

The anger washed over his face.

Eyes blackened to a raging storm color.

She noticed his fists clench, hanging at his sides until the whites of his knuckles threatened to fracture through the skin.

His chest expanded so much, testing the material of his shirt.

Nerves skittered down Nina's spine, and when Tomb threw his head back and roared, it only intensified those nerves.

"I'm going to kill that motherfucker. He's dead meat."

Okay. No talking about it then.

It was what she'd feared and the reason she'd asked to tell him here where he'd have his boys to hold him in check.

"Please, baby, listen to me a minute." She implored, moving deeper into his space until she could touch his rapidly moving chest.

She'd never seen him so mad.

He was snarling like he'd transformed into a lethal beast. All color was gone from his eyes, just black disks of fury staring at her as he let his head hang low on his neck. The words grated through his clenched teeth.

"This guy asked to fuck you?"

"Tomb, baby…"

"He. Asked. To. Fuck. My. Wife?"

Trembling, not from fear. She'd never be afraid of her husband, but she was worried for him and what he'd do. Nina nodded.

Another violent growl exploded.

"Where the fuck is he based? Tell me right now."

"I didn't tell you so you could go off half-cocked. It's nothing, I told that jerk where to go."

"Nothing?" he snarled, lip curling. Her sweet man receded into the background. This Tomb was a tall drink of pure animal. "Someone talking to my wife that way is not nothing. He's borrowing his last breaths. Where the fuck is he based, Nina?" but then he fired another snarked question. "How long has he been chasing you?"

"It's not like that. Conti sometimes drops by and taunts how bad it would be if I lost the salon. He's been increasing the rent dramatically for a couple of years and then started suggesting how it could be different if…" Nina swallowed hard when Tomb growled.

"It was when you gave me back my phone…" she watched Tomb's brow become more furrowed. "He called then, and that's when he… when he made it plain what I could do or lose my salon."

"Has he ever come to the salon with any Riot Brothers?" Asked Axel, leaning an elbow on the bar close to where Scarlett was sitting.

"Not that I know of. Conti usually has a driver and another guy with him, a bodyguard, maybe?"

"You talked to him while we were at the lodge?"

Tomb fired the words like a quiet whip, and the accusation hit her square in the belly. It sounded awful and deceitful when he put it like that.

Fuck, fuck, *fuck*.

It was so bad.

Staying quiet only compounded the problem. When would she fucking learn?

In her girl math, she'd thought ignoring it would make it go away, and now she'd made it so much fucking worse by not sharing it with him from the start.

"Let's talk about it, Tomb."

He only looked over her head toward Axel. "I need that address right now. Text it to me." Then, without speaking to her, he spun on his boots and started striding to the entryway like an avenging demon. It wouldn't have looked out of place on his broad shoulders if he wore a sweeping black cape.

For a fleeting moment, Nina gaped at his retreat, and then she sprang into action, shouting for him to stop. Tomb didn't look back, but he growled, "*Splice.*"

And then she felt arms banded around her waist, holding her back.

"Let me go," she screeched as Tomb got further away, and then he was out of sight, going to do God only knew what. "I swear I will break your bones if you don't let go of me, Ryan."

"Can't do it, Nina."

Splice released his hold once the motorcycle bellowed through the exit, and Nina rounded on him.

"Some fucking help you both were. You were supposed to hold Tomb back, not me!"

Axel flashed a sympathetic smile, like this was all fun and games. He stood to his full height, drawing back his arm around Scarlett's hip from where she sat perched on the bar top.

"Tomb's gotta do what he's gotta do, Nina. He'll be back."

"Yeah, in what? Prison orange? We have no idea what he'll do. I've never seen him this angry before." This *unstable*.

Nina was frightened for her husband. In the state he'd left in, he was capable of anything. And that *anything* made bile sloth around her uneasy belly.

Splice added. "Nah, he's smarter than that. You want a drink, Nina?"

"Piss off." She told the man she considered a close friend.

Axel gave her a shoulder pat and a look of understanding. "It'll be okay, Nina. Conti overstepped. Tomb can't ignore that. It's nothing I wouldn't do in his place."

"Men." Chimed in, Scarlett and Axel sent her a smoldering look.

"Yes, *men*. Kiss me, wildcat."

Scarlett fell onto Axel's lips for a fast kiss, and then Axel strode off, whistling for a prospect to follow him to the office. No doubt to find the address for Conti.

Fuck all the fucks. This wasn't good.

What was Tomb going to do?

And what trouble would he be in if it went too far?

Splice sidled up and nudged her shoulder in a friendly way. "If some tool told my woman he wanted to fuck her, and he did it in a sly fucking manipulative way Conti did, I'd react the same as Tomb, babe. Let your man handle this shit. You should've told him right away. Now it's worse."

Guilt made her glare at him.

"You'll never be in this position, Ryan, because you're incapable of monogamy." She accused.

"Hey! Don't you blame her for the shit a man does." Defended Scarlett, slipping down from the bar. She was no taller than Nina but popped her chin high to glower at Splice. He only shrugged indifferently.

"Can't argue with the truth, Scar. You all whine you want better communication, blah, blah, whatever. But you keep shit to yourself, the important shit, until it's too late, then expect us to wade in and fix it."

As he was about to walk off, leaving Nina with shoulders ladened with worry, he wasn't altogether wrong about what he said. He turned a sympathetic smile her way. "Relax, Nina, we have a cop on our payroll. If Tomb goes nuclear, she can clean it up, no problem."

His parting words didn't ease her in the slightest. It only intensified the worry about what Tomb might be about to do.

Scarlett threaded her arm through Nina's. "Let's go to the kitchen and make the best coffee, babe. We can let the boys do their thing and talk about how much we hate their overbearing behavior, but secretly love it."

Nina couldn't help but laugh at Scarlett's positivity.

After ten unanswered calls to Tomb, all Nina had left to do was wait and worry.

Tomb

The fuckhole's HQ address came through while Tomb idled at a stop sign. He gazed over Nina's stream of messages and missed calls, then shoved the phone into his pocket, powering the bike forward.

It took only minutes to reach the office block.

Tomb circled the block and parked on the corner, several storefronts away. While he wanted to storm in, guns blazing, he needed to pump the brakes on his temper, so he climbed down from his bike, sitting sideways on the seat. While he stared at the building, imagining decimating it brick by brick, he took black leather gloves out of his pocket and slid them onto his hands. Not leaving prints behind was lunatic 101.

Though, just his luck, the place would be rigged with cameras.

No fucking matter.

This was happening.

His blood burned when he pictured the cunt putting the moves on his Nina.

She hadn't told him.

That fucking burned deep in his gut.

But it wasn't Nina he was angry with.

She could accidentally firebomb a pet store, and he'd cradle her on his lap to comfort his sweet princess. Her silence over this would come with consequences, and he promised she'd love each one with screaming pleas.

Until then.

He pushed off his bike seat and started the quick stride down the street. The office building had an open-door policy, and he walked in unaided, passing by a reception desk.

He found what he was looking for, and Tomb's lip curled, anger bubbling beneath the surface. Emilio Conti: The gold CEO placard on the door.

Tomb didn't bother knocking. He wasn't here for a tea party. He was prepared to kick the fucking thing in if need be, but when he tried the handle, it turned, and he shoved it wide.

The outpouring of rage filled his torso seeing the blue suit-wearing fuckface behind a desk, in front of double windows. He wanted to see that face covered in bruises.

A male secretary at another desk looked all of a hundred pounds dripping wet. Wearing glasses and a smart suit, straight out of college.

Both heads rose on Tomb's entry. He knew the impression he gave with his size alone as he filled the doorway. Anyone who knew Tomb knew he wouldn't hurt a fly. Unless pushed. He'd been fucking *pushed*.

The college guy spoke, adjusting the glasses on his nose. "Sir, do you have an appointment? Is there a property you're interested in renting? I'd be happy to assist you."

Polite fucker.

Tomb would hate to break his bones if he got in the way, so he gave the college kid his full attention for a second. "I need words with your boss. Take an early lunch, kid."

It would be the only warning he gave. If the kid wanted to watch the show, so be it.

"What is this about?" Conti asked, and Tomb glared at him.

"Nina King. You recall that name?"

Conti showed recognition, and something changed in his face. *Fear*. It smelled fucking good in the air. He should be afraid.

"Ed, take your break early."

"Are you sure?" Glasses asked, clearly aware of the animosity rising from Tomb. But he grabbed his satchel. "Okay then, can I bring you anything back?"

"No."

Tomb moved deeper into the room and waited for the door to close. Leaving him alone with the man he wanted to tear to shreds.

"What can I help you with?" polite asshole.

"Nina King."

Conti chose his lane and went with a lie. "I do not recall the name. You can remind me. I know many people and rent hundreds of properties."

Tomb drew closer until he could see the whites of Conti's eyes. "*My wife*." He grated through his compressed teeth. "The woman you've been threatening to take away her salon."

Conti blinked and went to rise from his leather chair, but Tomb got there first and used a gloved hand to shove him down. "Listen to me, Mr. King. I do not know what this is about, but if my tenants have complaints, they can bring it to me."

"Slick motherfucker, aren't you? Bet you get a lot of side pussy with that accent, huh? Your woman at home, oblivious to what her husband is doing out of the house. Dirty coward putting his tiny prick around town. But you tried it on with *my wife*, Conti. You put her in a position where she had to listen to you proposition her. And that doesn't wash with me."

The denial spewing from Conti's quivering mouth fell on deaf ears. Tomb yanked the chair around to face him.

"You're saying you didn't tell Nina you wanted to fuck her? That you'd cancel the rent if she opened her legs for your pencil dick? You saying my wife is a fucking liar?"

Splutter. Splutter. Panic. The guy was a coward down to his marrow. "*Sí*, yes. It's not how you say. It's a misunderstanding. I speak not-so-good English. I spoke mistakenly, and she did not understand my meaning. Do you get it?"

It was funny how his accented speech pattern abruptly declined.

Tomb smirked and straightened to his height, rubbing his chin. "Yeah? So, this is all a big misunderstanding then, huh?"

A wash of relief entered Conti's eyes. "Yes, I'm an entrepreneur and a happily married man with children. I do not engage with another man's wife."

"Ah, maybe you're right." Tomb said, keeping his tone steady. "I guess I can forget all about this, but there is one thing you can answer for me."

A calmed Conti adjusted his necktie.

"Of course. I am happy to clear up any dispute with Mrs. King."

Conti wouldn't have working legs to stand on again to be in front of Nina.

Tomb's chest filled with air, sensing his control was ready to snap down the middle. "Do you think I could overlook you disrespecting *my wife*, you slimy cunt?"

Conti only had time to widen his eyes as Tomb cocked back his clenched fist and brought it home on the other man's face with the weight of all his unleashed anger.

Tomb couldn't say exactly what happened in the next few minutes.

It was like he tapped out of his body and stood by, watching himself destroy the suited Italian with one punch to his smug little face after another.

When Conti tried to evade, Tomb hit him harder until blood was his new skin color. When Conti fell to the floor and tried to crawl away from the punishing blows, Tomb stood on his knee and heard the bone snapping. And when Conti attempted to fight back, throwing a wayward arm out, hoping to unbalance Tomb, Tomb caught the watery-weak arm and put pressure on the wrist until Conti howled in agony. That bone became another puzzle piece for some lucky doctor to repair later.

Bar brawls were one thing. Spontaneous violence that came out of nowhere, was usually for a reason.

It was a completely different approach, causing someone to bleed on purpose until they couldn't see for the blood pouring into their eyeballs.

Tomb was out of control in those moments. Only hearing Nina's words rattling around his skull to fuel his hatred and rage.

When he sensed Conti had taken enough of a beating to learn his lesson, he stepped over the broken and bloody man, going down to a crouch near Conti's head. He grasped his chin to get him to focus. The sobbing douchebag could cry out for help as much as he wanted. Tomb wasn't the man for forgiveness.

"I was never here. Do you hear me, Conti? I'm leaving you alive. That's the only reprieve you get. You talk to the cops, and it'll get worse for you next time. And if anything blows back on my wife, you'll wake up dead."

Tomb sat for thirty minutes down the street, watching the building.

He saw when a black Mercedes pulled up, and a bomber jacket-wearing guy rushed inside with hurried steps like he'd been alerted to an emergency. Minutes went by until that same man brought Conti out to their car.

Tomb's gloves were awash with blood. Carefully peeling them off, he stuffed them into a dumpster nearby before climbing onto his bike. Before he rode off, he called Nina.

She answered after the first ring.

She sounded panicked and relieved. "Are you okay?"

"Where are you?"

"I came to the salon. I didn't know what else to do. You weren't answering."

"Stay there. I'm on my way." And he dropped the call.

Tomb

The howling wind blowing in his face went some way to calming Tomb's inner turmoil. But his simmering violence would only disappear when he could see Nina.

"Ohhhh, aren't we special getting a visit from the biker hubby?" Announced an overly happy Ross when Tomb strode into Nina's pink-decorated salon. It smelled of perfumes and chemicals. A radio station played the latest ear-splitting pop songs, and every pair of female eyes turned to look at him.

But he only saw Nina. She stared at him, looking so strong-willed and uncertain.

His queen in this life and the next was the toughest of all women, but he was the lucky SOB who was allowed beneath the surface to see her vulnerabilities.

From her expression and how she locked her fingers together, she expected a showdown and gestured for him to follow her into the back office, where he closed the door with a quiet snick of the lock.

"Let me speak first, okay? I know you'll yell at me, and I suppose I deserve it…"

Tomb stopped Nina mid-flow by sliding a hand to the back of her neck and hauled her into his chest, where he could lower his head and smash their lips together. She gasped, and that was his opening to get inside, to find her tongue for a deep taste of heaven. One second, and then Nina hummed, relaxing fully in his arms, winding hers around his neck, and she kissed him with the same passion.

She tasted of sweetness and coffee.

She tasted of forever. *His forever.*

"I need to have you," he spoke against her chasing lips, groaning when she caught his tongue and sucked hard. "I need to be joined to you. Right now, Nina." Even to his ears, he sounded like a desperate man. The fact was that some fool had approached Nina more than once and scared her. Made her fucking worry, and to keep it secret from him, made his blood run cold, and his surge of possessiveness was at an all-time high.

Nina was his woman. *His wife.*

Being inside her was his piece of paradise no man like him should ever deserve. Her skin should've remained untainted by his dirty hands, but there wasn't a soul in the world who could rip him away from her.

And it was that paradise he was about to chase like a junkie.

"What happened?" she questioned, wide-eyed. "Is everything okay with Conti?"

"It's fine, baby."

"Truly?"

He'd tell her everything later. "Get out of those jeans," he issued roughly, afraid if he undressed her, he'd rip the clothes to tatters. Her reaction was fucking mouth-watering when he saw her tremble, eyes all wide and lust-filled. And when her nipples poked through the shirt, his perverted side howled with satisfaction.

"Nina." He growled when she was taking too long.

Her shaking fingers reached down and unbuttoned the jeans. His eyes stalked the movements of her trembling fingers, all but snarling to get at his peace.

Only Nina's presence had ever reached directly into his chest to find the hollowness, filling it with her spirit. Tomb didn't know how it worked or why. He didn't need that answer. Deep in his marrow, all he understood was that this woman was made to be his.

He was carved from stone so he could be hers.

He'd had the most significant wake-up call recently and would never sleep on their relationship again.

Down went the jeans, and his thirsty eyes roamed over her legs.

"Are you mad at me?"

"Am I ever mad at you? You're my whole fucking world. The center of my chest."

She inhaled, her eyes glistening with unshed tears. "You look like a beast about to rip out of your clothes."

"You're about to appease my beast cock. Now, turn around, baby, and press your hands on the desk. I wanna see you tip your ass back and offer me that perfect wet cunt."

"*Oh, God.*"

"I wish God were here to help you, but it's only me. Come on, get a move on. We don't have time to waste."

"Okay, *okay.*" She wheezed, shuffling out of the tightest jeans until he spotted her soft panties. He wouldn't rip them off. He enjoyed defiling his wife while she was dressed, leaving her with a dripping pussy full of his come.

It took a moment to free his cock. To position himself behind her, to hold on to her hip while he found her drenched hole, keenly trying to entice him in with little flutters.

One shove and peace was upon him. "*Christ.* There we go," he groaned into the side of Nina's neck. "You clasp onto that dick tight, princess. It's the only fucking way to bring me peace now." Bent over the table, she garbled nonsense. Tomb grinned, knowing her love for his deepest fucks. His perfect woman in and out of bed. "This happens when my wife doesn't confide in me or give me her problems. She gets a good dicking."

"Please, Rome. *Yes.*" she purred.

Tomb couldn't alter his abrasive tone, not when he felt like he'd fallen into heaven, one thrust at a time. There wasn't gentleness either. It was *impossible*. He felt out of control. And when Nina grew increasingly louder with her moans, he put a hand over her mouth.

"Those screams are only mine."

"Yours," she muffled around his fingers, looking back at him through lust-drunk, lowered lids, and his dirty little wife pushed back her ass, asking for more. When each shove took his dick deeper inside of her, he knew he was using her body, but he couldn't stop. Not until Nina pulsated around him was it the beginning of the end.

Frantic fucking.

Sordid thoughts pounded in his temples.

The insane ways he could truly work her over, to see stars and moons, if he had her somewhere private, and when he wasn't trying to appease his internal chaos.

Tomb wanted to gorge on Nina's cries. Swallow them whole, feel them rattling around his chest while she dug her nails into his shoulders and took the fuck of a lifetime.

Starved, raspy words pressed into her neck as he angled over her prone body and gave her everything he had. The end of Nina's climax was the kick-start to his own. Tomb grunted harshly, sinking his teeth into her shoulder while his orgasm was torn out of him in hot ropes.

Though he trusted her staff not to burst in uninvited, he wouldn't allow Nina to remain without clothes for long, as he crouched down, not long after, to put her panties and jeans right again.

"What a sticky delight that's going to be for me to deal with today," she said with her lips curved, eyes glinting from her orgasm.

"It'll dry," he appeased with a smirk. Rising to his feet, Tomb took her face and kissed her lightly. "I'll shower my come off you when you get home tonight."

"Something to look forward to then," she smiled, swaying on her feet, and Tomb carried her around the desk to plonk his ass in her leather chair. Snuggled on his lap, he kissed her temple. "This office needs a couch."

"Why? So you can fuck me here more often."

"If my wife needs an afternoon fuck, she gets it. I'll have my cock on 24/7 call."

"Sweet man." She chuckled, tugging at his beard. "I love you, Rome."

"I love you, too, princess."

"You do?"

Agony hit his solar plexus, hearing her surprise. He should have been saying it more often.

"Yeah. Always have, always will, until I'm worm food."

He was a bastard to get off on her softer, vulnerable side. It made his libido sing like a church choir.

"Maybe even after that?" she whispered, and Tomb grinned against her temple, giving her hip a nice little squeeze.

"No doubt. You're stuck with me now. And when you get pissed at me, we'll work on it. Ride it out on my cock. We can take it like a champ. Any time you wanna get angry at me, climb into my lap, baby."

"Mmm." After a minute, she stirred. "I should get back on the salon floor."

Yeah, he had shit to do, too.

It wasn't guaranteed Conti wouldn't get the cops involved, and Tomb needed to be prepared for that.

With a promise to see her soon, Tomb left Nina after a tingling kiss as he strode through her salon. Ignoring the knowing grins from her staff, he headed back to the clubhouse.

Once Axel caught up with the details, he was about to send a probie to scope out the hospital, but Bash volunteered instead. Likely to see the ER nurse he couldn't get a date with.

Bash reported Conti checked himself out of the hospital later that night, his body in plaster and stitches, and was aided to his G-Wagon by his men.

A prospect watched Conti's house for days.

No cops were involved.

The weasel had a decent brain cell left, after all.

Tomb

It wasn't often his Nina made house calls.

Only to one client.

Currently, Tomb had his ass parked on the second from bottom step, leading to Ruin and Rory's townhouse. Ruin's superstar old lady had agoraphobia and didn't leave the house much. She'd improved in the past year, but since Nina and the other old ladies got to know her, Nina came by every four weeks to do some female shit with Rory's hair.

Since Ruin was still being a petty jackass over some dumb shit Tomb joked about ages ago about Rory, Tomb wasn't welcome in their house.

Fine by him. He was too goddamn exhausted to be social with people, anyway. Cracking a wide yawn, he rested both arms on his knees. Nina should be done any time. He'd let her know he was waiting outside. They'd get dinner at a barbecue place in town, and then he'd spend the night watching one of her shows while she laid across his lap.

Domestic euphoria, Nina called it.

Whatever its name, it pleased Tomb. Entirely.

They were learning each other all over again. Discovering what the other needed most from their relationship. It turned out that he and Nina were competitive because each tried to be the victor in *pleasing*. It was satisfying bearing witness to his spit and vinegar-mouthed wife succumbing to his overbearing demands because she *wanted* it, too.

Tomb hadn't held back. He promised he wouldn't.

No one said he was correct in how he acted now.

But it worked for them.

Being under Nina's thumb was not the wrong place to be, not for Tomb. He was happy as a fat bull in a field full of horny cows. Giving him the decision-making responsibility made her feel at ease and reduced her stress.

He only had to eavesdrop on a call with Monroe to find out her wholesalers had shafted her two months running with supplies. Tomb tagged himself in. He spoke personally to the prick to resolve the issue ASAP and to refund the difference while warning them never to mess with his wife's business again.

If it made him an arrogant twat, Tomb's one job was to take care of Nina. Beginning and end. His methods didn't need a moral compass.

Rory's one-way street was quiet, so Tomb's hearing perked when he caught the distant tone of a male voice heading down the avenue toward him.

"Leonard, we're not out in the fucking cold for the good of my health. You wanna take a piss sometime this century?"

Tomb recognized that hoarse voice.

Sure enough, when he leaned toward the left, he saw Ruin sauntering back toward his house.

At his side, hooked up to a harness and leash, was Rory's pet teacup piglet. Instantly, a smirk tugged Tomb's mouth, seeing the pig dressed in a bright red sweater, rubber booties, and a hat. A fucking hat. Ruin barely moved because the pig had to snuffle excitedly around each tree along the sidewalk.

People always thought of Ruin as a psycho.

Tomb wasn't so sure about that.

Sure, the guy had odd behavior. Being the club enforcer, he'd dealt with more darkness than anyone, which had to affect even the most closed-off man. Ruin only spoke to his twin brother for years and grunted at everyone else. It'd been no kept secret that, back then, in order for Ruin to get some action, Reno had to be there fucking the same woman.

That incestuously close activity changed when they both hooked up with their old ladies within months of each other.

But Tomb saw through Ruin's aloof demeanor. The guy observed his environment and its people better than a birdwatcher searching out a bald eagle.

When Tomb chuckled at the pig's antics, Ruin's head reared up, and he scowled.

Yep, that big bastard was still sour with him.

"How's it going, Ruin? Lenny not cooperating tonight, huh?"

Leonard charged over at the sound of his voice, dancing at Tomb's feet, waiting for the chin scratch he gave the pig. Then he shot off to a nearby tree and started pissing.

Ruin only grunted at Tomb.

"I'm waiting on Nina."

"I know."

Ruin stood with his back to Tomb, in no hurry, watching the pig, letting the animal play as long as he wanted. Another trait of the club enforcer was endless patience and a stillness that freaked people out.

Psychos were born, Tomb thought. But Ruin had made himself into one to endure, to ensure his twin brother survived by any means necessary. Not that Tomb would say any of that to Ruin's face. He was likely to catch a fist to the mouth again. Tomb's teeth still hadn't recovered from that brutal trauma.

Facing the elephant in the room, he asked. "You ever gonna be good with me again, brother?"

Ruin turned around and angled an eyebrow.

"I think your old lady is a nice girl. What I said was a joke, a shitty one, but I know I fucked up."

Tomb shook his head. He painted his woman's toenails once, and now look at him, baring his soul for a brother to forgive his stupid mistake.

"Nina likes Rory." He started, knowing Ruin was listening, even if he'd turned his back again. "She enjoys visiting, even without all the hair shit. I think she wants to invite you guys to our place. She's kicked my ass more than once to make it right with you, Ruin. What do you say? Can we put it in the past? My dumb mouth won't say any shit to your woman." Silence. "I know what it's like to be protective. Women make you insane, like you lost your mind most of the time. But I wouldn't change it."

Fuck's sake, he was like a little girl now on the first day of kindergarten. But he'd promised Nina he'd try to make it right with Ruin.

What Nina asked for, Nina got.

"You heard gossip around the club about Nina and me? How we nearly came to quits. Or that's what she thought. I'd chase my wife through a field of bees, and I'm fucking allergic to them." He caught Ruin's snort.

"What I feel for Nina isn't the same offhanded bullshit people crow about. Love is thrown around like confetti. It's meaningless. She burns right through me. Fucking consumes me. One look from her splits me open and leaves me feral. Nothing has been the same since meeting Nina because my thoughts, my fucking air, are infected with her presence. You think I'd drag my nasty eyes off my woman to look at yours, brother? I'm sharing this with you, so you understand, yeah? When Nina is near, no one else exists for me. But I don't have to explain, do I? You get that now. Your old lady makes you feel the same way."

Another wave of silence and Tomb stopped flapping his gums. He'd tried like a pussy. Now, he'd have to tell Nina Ruin had broken up with him for good.

At that, Ruin strode up the steps with Leonard under his arm; he moved by Tomb without a word.

At the top, he heard.

"You can come in." A deep furrow was etched on Ruin's face, like it hurt him to let anyone else inside with his woman. Ruin added. "You don't touch my old lady, Tomb."

Tomb rose and climbed the steps. His eyebrows hitched into his hair. What the fuck did the enforcer think he was going to do, dry hump another man's wife?

"I wasn't planning on it."

With a deeper frown, Ruin hesitated, opening the door. "Aurora likes people. She gives out hugs like free goodie bags. *I don't like it.* Just don't go near her." His *or else* was strongly implied.

Ah, he got it and nodded. "You wanna kiss and make-up now?" Asked Tomb, holding his arms out wide. His smile even wider. Braced for a punch.

"Not unless you want to pitch down those steps head first."

Tomb barked a laugh and followed Ruin inside.

Nina

Living on a diet of Tomb sex left a woman feeling weakened some days.

After soaking in a hot bubble bath her man of action had made for her, she sipped the last of a glass of Merlot and climbed out, fully recharged and ready for dinner.

Over three weeks had passed since they returned from the lodge, and Nina had been anxiously dreading for the police to arrest Tomb. The boys had channels to monitor the police, and as yet, no reports had been put through the system. Even better, Conti wasn't around the office when she dropped off the rent check this month.

"You look relaxed," mentioned Tomb, sending her a look over his shoulder while he sprinkled salt and pepper on two steaks ready to throw on the grill.

"Hot water and red wine do wonders for a woman's body."

When he raked his predator gaze slowly up and down her body, smiling at her, shudders raced along Nina's spine.

He was so handsome, so fixated on her these days. It was utterly invigorating. And he'd been merciless in his pursuit to show Nina what she meant to him.

It all made sense now that she was out of the other end of her marriage crisis. Sometimes, two people had to fall apart to come back together with more vital values and a renewed love and respect for each other.

It was never about fixing a broken relationship but building something new, something impenetrable.

Something better. More authentic, relying on trust and love.

Sliding her arms around Tomb's waist from behind, she kissed his t-shirt-covered spine. "I spoke to Casey earlier. She's going stir-crazy about being sequestered at the clubhouse. Denver won't let them out of his sight."

"She's got a sound head on her shoulders and will hold out until we figure out how to neutralize her brother."

"Do you think he'll try to snatch her back?"

Washing his hands, Tomb dried them on a towel and turned to face her. Lack of answer was answer enough. And that caused worry for her friend.

Tomb slipped a hand underneath her hair and dotted kisses on her forehead. The affection swam deep in her blood. She was about to suggest they hurry with dinner so they could go to bed when they heard the pipes of a motorcycle pulling into their carport.

Tomb strode to the window to see who it was. "Ruin? What's he doing here?"

"And why? He's never been to the house before." She added, confused. Ruin was only social with his wife and brother. She always thought he just tolerated everyone else associated with the Diablos MC. But she couldn't deny his utter devotion toward Rory. Seeing that big man fold under his wife's thumb was stomach-achingly sweet.

"Invite him in."

"He won't come in," said Tomb. Another kiss on her forehead. "I'll go see what this is about."

Sure enough, Ruin was waiting by his bike when Tomb strolled outside. Nina unapologetically spied on the scene from the window, but couldn't hear the two men talking.

They looked serious, their mouths moving. There were signs of surprise on Tomb's face, and then he laughed. Ruin smirked. Tomb whacked Ruin on the shoulder and gave him a manly half-hug.

For Tomb to hug Ruin and the other man, not to put Tomb into an early grave, it had to be something good. More than curious to know what was going on. She nearly pounced when Tomb came back through the door. "You hugged Ruin! What's going on?"

Smirking, Tomb took her face and kissed her so damn deep she nearly floated off the floor. He left her in the middle of the kitchen all tingly and still with no answer while he returned to the steaks, tossing them on a tray ready to carry outside.

"Rome! What was it?"

"Put it this way, Conti won't be a problem anymore."

Frowning, she was none the wiser. "What does that mean?"

He cocked a look over his shoulder. "Do you really wanna know details, baby? Or trust me when I say he's no longer an issue for you."

Oh.

Oh, shit.

If she was catching his covert gist, then no, she didn't need details of what Ruin had done. Or if Tomb asked for it to be done.

"I'll trust you."

"Good, now get your ass over and pay me some tax."

"Again? I swear not even the IRS rides my ass this hard during tax season." She huffed, shuffling across the kitchen to lean up as Tomb bent his head so she could kiss him again.

"Now he's gone. All Conti's holdings will transfer to his wife or sons." Stated Tomb. "I'm going to send our lawyer a message. I want your salon out of their clutches."

Nina blinked, goggled by what he was saying. "But…"

"No buts, Nina. That's *your* fucking salon. I should have bought it for you years ago."

His eyes narrowed like he expected an argument from her.

This 2.0 version of Tomb wasn't in a compromising mood, if he ever was. He'd told her he wanted to take her over. This was the tip of the iceberg and didn't need a compromise.

Nina didn't want to argue.

She wanted her salon.

Leaning up on her tiptoes, she wound her arms around his shoulders. They melted any tension as she kissed him. "Thank you, love." Drawing back, she smiled against his mouth. "Take that from my next tax bill. I love you."

He smirked. "Yeah, I know. Let's eat."

So they grilled steaks and then had an early night.

Tomb

It was more than obvious Denver was pissed that he needed a convoy of protection to go to his final hospital appointment.

Being the Road Captain instinctively put Tomb in front, so he stepped off his Harley first. Bash made up the other end of the protective sandwich and parked next to Denver.

"This is bullshit. I don't need babysitters."

"Harvey's boys' already got the jump on you once, brother," Bash mentioned, rubbing salt in Denver's angry disposition.

For weeks, he'd kept his family under lock and key, safe from a Riot Brother's ambush. As hardcore as he went for his family, it didn't mean he wasn't spitting mad about it all.

Tomb didn't expect Denver's deranged brother-in-law to attack him again at a hospital. But they weren't taking chances with security.

Axel held a cautious meeting with Harvey, who seemed just as surprised by the attack, and said he would yank his guy in line.

No one trusted Harvey.

As a formation of three, they cut through the ER department to get to where Denver needed to be. Tomb grinned to himself as Bash sought his defying nurse. Splice owed him fifty bucks. He bet Tomb, the woman Bash had been chasing for a year, would smile at him today.

So wrong.

Dressed in her scrubs, she was holding a bunch of folders. Like she'd caught Bash's scent, she swung around to glare. But a man would have to be dead in his coffin to miss the flash of interest in her eyes as she scrambled to put the reception desk between them.

It didn't stop Bash from advancing; he only had one mission: to climb into those scrubs with her.

Tomb tapped him on the shoulder, leaning in. "Relax, brother, you'll get arrested for rutting in public if you keep staring at her like you wanna eat her up."

Bash shrugged him off, his gaze only in one place: the woman attempting to ignore him.

Tomb thanked God for his Nina. He'd hate to be out in these streets doing the mating dance to catch a woman's attention.

Denver told them to wait, and he stalked down the hallway to find the department he needed for his final checkup.

Tomb found a seat and flipped through an old magazine that looked like it was from the 80s. Giving up trying to gain his nurse's attention, Bash threw himself down in the chair next to Tomb.

"Not wearing her down today then, huh, buddy? Move on. You gave it your best shot."

"She wants me," he growled low.

Bash proved how easily he'd lost it over the nurse when a male doctor got mouthy with her for not bringing a chart to him quickly enough. They watched Charlotte edge away from the oily doctor, crowding her personal space while he criticized her.

Bash jumped up from his seat so fast Tomb couldn't stop him.

"Here we fucking go," he muttered, shaking his head. No doubt they were going to get kicked out by security.

Bash cornered the white-coated doctor, blocking his exit, and then he made shit worse by locking a hand around the guy's throat.

"You ever get in Charlotte's fucking space like that again, and I'll break every goddamn finger and shove them up your ass. She's a no-go area for you."

Every word dripped with a violent promise.

When Tomb relayed the story to the other brothers later, he added how the doctor had turned blue before Bash let him go.

And as predicted, they were tossed out of the ER waiting area.

Charlotte saw it happen, and she scowled at Bash the whole time. Her reluctance to date him was because she already thought all bikers were bastards. Bash's little power showdown didn't help his campaign to win her around.

Denver got home to his family unscathed. There was no lasting damage to his body from the knife wound, so some good happened that day.

He was still in a pissy mood, though.

But now, so was Bash.

Tomb

With Axel and Scarlett taking a trip to Denver to visit his daughter and her family, Chains was in charge of the club.

The VP was in Axel's office, with his feet up on the desk, enjoying dumb videos on his phone.

"Wondered how long it'd take you, brother." He addressed Tomb without looking up. "You lasted longer than I thought. I owe Diamond a Benjamin."

Tomb could have faked understanding what the VP was crowing about, but how closely he kept tabs on his wife was well known. They thought his deranged behavior was fucking hilarious.

"The girls have only been out for a few hours. You gonna break up their night? Nina will rip your balls off."

Nina was out with Chains' old lady, Monroe. She made him promise not to send Splice to keep watch on her, but he promised nothing about Forger. And when he got word that a dope had been trying to buy the girls' drinks, Tomb's trigger had been pressed.

"I was only giving you the heads up if you wanna tag along."

Chains looked over and smirked knowingly. He threw his legs down on the floor and climbed to his feet. "What the hell. It's been a while since I got a hate-fuck, might as well rile my old lady while we got the house to ourselves."

When Chains married Monroe, she came with three sisters; one unfortunately died, and now he catered to the other two like they were his kids, keeping them protected and spoiled. It wasn't uncommon to see Chains being trailed by those girls.

Tomb handed the probie a hundred bucks to enjoy his night once they arrived at the bar.

Nina's shocked, parted lips shouldn't have turned him on when she saw him.

Or the scowl that came right on its tail.

But it did, so he flashed his wife a smile as he trekked across the bar and kissed her slack lips. "Hey, princess. Point out the guy who tried buying you a drink."

"Hell no, Rome, I won't." She laughed, her little diva temper bursting as he crowded into the booth beside her. He sent Monroe a smile across the table, silently apologizing for muscling in on their night out. But she was mauling Chains with her mouth.

"Is that why you're here? I'll knuckle-punch Forger; I told him to shut his big mouth. We dealt with it. The guy was trying to charm Monroe, anyway." Nina shuffled the inch separating them and slid her hand across his stomach, dipping her fingers beneath the material to touch skin.

Look at his woman, trying to be all tough and bold, pretending she was mad at him, but she was just as addicted and couldn't stand so much time apart.

It made him a pig.

A domineering asshole.

But ask Tomb if he was sorry.

Nina was everything good, his tether to the world.

"I hope you're happy with yourself, Rome King."

He dropped his mouth to rub over her silky hair. "I'm the happiest man on earth, princess."

Being so close, he heard Nina's sigh, and then those seeking fingers closed over his growing dick, making it harder than steel. Grunting, he grasped her face, turning it toward him.

Oh, yeah. There was his teasing witch, seducing him with a smile.

Not giving a fuck where they were, he took her lips, prying them open until she moaned around his tongue.

"For your gatecrashing crimes, you can buy the drinks for the rest of the night, Rome King. And we're dancing." She informed him, daring him to deny her.

Like he would.

Tomb was full and satisfied if Nina's wishes were attended to.

"We're gonna head home, Nina." A blushing Monroe told them, clinging to Chains' hand, they'd already climbed out of the booth. Chains was smirking, rolling a hand over his mohawk, and Tomb got the message.

"No! You can't go. Tomb is going to spend a fortune to say sorry."

"I'll take care of the bill." He piped in like a giving asshole so his buddy could get his woman home to bed. Chains nodded, ushering his old lady to get moving.

"I'm sorry." A smiling Monroe looked less than sorry. She was about to get laid. Tomb couldn't blame her. He wanted to rush Nina home to bed, too. "We have the house tonight, Nina..." she left the rest hanging, and Tomb's old lady chuckled.

"Fine, rock your brains out."

"Thanks, babe! I'll call you tomorrow." The two women leaned across the table to hug.

And then they were gone.

Leaving Tomb with his hand crawling up his wife's tiny skirt, her thigh was soft and warm, inviting him to sin right there in public.

"Well, you got your way, me all to yourself, you possessive thug." She nuzzled his beard, pawing over his chest, sliding her hand into his club cut.

He couldn't stop staring at her or keep his hands to himself.

No question about it. He'd die without Nina.

Tomb wouldn't want to live without her if she wasn't in the world. He already had a plan if she was taken before him in their old age, and he prayed she wasn't. He couldn't watch that. It would destroy him. But if that day came, the second Nina took her last breath, Tomb would follow her.

It was the only secret he kept from her because if she knew, she'd kick his ass from one end of the house to the other. Even the imagery of their mental battles made his dick jerk.

Nuzzling her neck, Nina arched for more of his seeking mouth.

"You might think I'm overbearing by needing to control the outcome of things, princess. But everything I do stems from love. I own you, and you possess every inch of my heart. I'm hollow without you."

Tomb knew his girl relented when she huffed and curled deeper into his side.

"You finished being in a mood with me?"

"Holding a grudge is a woman's rite of passage, Rome. Deal with it."

"A nice decent fuck would fix that," he said, chuckling.

"Tomb." She whimpered. Desperation in his name.

His heart pounded, and there was no inch of his body that arousal didn't touch. Groaning with a curse, Tomb grazed his teeth over Nina's neck. "You're so goddamn compliant, princess. Such a fucking treasure, worth more than any money a man could fight for."

The kiss she attacked him with was energetic and heated. His desire for Nina grew with every kiss and lick, overpowering the restraint of his denim jeans.

"There," she smirked, nuzzling his lips. "Now that's fair."

Blinded by pleasure and her taste, he asked, "What is?"

"How much you turn me on, no matter what you do."

Tomb let go of a quick burst of laughter. "Never doubt it. You're vital, wife. My hot little piece, and now we're going home, or I fuck you here."

"God, yes." She latched onto his mouth again before he could move. "I love you."

Love was a tame word for how he felt about Nina.

Crucial.

Beginning and end. She was crucial to every part of his immoral life.

As Nina poked him in the ribs to get him moving, trusting him to get them home safely, anticipating how she'd paw him like a wild animal the entire ride home.

Yeah, he smirked, an arm slung low on his wife's waist, his fingers playing with the edge of the skirt he wanted to lift to get at her pink, wet skin.

He'd won the mouthy princess lottery long ago.

Nina
A YEAR LATER

Tomb was the most competent, gets shit done without complaint, kind of man, and it always affected her internally when she saw him doing manual labor.

Pausing in the nook in their house between the kitchen and living room, she bit the corner of her lip.

"I feel sexually objectified, Nina." He said sardonically, kneeling next to the massive 12-foot artificial Christmas tree he'd secured into the stand. The thing was as wide as a bear.

"So you should, my love. I'm ogling you hard. It looks incredible."

Tomb set an amused glance over his shoulder. Dark hair, wet and glistening still from his shower, before she tasked him into the basement to bring up all the Christmas stuff.

"The tree or my ass?"

His ass was yummy in the stretched denim.

She sent him a saucy answering grin, and he rose to his feet without groaning or creaking noises as someone their age would make.

He headed for her with *sexual intent*. She had to laugh, warding him off with a hand, which he ignored because he pulled her against his chest. His hand covered her ass.

"There's no time for that. I have to decorate. And you have holiday bins to bring up from the basement."

That dark head descended anyway, like she hadn't spoken, kissing her into submission, leaving Nina's head spiraling.

"Every December, you turn into a drill sergeant until it looks like Lapland puked up in here."

Stroking over his veiny forearms, Nina stopped at his biceps and squeezed. "What's the point of having these big guns if I don't use their strength? It's why I'm the smart one. Leave the logistic planning to me, love."

She earned a butt smack, and she laughed. "Hey, no funny business. Your mom and brother will be here in a few hours, and I need everything looking amazing. I want jaws to drop in awe."

"I could still be in bed with my head between your legs. Think about that when you're barking orders down the basement at me."

It was the perfect way to wake up on December 1. She was still experiencing the orgasmic endorphin high hours later. Tomb was always so *giving*.

Not only with sex.

Every part of their lives seemed to operate on the motto 'if it made his wife happy.' The more Tomb gave or did for her, the more satisfaction pulsed out of his colossal body in blistering rays. She'd gotten used to his ways now. She could hardly mention something without it being done days later.

He was insane. He was so fucking *incredible*.

If the love language, acts of service, had a poster boy, it would be Tomb.

It wasn't rocket science. The secret to a happy marriage was having two bathroom sinks, having regular sex, and talking about everything. Oh, and to make each other laugh. When Tomb was in one of his teasing moods, he made Nina roll on the floor; she was never more attracted to him than in those moments.

Through hard work, they nurtured and improved their relationship. Their marriage was vital to them.

"I appreciate your dedication to the cause, love." She teased, stroking his chest all over. His body pleased her immensely. But it was his heart she belonged to.

They'd agreed years ago that Christmas was her domain, to go as high maintenance and over the top as she pleased. Tomb took care of their New Year's Eve plans. This year, they were heading to the lodge. It was their new favorite getaway spot. Only this time, they were going with five other couples.

She'd jokingly asked what happened if it was a key-in-a-bowl situation. Nothing riled her man faster than the thought of someone else touching her. She'd been tied to the bedposts so quickly and spanked for her loose lips. She'd laughed and moaned through each spank of his meaty hand until he'd brought on an orgasm speeding through her.

"Princess, you need to put pants on."

She looked down at her bare legs. "Why?"

"You either want me to lug all this Christmas shit all over the house or to fuck. Watching your ass wiggle from side to side in only panties has all the blood in my head rushing down to my dick."

She considered teasing Tomb. But she wanted her décor bins brought up from the basement. Jaws must drop in awe!

Their three-year-old nephew, Will, had sped into the house when his dad parked the truck hours later. Nina swept the solid little boy up in her arms after he'd screamed her name, acting like it hadn't only been days since she'd last seen him at Thanksgiving.

They all adored that kid, and he looked enough like Tomb; her heart fluttered. Thank Moses, the broody feeling never lasted. She was happy being the favorite auntie who could return the kids to their parents.

"How's my best boy?" she blew kisses on his neck and made the kid writhe with giggles.

"Santa's coming, Aun' Neens!"

"I know he is. Have you been good? You know he's watching, right?"

The boy's eyes went round as a tire, and he nodded emphatically. "I good."

"Yeah, right." Muttered Austin, striding in with a smile, then kissed Nina's cheek. "Hey, sis."

"I good boy, daddy!" scowled Will, stomping his foot. "Aun' Needs says so."

"Well, I can't argue with Aunt Neens, can I?"

"No, you can't." piped in her over-protective hubby as the brothers hugged.

Will had come to their family as a massive surprise.

One they all loved without question.

Austin's one-night stand reappeared with a two-month-old baby one day. She didn't want the baby and gave Austin the option of taking him before handing him over to the state.

A perpetual bachelor who wanted only a life free of responsibilities suddenly became all about that baby.

Hours later, Nina thought Tomb was out the back, showing Austin and Lori's boyfriend his new Harley, when a hand skimmed around her waist. Then she felt his warmth up against her back, and she smiled.

"You'll have to make it quick," she said. "My husband will be back soon, and he's wildly possessive of me."

"Woman, you'll be the death of me, having me kill imaginary men." He growled in her ear.

"I love you being feisty."

"You love me insane."

Mmm, that she did. He was the most gorgeous man on the planet when he was slightly unhinged and in ultra-possessive mode. It was rare for them to have a date night without him glowering at some poor person who he thought had *looked* at Nina for four seconds too long. Most often, once they got outside or into their truck, he'd have his mouth latched onto hers and his hand down her pants, marking his territory. Because she loved getting his angry mauling way too much, she never reminded him she was not a forty-two-year-old supermodel, and men didn't stare at her as often as he thought.

"What's under this little red thing, hm?" he fingered the hem of her knee-length Christmas dress.

She bumped back into Tomb, grazing his crotch, and he grunted sex-heavy noises. "You'll find out when everyone has gone home."

"Too long."

She turned in his arms and reached up to kiss him on the bearded chin. "I'll make it worth the wait."

She watched as his eyes flared with want glowing back at her.

Their spark never dimmed. It burned brighter than ever, and it was cliché to say they couldn't keep their hands off each other.

Very true, though.

They were not a fairytale, far from it.

Their yelling fights still happened, and sometimes they clashed and couldn't agree, but love was never far away, even throughout those arguments.

But prioritizing each other was key. Reconnecting despite their busy schedules.

Who knew communication was life's secret to a happy, healthy, mutually obsessive relationship?

Pouring all her love through her arms as she cuddled close to Tomb's broad chest, she felt peaceful, content to stay there for the rest of the day.

Nina wondered how long Tomb would stay happy once he found out she'd volunteered him to help decorate the salon tomorrow.

She'd have to drop that little nugget of info while she had his dick in her later. Wasn't sexual manipulation part of everyone's arsenal? Tomb used it on her if his heavy-handed, bossy tactics initially didn't work.

His motto was that it was better to ask for forgiveness (which he never did because he was never sorry for his demands) than to ask for permission.

"I can hear you thinking, princess." He said with his mouth brushing against her hair.

Nina blinked innocently up at him and watched Tomb's eyebrow wing up. "I was thinking about how much I love you and how I married the best guy."

"*Christ*." he gusted a sigh. "Whatever the new scheme is, wait until you're sucking my cock to tell me."

He knew her so well.

And nothing in the world felt better than that. She was back on the same page as her biker husband, knowing they worked hard to make their marriage the best it could be.

Give and take.

Take and give.

Compromise.

And love each other through the challenging times.

Looking back now at those harsh, painful months when she considered leaving him, it felt like an out-of-body experience. Through months of effort, they successfully resolved their differences and understood each other better. They'd found a happy medium that pleased them both.

She couldn't imagine a life without Tomb. Laughing at silly things, reading his texts, riding his bike, feeling wild at her age.

"I forgot to say," Tomb said, drawing back, a twinkle of mischief in his eyes. Nina was instantly suspicious of what he'd say next. And she was right to be. "You owe me three days of Christmas tax."

She mock gasped. "You're a piece of work, do you know that? You're going to leave me destitute, taxing me so much."

Those big shoulders shrugged, and his grin was oh-so-boyish. "Times are hard, baby." He pressed his pelvis into her. "Very. Fucking. Hard."

"Can I give you an IOU?"

"Nope. Need paying now or…"

"Or what?" She shouldn't be this turned on while her in-laws enjoyed eggnog and board games in the next room.

She *appreciated* this man more than she had words to express. Every day, he showed her with actions how much he loved her, but man, he was a smooth con artist.

"Or I'll push you into the nearest closet," his voice turned rusty with desire. The sound of it skipped all over Nina's skin, sending her senses reeling. "And discover what's under this dick-teasing dress while I exact my tax out on you."

"You'd have to cover my mouth," she muttered. "You know how loud I can be when you're being filthy."

His eyes darkened, and Tomb cursed. "*Fuck.* You play dirty, wife."

Smiling, she tugged at his shoulder, "Bring that mouth down here, love, let me pay my debts."

Their mouths met, and Tomb licked his way inside in that hypnotic way he had of kissing her, which made every thought fall from Nina's mind.

"Uncle Rome is kissing Aun' Neens again," Will snitched from the couch, having woken from his nap.

"Boy, I'm gonna drop you off at the nearest reindeer zoo and let them shi—poop on your head." Threatened Tomb, making the boy explode into hysterical giggles. Tomb dropped another kiss to her wet lips and strode across the room to hang their cackling nephew upside down.

Even while teasing Will, Tomb's haunting eyes stretched across the room to find her with his sinful lips curved. They shared a look of love and partnership, hinting at a romantic evening ahead.

Family meant everything to them, especially Nina, who'd created her family with some of the most wonderful people ever.

But they'd forever be each other's obsession.

And that's why she never asked Santa for anything.

She'd already gotten her best gift.

A big, bearded drink of biker water, who would fight through fire and brimstone to make her happy.

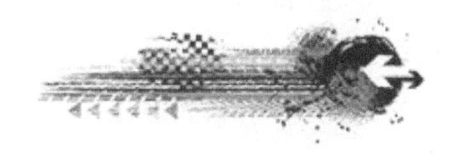

Nina
TWELVE YEARS LATER

Raising a teen boy was pure hell.

They smelled of boy, no matter how many times they showered. They were lazy, uncooperative, had a mile-long attitude, and never stopped wanting things.

But then there were these pockets of moments where that teen boy was the sweet little boy she adored and who would smile at her like she hung the stars.

Those times were few, and she'd mark it down on the family calendar in the kitchen that December 24 was a miracle day because Will hadn't grunted once yet. However, the day was still early.

No one could have predicted that twelve years ago, the day after New Year's Day, a drunk driver would swipe Austin's truck off the road, killing Tomb's brother instantly. Or that he'd named them in his will to become Will's guardians.

Of course, it was a non-question. They took the boy.

It had been a complicated adjustment period for all.

They hadn't known how to be parents to anyone, least of all a grieving boy who didn't understand why his daddy wasn't with him. Tomb had been devastated to lose his brother, as they all were.

Somehow, they'd gotten through together.

But Will had never been the same.

He'd stopped talking for years. Therapists said it was the shock. *No shit, Sherlock*, and to give him time to heal. At first, they'd tried to coax him into talking again. They showered him with love, activities, trips, and bribes. Nothing worked. And then they decided just to let him be.

Even being nonverbal, all his teachers reported how book-smart Will was. He excelled at every level, loved to read everything he could, and even skipped a few grades.

Slowly, he'd come back to them, being the fun-loving boy as he'd aged.

But he'd yet to speak again. And that was okay with them all. Will was the most loved person in their family. His favorite thing to do was tagging along with Tomb to go to the MC. He shadowed every biker there, soaking up whatever they showed him.

He was a born biker, Axel said.

Nina didn't know yet what fifteen-year-old Will would be as an adult. Right now, he was a moody little shit with an attitude, and if he still believed in Santa Claus, she sure as hell would bring out the threat of him not coming.

Nina went all out making breakfast every Sunday — family day — and each Christmas Eve. She was finishing cutting the strata casserole and piling a stack of white chocolate chip pancakes when the boy in question sloped in. Looking like he'd slept for days, his dark hair stood up in tufts all over his head.

She loved her boy, even when he infuriated the life out of her.

At the rate he grew, he'd be as tall as Tomb in a few years. He already towered over her with his lean frame.

"Happy Christmas Eve, sweetheart."

He grunted in return. It was a good grunt, though. With his mouth already half-full with a piece of honey-glazed bacon, Nina pointed a spatula at Will. "Rome is out in the garage. He said he was fixing his bike, but he's doing something with my gifts. You wanna go let him know breakfast is done, and I'll be pissed if it gets cold?"

Will chuckled and grabbed another piece of bacon before nodding.

Minutes later, two laughing boys came through the back door. Will headed right for the food, filling his plate high. Tomb wrapped an arm around her waist, bringing the scent of snow with him.

"You summoned me, princess?"

"And you came." She smiled as Tomb lowered his head to meet their mouths.

"Always." And then they fell into a tame Christmas Eve kiss.

Behind them, they heard a gagging sound. Without raising his head, Tomb said calmly. "You know it's not too late to return that expensive video game shit, Will."

It was followed by Will chuckling. He never took Tomb's threats seriously because he knew he could get away with it. To a point. He was an intelligent brat.

They loved him so much.

And they loved each other to distraction. *Entirely*. Without walls or boundaries.

Nina's salon was thriving, and she was home on a snowy Christmas Eve with her two boys.

Nothing in life was as good.

He made her feel like the lyrics of a Celine Dion song.

Like they were the only two people in the world.

Tomb's love and devotion to their marriage made Nina the luckiest bitch in Manolo Blahnik.

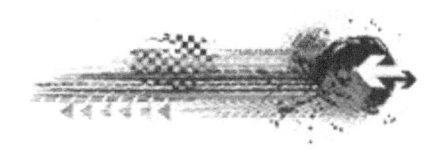

Tomb
A YEAR LATER

Blind pleasure rode heavily down Tomb's spine.

With his chest plastered to Nina's damp back, his fingers cuffed around the front of her throat, Tomb could watch through the mirror how the bliss hit her when he plunged his dick deep.

There was nothing better than hearing how aroused Nina was, even when her voice was muffled. The way her breath puffed in and out with quickness and her skin turned pink all over. She was a fucking vision, even better with age.

The woman of his dreams was still hot for him, and he never complained about it.

Tomb was no fool. In some ways, sure.

But not where Nina's needs were concerned.

Following her into the shower this morning had been a clever idea, because she greeted him with outstretched hands and a welcoming mouth.

His wife was easy to arouse.

Sometimes, all it took was a few depraved words in her ear or a text message, and she would be a feral animal all over him. She *loved* filthy messages. The way she demanded to be fucked tasted like chocolate in his mouth.

Sex was easy for them. The easiest thing he'd ever done with anyone.

And in front of their fogged bathroom vanity mirror, he gave it to his gorgeous wife, one ladened thrust after another. Biting the inside of his cheek to stave off his rushing climax, he worked in deeper, her tight walls strangling his cock in the best way while his fingers glided over her slippery clit.

Nina whined. The vibrations felt against his palm were like a drug. Something he couldn't get enough of. He lived for it.

If obsession had a face, it would carry Nina's.

If heaven existed, she was it.

Nothing had waned between them.

Their fires burned brighter, more so when he was wringing pleasure from her addictive body.

Her eyes locked with Tomb's in the mirror, and a sharp zip of bliss curled his gut. He was close to exploding and needed his wife to go first.

"Look at you, taking it like my best fucking princess, aren't you?" he husked low in her ear. Those were the magic words for Tomb to feel her clamp around his strangled cock, and her orgasm gushed so fucking scalding. He was blinded by his climax right after.

"Fuck, just like that." Groaning, he remained buried.

"If Santa had sex like that on Christmas Eve, he wouldn't need all those cookies," murmured Nina as she turned in his arms. The sight of his semen and her wet pleasure coating the inside of her thighs never ceased to rev his engines.

He was a sick motherfucker who got off on messing up his wife.

She nestled into his chest, all soft and warm, and Tomb knew he'd started their Christmas Eve just right. After their quiet moment, Nina would go at warped speed for the rest of the day, making their family time as magical as she always did.

"We've filled each other with wonderful memories, haven't we, Rome?"

"Still got a long way to go, princess." He tapped a kiss on her forehead as she swayed in his arms.

Nina was his soul. If he had one, she was it.

Making her happy was his center.

"We should get going." She said, making no move to leave his arms.

"Get back in the shower, baby. Gotta clean you up. Unless you wanna wear my come all day?" a satisfied growl rattled around his chest. Yeah, he'd like that.

Scolding, she pinched the skin on his side. "Don't be dirty. Get in the shower. I might let you get on your knees and clean me."

Her suggestion reached down to his half-hard cock. Her eyes were sparkling when he pulled away to look at her.

"Now, who's the dirty one, huh? You want to watch me lick up the mess we made together?"

The tremble that visibly went through Nina was his answer as he got them into the shower. Tomb lowering to his knees meant they weren't finished.

No one could tell that Tomb had violated his wife earlier that day. She was effortlessly beautiful and put together stylishly.

But Tomb would know.

Will was already out of bed, and in an even bigger shock, his punk kid was shoveling snow from the walkway.

"He's giving a last push to get that dirt bike," chuckled Nina, a steaming cup of coffee held in her hands as they watched Will through the window.

Tomb grunted. Will had been lobbying for his Christmas gift and working hard to earn it. The bike was waiting for him at the clubhouse.

Will wasn't a bad kid. He could sure be worse, Tomb reckoned.

He loved that kid. And couldn't picture him not being part of their family, but Tomb still, to this day, wished to God Austin was around to be Will's dad.

The grief got more manageable, but the wound of losing Austin never fully healed. He lived with it, and every time he looked at Will, he saw his brother in his features and mannerisms. It helped to know Austin was still with them.

Coming through the back door, bringing the cold with him, Will pulled off the sheepskin gloves and beanie hat to run his hand over his hair.

"Happy Christmas Eve, sweetheart." Greeted Nina, her arms open.

The boy groaned but sloped over to be hugged by his aunt. Will knew better than to refuse affection from Nina.

"Happy Christmas Eve, Neens."

It surprised everyone early in spring when Will spoke again.

Will's reason for speaking didn't come as a surprise because he had a protective nature. During a club party, he witnessed someone bothering his lifelong friend Samantha. Will had burst through the crowd to rip the guy off her, and he screamed in his face, "*Keep your fucking hands off her!*"

Nina had been too busy bawling into Tomb's chest to realize their boy had cursed.

All was good, and Tomb couldn't ask for anything more.

He had a kid that was a star quarterback and a wife who owned the land to his fucking being. The club was going through good times, too.

Yeah, he smiled as he roped Nina in and got her curled up against his ribs.

He was in no doubt that he'd be in for a fight tomorrow when Tomb informed Nina he was taking her away for a few weeks. All these years later, she sometimes pushed up against him.

She needed the break; he'd waited as long as his overbearing self could.

Nina took care of everyone else.

Tomb took care of her.

And that's how it would forever be.

He'd rise from the fucking grave to accomplish his job.

A man needed a reason to live fully, cramming it with every bliss-inducing inclination and hedonistic decision.

Nina King was his reason.

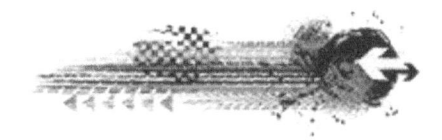

Tomb
MORE YEARS LATER

"I think I got a girl pregnant."

"You think, or you know?"

Will dragged a hand through his black hair, tattoos gracing his fingers and the back of his hands. Tomb had been with him to get his first piece of ink. It was a map of Austin, dedicated to his dad.

Some tattoos covering his body were dedicated to Nina, and Tomb couldn't love the boy more for that. Will had been under Nina's thumb as much time as Tomb. They might clash like thunderbolts, but if there was one thing Tomb and Will could agree on, it was how much they protected Nina.

"I know. She told me tonight. What the fuck am I gonna do, Rome? I can't have a kid. I'm only twenty."

Tomb couldn't say he wasn't shocked; he thought he'd instilled in his boy the importance of wrapping his dick up. But now wasn't the time to dress him down when Will was going through some shit. Tomb palmed his shoulder and drew his kid in.

"I don't know how it happened."

Despite the situation, Tomb chuckled. "I think we had the sex talk with you years ago."

"*Sleeping* with her. I don't remember it. At fucking all, Rome. I woke up in her bed after a party, but that's all I know. That was weeks ago, and I got out of there and forgot all about it."

"Then there's a chance it isn't yours."

"She says it is." He scrubbed a hand down his sick-with-worry face.

"Son, I won't blow smoke up your ass and say it's going to be easy. If this is your baby, then you have to be strong about it. I know it's not how you saw your future."

"No shit."

Tomb one arm-hugged his boy. "Don't freak out. You know Nina and me will be here for you."

Across the room, the woman in question laughed at something the young girl she was talking to said, and Tomb and Will looked up simultaneously.

Will cursed. "Fuck. *Fuck*. How do I tell Samantha this?"

Sammie was the girl with Nina. A sweet, quiet, bookish girl. She'd been Will's friend for a long time, but the agony on his son's face as he stared across at Sammie told Tomb it was more.

"I'll lose her. She won't stick around for this shit."

"You and Sammie? I thought you were only friends."

"We are."

"Sure about that?"

Will dragged his eyes away, but Tomb understood what Will couldn't answer. Whatever he felt for Sammie, it was more than friendship.

"I need to ride and clear my head. You won't say anything yet, will you?"

"It's not mine to tell, son. Ride safe, yeah?"

Will swung into his jacket before striding out of the clubhouse.

He wasn't aware that Sammie was following his every step, her wide-open feelings shining from her begging eyes.

Yeah, Tomb thought, his kid had a complicated situation on his hands.

<u>Coming up is Bash's story.</u>

Renegade Souls MC Series:

Dirty Salvation

Preacher Man

Tracking Luxe

Hades Novella

Filthy Love

Finally Winter

Mistletoe and Outlaws Novella

Resurfaced Passion

Intimately Faithful Novella

Indecent Lies

Law Maker Novella

Savage Outlaw

Renegade Souls MC Collection Boxset 1-3

Prince Charming

Forever Zara Novella

Veiled Amor

Renegade Souls MC Collection Boxset 4-6

Blazing Hope
Darling Psycho

Taboo Love Duet:
It Was Love
It Was Always Love
Taboo Love Collection
Forever Love Companion

From Manhattan Series:
Manhattan Sugar
Manhattan Bet
Manhattan Storm
Manhattan Secret
Manhattan Heart
Manhattan Target
Manhattan Tormentor
Manhattan Muse
Manhattan Protector

Naughty Irish Series:
Naughty Irish Liar

Diablo Disciples MC:
Chains
Reno

**Axel
Ruin**

Website: www.VTheiaBooks.com
Author Facebook: www.facebook.com/VTheia
Readers Group: Vs Biker Babes

Be the first to know when V. Theia's next book is available. Follow her on <u>Bookbub</u> to get an alert whenever she has a new release.

Tomb

Made in United States
Cleveland, OH
11 March 2025